DESIRING THE HIGHLAND LAIRD

Highland Destiny
Book 1

Michelle Miles

ARE YOU SIGNED UP FOR DRAGONBLADE'S BLOG?

You'll get the latest news and information on exclusive giveaways, exclusive excerpts, coming releases, sales, free books, cover reveals and more.

Check out our complete list of authors, too!

No spam, no junk. That's a promise!

Sign Up Here

www.dragonbladepublishing.com

Dearest Reader;

Thank you for your support of a small press. At Dragonblade Publishing, we strive to bring you the highest quality Historical Romance from some of the best authors in the business. Without your support, there is no 'us', so we sincerely hope you adore these stories and find some new favorite authors along the way.

Happy Reading!

CEO, Dragonblade Publishing

CHAPTER ONE

EVANGELINE "EVIE" SINCLAIR exited the Edinburgh International Airport with a raging headache and the worst hangover of her life. She hated flying. Even more, she hated flying over ten hours.

She managed to sleep on the long first flight with the aid of copious amounts of alcohol and a handful of melatonin, knowing all the while she would regret her decision later. She did when she had to sprint to the gate at Heathrow to catch her connection to Edinburgh. Now, her stomach roiled, and her head pounded as she dodged throngs of visitors.

But her twin sister, Chloe, was worth it. She wouldn't miss her first big fund-raising gala for anything in the world.

She hadn't seen her sister in nearly a year. Not since Chloe took on a job as the director of public programs at one of the more prestigious history museums in Edinburgh. It had taken some time for her work visa to come through, but when it did, she packed up her American life and headed to Scotland, leaving her behind. Evie was happy for her but at the same time, she wallowed in self-pity when Chloe left. She was, after all, all the family she had left.

Well, except for their older sister, Brianna. She was a free spirit and an underwater photographer living her best life in the Caribbean. Years had passed since she'd seen Brianna.

Evie made her way out of the terminal, her stomach roiling

from the travel and the booze still swimming through her veins. She hated to admit how pukey she felt.

When she saw Chloe standing on the sidewalk, though, all that disappeared.

She and Chloe were fraternal twins, and, by Evie's account, Chloe got all the looks *and* brains. It wasn't fair.

Chloe was always effortlessly stunning. Tall and graceful, her long auburn hair tumbled over her shoulders and down her back, the strands catching the light in a way that showed off her golden highlights. And those eyes—huge, striking emerald eyes framed in dark lashes Evie envied her entire life. She never got over how naturally beautiful Chloe was, never needing a drop of make-up on her porcelain skin which was smooth and perfect without even trying. Not even a blemish in sight, even during their awkward teenage years while Evie battled every breakout. Even the smattering of freckles across the bridge of her nose and cheeks was charming.

Evie, however, earned the nickname Freckle Face in third grade. It dogged her throughout her entire school career. It didn't help that she had vibrant red-and-gold hair as brilliant as the sun, making her stand out even more. And her eyes were more like the color of a mud puddle.

When Chloe caught sight of her, she gave an enormous wave, her face splitting into a bright, happy smile. It was hard to feel crummy when Evie looked at that joyful face.

"You made it!"

Chloe enveloped her in a hug that nearly stole her breath. It was good to hug her sister again. When she pulled back, holding her at arm's length, she looked her over, then frowned.

"You look like crap," she said.

"Thanks, it's good to see you, too," Evie replied.

"Bad flight?" Chloe asked, ignoring her quip.

"The flight was fine."

She didn't want to tell her sister she was hungover or that the mad dash through Heathrow had drained every ounce of energy she had left. Or that all she wanted to do was crawl into bed, pull the covers over her head, and sleep for a week.

Chloe took her suitcase from her, which was nothing more than a carry-on. "Is this all your luggage?"

"I travel light," Evie said.

Chloe lifted an auburn brow. "You didn't check a bag? You'll be here for nearly ten days."

"I have a terrible fear of lost luggage." Evie hooked her arm with her sister's. "You know that."

"Yes, but…ten days, Eve."

"Dinnae fash yerself, lassie," Evie said in her best Scottish accent, which was terrible.

Chloe laughed, a bright happy sound that made Evie grin. "Come on. Let's get you settled and then I'll introduce you to Bruce."

That stopped her cold. She halted in the middle of the sidewalk, her gut clenching and her hangover threatening to rear its ugly head.

"Who the hell is Bruce?"

Chloe flushed, her cheeks turning a pale, lovely pink. "I didn't want to tell you on the phone. I was afraid you'd back out."

This didn't sound good. Not at all. She didn't like where it was going. "Tell me what?"

"I met someone." She said it as though it were a secret she was afraid to release into the world.

"His name is Bruce?"

"Yes." She took her by the hand and tugged her down the sidewalk. "We can discuss it on the way to my flat."

Evie had no choice but to follow her sister, her mind swirling with questions. She was gone less than a year and now she had a flat *and* a boyfriend?

What had Evie been doing the last few months? Nothing except for throwing herself the biggest pity party on the face of the planet. All because she missed her twin with a ferociousness she had never expected to feel.

She blamed it, too, on the fact that Brianna was so far away, and they rarely talked. Having Chloe move over four-thousand-miles away was like having her heart ripped from her chest and stomped on. It was the worst day of her life when she left but she didn't dare stop her. She couldn't. Not for selfish reasons. Even though Chloe had asked her what she thought when she was offered the job.

In fact, Evie talked her into taking it. Telling her she would be fine. She could manage on her own.

They had never been separated for so long or been so far apart in their entire lives. They spent every moment together growing up. They shared a room. They leaned heavily on each other when their parents died at fifteen and Brianna, ten years their senior, became their legal guardian. Evie suspected Brianna was angry at having to give up her life to return home and take care of them until they were out of high school.

Then, later, when they were independent and Brianna had returned to her beachy ways, they shared an apartment.

Until Chloe left.

Chloe loaded her small suitcase into the back of a compact car.

"Evie." There was a terse note in her voice. "You haven't listened to anything I said."

Evie realized Chloe was talking nonstop and she hadn't heard a word.

"I'm sorry," she said, flushing hot. She hadn't meant to ignore her. She was lost in thought.

"I know that look." Chloe motioned to the passenger side.

But Evie hesitated as she stared at the small car. "You can…drive? Here?"

She gave her a bright smile. "Sure."

But Evie wasn't so sure. "But it's on the wrong side of the road, Chlo."

"The right side if you're talking to a Scot." She giggled and motioned to the passenger side again. "Hop in."

With reluctance, Evie slid into the passenger seat. "I didn't know you were driving here."

"Well, with the work visa, I was able to get a driving permit."

Her sister pulled into traffic on the left side of the road, merging with ease. Evie gripped the door so hard, her fingers ached. Traffic was heavy as they moved down the narrow road, the other side of cars zooming by at an alarming rate. It didn't seem to bother Chloe.

Evie cut a glance at her sister as she navigated the streets as though she'd been doing it her whole life. She was definitely the prettier of the two of them. It was hard to be jealous of her when she was so damn likeable. She was the popular one in school. The class president. The one voted Most Likely to Succeed. Homecoming queen. Prom queen.

Then, in college, she took her classes seriously. So serious, in fact, she dumped a guy who wanted her to move in with him, get married, and drop out. Chloe was not going to let anyone stand in her way. Chloe wasn't in love with him. She was in love with her studies and history.

"I missed you, Chlo," she said finally.

Chloe gave her a sideways glance and smiled. That grin that said everything was going to be all right now that they were back together. "I missed you, too, Eve."

She clasped her hands in her lap and watched as the city flashed by the window. Chloe sped round a roundabout like she had driven them all her life. Evie gritted her teeth and tried not to cry out with sheer terror as they took the corner on what felt like two wheels. She tried conversation to keep her mind off the road.

"Did you ask Bri to come?"

Her sister stiffened at the mention of their older sibling's name. Her hands clutched the steering wheel so tight her knuckles turned white.

"I didn't."

Though she knew the answer, she asked, "Why not?"

"Eve, you know why. She couldn't wait to get back to her

beaches and her dolphins." Chloe didn't bother to hide the animosity in her voice.

She understood. The moment they graduated high school and sold their parents' house, Brianna packed up and left them on their own. It was a struggle, but Chloe was determined to go to college. Evie never cared one way or another. Evie was the one who encouraged her to follow her dreams while she made sure they had a place to live and food to eat. They'd managed to save some of the money from the sale of the house, but even so, Evie went to work to help pay the bills so they wouldn't exhaust their savings.

"Brianna is built different than us," Evie said.

"Don't make excuses for her," Chloe snapped. "She took care of us because she was forced to."

It was a bone of contention with Chloe. Evie, though, tried to forgive her.

"It's like she didn't even care when Mom and Dad died."

"Don't say that," Evie admonished. "She was as sad as we were."

"Was she? You know she blew through her part of the inheritance already, don't you?"

"I didn't."

Evie shifted in the seat and regretted asking about Brianna. It wasn't a lot of money, but it was enough to sustain them and help pay for Chloe's college. Evie thought it was important she go because she was so much smarter than her and deserved the chance to live out her dreams. Evie never dreamed of a career. She floated from one job to another without any purpose or direction.

Chloe blew out a breath as if she were defeated. "I'm sorry, Eve. I don't mean to sound so defensive about her."

"You hold grudges. I get it."

When Chloe cast her a sideways glance, Evie grinned at her. "God forbid we get into a fight and you hold one against me."

"That will never happen."

She took another roundabout at breakneck speed. Evie held on for dear life.

"Tell me about Bruce," she said through clenched teeth, trying to take her mind off her sister's driving. She was never great at it—at least that was something Evie was better at—and this driving on the wrong side of the road set her nerves on fire.

"I can't wait for you to meet him at dinner," Chloe said.

"Dinner? Tonight?"

"I told him we'd meet him at the pub."

"Pub?" Evie reached for the door handle and hung on, her nails digging into it.

"Yeah, he and his band play there every Tuesday night."

"Band?"

What the hell was going on? Chloe was not the type of girl to fall for a guy in a band. Chloe was the type of girl who made straight A's and aced all her exams. The type of girl who was in bed by nine and never missed a deadline. The type of girl who worked hard and sometimes enjoyed a glass of wine.

All this talk about a pub and a band and some guy was unnerving.

"Not like a rock band or anything," she said. "More like…traditional music."

"So, no AC/DC or anything?" she asked.

Chloe laughed. "Nothing like that. Here we are!"

She took a turn into a cramped car park that had narrow spaces. But Chloe seemed unfazed by it as she threw the car into reverse and backed in like a professional driver. Evie was impressed. It was clear her sister was eager to get out and show Evie her flat. And she was eager for that, too.

Right after a nap and a couple of ibuprofen.

Chloe pulled her suitcase out from the backseat and waved at her to hurry and follow. Evie trudged after her sister, the long flight and her hangover finally catching up to her.

Inside, the flat was spacious yet cozy, with a tiny kitchen, living area and dining room.

"Two bedrooms," Chloe exclaimed. "This is your room."

Between the bedrooms was a modest yet functional bathroom. Stepping inside, the space was compact but thoughtfully arranged. The sleek, white sink sat beneath a mirrored cabinet. Below that, a shelf for her smaller items like her toothbrush and face cream. Over the shower-tub combo, there was a frosted window that let in filtered light. The walls were a neutral shade, making the space feel clean and bright.

Her gaze wandered to the toilet—a bit different than what she was used to in the States. It had a dual-flush button on top, an eco-friendly design which was likely common in this country. It felt lower to the ground than what she expected but it was oddly practical, like the rest of the bathroom.

"You got the place furnished?" she asked.

"I did. It was better than trying to furnish it myself."

She stood at the foot of the full-size bed, her hands on her hips as she looked around the room, as if seeing it for the first time. There was one window with the blinds open that let in shafts of light. Along with the bed, there was a small nightstand with one lamp. Across from the bed, a desk and small chest of drawers.

"It's not my taste, but I decided I didn't care after a while." She grinned.

"It's great," Evie said, stifling a yawn.

"We'll meet Bruce in a few hours. That should give you time to rest."

She headed for the door.

"Chlo?"

She paused, her hand on the knob.

Evie grinned at her, a sense of happiness coming over her. "I'm glad I'm here."

She returned her smile. "I'm glad you're here, too."

When she closed the door, Evie fell onto the bed, kicking off her shoes at the same time. It wasn't long before she was fast asleep.

CHAPTER TWO

THE DREAM CAME to her immediately after falling asleep. She ran toward a castle in the dead of night. Lightning split the blackened sky as it streaked across it. She halted a moment, breathless, thunder rumbling in its wake. Ahead of her, the towers soared into the night sky. Thick, high walls encircled those towers. Fat raindrops dotted her head. She started running again, heading for the portcullis, but the gate was closed.

Then the dream morphed into something else. She was inside. There was a warm fire blazing in a hearth and no other light. It illuminated the bedroom she was in. She was on the four-poster bed with thick, velvet curtains at each post. A man lounged in a chair by the fire. He was shirtless. His chest was broad and muscular with a sprinkling of dark hair across it. His long legs were stretched out in front of him. There was mud on his boots. His arms rested on the chair, his hands dangling. His head rested against the back of the chair. His eyes were closed. His chest rose and fell with rhythmic breaths.

He was devastatingly handsome with a strong square jaw covered in stubble. Long hair plaited on either side of his head.

She climbed out of the bed and padded toward the chair. Her bare feet were silent on the cold stone flooring. When she reached his side, his eyes fluttered open. He looked up at her with the bluest eyes she had ever seen. Desire flickered through the depths. Dark brows lifted in question as he looked up at her.

She pulled off her shift and dropped it to the floor, standing naked before him.

"Och, lass…"

His voice was deep, dark, dangerous and oh, so sexy. She moved to stand in front of him. He sat up, his gaze moving over her flesh with a look of reverence and yearning. His long hair fell across his massive shoulders.

"Don't turn me away," she said. "I'm here for you."

He reached for her, his warm, calloused hands landing on her hips as he pulled her to him. He shifted in the chair to be closer to her. His mouth, hot and damp, landed on the flat plane of her stomach. Her eyes fluttered closed as he placed long, slow kisses along her abdomen.

A breath shuddered out of her as he moved downward.

And then she woke up.

Evie sat straight up in the bed, sweating. Her heart beat at a rapid pace. The dream had seemed so real. So lifelike. She was certain she had felt the man's kisses on her flesh. She glanced down to make sure she was still dressed.

Her clothes clung to her damp body. She pushed herself off the bed and stood, wobbling a bit on her feet.

The dream was more than a dream. It was as if it were a memory. She swore she still felt his roughened hands on her hips and his soft, warm lips moving along her skin. Her eyes fluttered closed as a mewl escaped her.

A rapid knock on the door made her nearly jump out of her skin. Her eyes flew open as the door pushed open and Chloe stuck in her head.

"Oh, good. You're awake! Ready to meet Bruce?"

"Ah…"

Her brows drew together. "Are you all right? You look a bit flustered."

"Fine. Just, um, give me a minute to change and freshen up a bit?"

"Sure."

She closed the door with a snap. Evie sank to the bed. She pressed trembling fingers against her lips. It was hard to dismiss the dream because, for whatever reason, it felt real.

EVIE MANAGED TO pull herself together for the dinner with the mysterious Bruce. She changed into clean, dry clothes and combed her hair. Then she managed to freshen her makeup with a swipe of her favorite lip gloss. There were still bags under her eyes but there wasn't much she could do about that. She felt like she needed a week's worth of sleep.

She grabbed her small handbag and headed out of her room. Her sister put on a bright smile when she entered the living room. She popped up to her feet.

"Ready?"

Evie nodded. She tried to turn her thoughts away from the erotic dream she had had of the hot guy, but it was hard for her to focus.

"Earth to Evie," Chloe said.

She shook herself out of her thoughts. "I'm sorry. What?"

"Again, you're not listening to me."

She flushed, her cheeks turning warm. "Sorry."

Chloe ushered her out of the apartment, closing and locking the door behind her. "You had a long flight. I shouldn't be dragging you out to the pub."

"It's fine." Evie put her on her best smile. She hooked her arm with her sister's. "I'm looking forward to it."

"I can't wait for you to meet Bruce," she said.

Instead of driving, they made their way out of the apartment to the pub down the street. Even early in the evening on a weekday, the place was packed. Every barstool and every table was filled. There were two men on the stage under bright lights, one playing a banjo and the other a guitar. The guitar player lifted his gaze as Chloe passed close to the stage and his face lit into a bright smile.

That must be her Bruce.

He was classically handsome with a swath of dark hair that fell over his forehead and a goatee gracing his chin.

Chloe made her way to the one empty table at the back of the pub. Her gaze was on the guitar player on the stage, a light of joy in her eyes. Evie hadn't seen her sister that happy in ages. It made her heart swell as she took her seat.

The duo finished their song and then took a break. It wasn't long before the guitarist made his way to their table. It was clear to Evie that this was definitely Bruce, for his steely blue-eyed gaze never left her sister's face.

Before he made it to the table, Chloe jumped up and rounded it. She fell into his waiting arms as they embraced, then paused for a quick kiss.

"You made it," he said, clutching her hands. His voice was deep yet soothing. Perhaps that's what made him such a good singer.

"I told you we would." Her gaze swept from him to Evie. "This is my sister, Evie."

"Och, Evie. I've heard a lot about ye, lass."

She rose as he extended his hand and they shook. "Have you?"

As they shook hands, though, she got a strange feeling in the pit of her stomach. Like something about him was off even though he seemed cordial enough. She, however, had learned over the years to trust her gut.

"Evie, this is Bruce MacDonald." Chloe clutched his arm and gazed up at him with adoring eyes.

Evie was uncomfortable in their presence. She lowered back down to her chair and scooted closer to the table. Taking that as a cue, Bruce and Chloe did the same.

"Where did you two meet?" she asked, trying to make conversation.

"At the museum," Chloe said. "One day he came in and, well… the rest is history."

She sat close to him, her hand still on his arm. He brushed the back of his hand across her cheek, grinning.

"I couldna take my eyes off her," he said.

Evie shifted in her seat, unsure what to say next. Thankfully, she didn't have to come up with more small talk when the waitress bustled over to take their orders. He waved her off, but Chloe ordered a pint of Tennent's.

"Beer?" Evie cut her a surprised glance.

"Bruce turned me onto it." She grinned at him.

"And for you?"

It took a moment to realize the waitress was speaking to her.

"Oh, water for me." She was still jet lagged and hungover from her bender on the plane.

"Break time's over." He kissed Chloe on the cheek. "I'll see ye after," he said, and then returned to the stage.

"Isn't he dreamy?" she asked as he walked away.

"He is," she agreed, watching as he picked up his guitar and laughed at something the banjo player said.

"I think he's the one, Eve." She said it on a wistful sigh.

Evie peered at the guy on the stage. While he was handsome, and he played a mean guitar, she knew nothing else about him.

"How long have you been dating?"

"A few months."

"And you know already he's *the one*?"

Chloe gave her a thin-lipped frown. "Yes. What's wrong with that?"

She shrugged, lifting one shoulder. "I don't know. It seems…fast."

"Sometimes true love *is* fast, Evie. You'll get to know him and realize how perfect we are for each other in no time."

When their drinks arrived, Evie wished she had ordered something stronger.

"I guess so," she finally said.

"Just because you don't believe in love at first sight, doesn't mean I don't," Chloe said. She took a sip of her pint.

"It's not that… it's…" It was hard for her to tell her sister she thought she was rushing into things a bit.

Perhaps it was because she was in another country and the man had a terrific accent. Who wouldn't fall for that Scottish brogue? She suspected Chloe had fallen in love with the idea of falling in love with a Scotsman, rather than the Scotsman himself.

She didn't know and she didn't want to seem like a doubter. She wanted to be supportive of her sister, who frowned into her beer.

"You don't have to like him," she muttered. "But I would like it if you got along."

Evie reached for her hand, grasped it. "Chlo, I don't know him." Then she glanced over at the man on stage, singing his lungs out and playing his guitar. "But I'm sure I will like him in time." She squeezed her hand to press her point.

That seemed to perk her up a bit and she smiled. "Good. Tomorrow, he's taking us shopping on the Royal Mile. You'll get to spend some time with him then and get to know him better."

She clenched to jaw to bite off the acid retort that she came to see her sister, not her sister and her boyfriend. Instead, she gave her a bright smile.

"I can't wait."

CHAPTER THREE

T HE NEXT DAY, they were up early despite a late night at the pub. Chloe was having the time of her life, so it was difficult for Evie to tell her she was exhausted and wanted to go back to the apartment to sleep. They finally arrived back in the wee hours of the morning.

After a few hours' sleep, she was still dragging, despite a pot of coffee, when Bruce showed up to take them shopping. Chloe, meanwhile, had a bounce in her step and the light of excitement in her eyes. In fact, she hadn't seen her sister this happy since she was a little girl when they were promised an ice cream cone after school.

Evie, meanwhile, tried hard not to be cranky even though her sister's sunny disposition was raking on her last nerves.

As they wandered through Old Town, Evie's mood lifted. Though she still felt like death warmed over, she managed to make the best of it and ignore the gushing between Bruce and Chloe.

They navigated the throngs of people headed to the shops and up the Royal Mile to visit Edinburgh Castle. It was a highlight when she spotted the castle rising up at the top of the hill. A piper stood on one side playing his pipes. People dropped both dollars and pounds as well as coins into the case in front of him.

They passed St. Giles' Cathedral as they made their way down High Street. She spied a small shop between a cigar merchant and a shop specializing in cashmere and lambswool that caught her attention. The name, Mystic Treasures, was in gold letters over the door. Her heart started to beat at a rapid pace. Something told her she had to go in there.

"I'm famished," Chloe said. "Let's grab some lunch. What do you say, Evie?"

But she was staring at the small shop with her heart in her throat. Such a strange reaction.

"Evie?" Her sister nudged her.

"Yes, of course," she said. "You two go ahead. I'll catch up."

"Are ye sure, lass?" Bruce asked.

She focused on his face, trying desperately to ignore the pull of the shop across the street. She managed a smile. "I'm sure. I want to look at something and then I'll meet you after."

"We're in no hurry," Chloe said, clutching his arm. "We'll come with you."

Irritation clawed through her, though she couldn't explain why. "No, you go on. I'll only be a moment."

Without waiting for a reply, she dashed across the street, leaving them behind. As she hurried away, her phone vibrated. A quick glance at the screen showed her a message from Chloe telling her where they would be. She stuffed the phone back into her pocket and pushed open the door.

The tiny bell tinkled, announcing her arrival. As soon as she was inside with the door closing behind her, she realized she was in a narrow antique store. She stood there a moment as her eyes took in the small shop. It was crammed full with all sorts of trinkets, furniture, and the like.

Why was she drawn to this shop? She had no explanation for it other than her feet moved her as though they had a mind of their own, pulling her closer and deeper inside. A faint tug in the center of her chest urged her forward. Something about the place called to her. It made no sense. Yet, here she was, standing at the entrance with her heart pounding in strange anticipation.

The air was warm and scented with the faint, comforting

blend of lavender and old wood. The quiet hum of distant chatter and soft music wrapped around her in a gentle embrace. The weight on her chest lightened, her aching soul finding a moment of peace within the cozy walls. Something about this place, with its soft lighting and the familiar scent of ancient items, eased the tension she hadn't even realized she was holding.

"Good morning," the shopkeeper called.

The woman had hair so pale it seemed to glow, cascading in soft waves down her back and over her shoulders. Her bright blue eyes caught the light, sparkling with a warmth that drew Evie in. On a second look, though, it wasn't a trick of light—her eyes shimmered as though they held a trace of starlight within them. When she smiled, one cheek hosted a dimple. Though she wasn't tall, there was something about her presence that gave her a larger-than-life appearance that bespoke of an ageless power. When she met the woman's gaze, she sensed an ancient strength beneath her friendly exterior. Her name tag read Moira.

"Hello," Evie said, finding her voice.

"Can I help you?" she asked.

"Just browsing," she said.

Moira looked her over, a small smile on her lips which sent a strange sensation through Evie, as though the woman scrutinized her.

"I know your face," she said.

Evie's pulse quickened at the odd phrasing. "I'm sorry?"

"Clan Sinclair," she said. "I know the look of you anywhere. I knew you'd come."

Evie shifted from one foot to the other, a sense of unease flickering through her. "Do I know you?"

The woman chuckled. A faint grin flickered over her lips. "Not yet. Where are your sisters?"

A tingling sensation skittered over the base of her neck as she gaped. How did she know she had sisters?

"My…sisters?"

She waved away the thought. "No matter. I'll see them in

time. Time is all I have. I'll leave you be to browse."

Evie watched her walk away as an eeriness pressed through her. The woman disappeared toward the back, leaving her to her own devices. It was the strangest conversation she'd ever had.

Evie walked around the shop, trying her best not to disturb any of the pieces. There was an old chair in one corner with a side table that had seen better days, on top of the table, an antique lamp made out of solid brass.

Moving deeper into the shop, she sensed a power somewhere within her reach. A humming power thrumming through her, calling to her. A power she could not ignore. She glanced around, looking for it.

On the far wall was a glass case. She headed there, her senses prickling as she moved closer. Inside the case were small items. Some she recognized. Others she didn't. Celtic symbols such as a cross, knotwork, and other things she didn't know.

Then she saw it.

A smooth stone in an odd shape with jagged edge pieces that seemed to be part of a puzzle. As if it was broken off from a larger piece. On it was carved a strange looking arc with another arc through it, appearing to be part of a larger symbol. Perhaps the missing pieces?

She peered at it through the glass, her heart ramming hard in her chest. She was certain this was the item calling to her. But why?

"Och, I see you've found our most unusual collection," Moira said, a smile in her voice.

When she spoke, Evie jumped. She was so lost in her own thoughts she hadn't heard the woman approach. She pressed a hand against her racing heart but tried hard to maintain her composure.

"Yes," she said at last. "What is it?"

She paused next to her, looking into the case. "Bits and pieces that were brought from all over Scotland."

Evie glanced back into the case. She pointed to the stone that caught her attention. "What can you tell me about that one?"

Her smile widened. "That one. Aye, you'd be interested in that one."

Another strange response. Evie gave her a sideways glance, unsure what she meant. "What's the symbol on it?"

"It's one point of a triquetra with a circle going through it."

"A triquetra?" Her brows drew together in question.

She grinned. "It's a tri-pointed symbol with overlapping and interconnecting arcs. That is one of the pointed arcs." She looked back at the stone.

Evie stared at it long and hard, unable to deny the burst of desire she had coursing through her. It was the oddest sensation, too. As odd as the shopkeeper. She had no idea what or how or why she felt that way about a simple little stone.

The woman turned away and picked up something, then showed it to her. "It looks like this."

She glanced down at the object in the woman's hand, which looked like a pendant. The triquetra indeed had three points that arched and overlapped. A circle went through the middle of it. She glanced back at the stone. The woman was right. The one point on the stone mimicked that of the pendant in her hand.

"Is the stone for sale?" she asked.

"Everything in my shop is for sale," she said with a grin as she replaced the pendant. "But that stone I'll give to you for free."

"Oh, no, I couldn't—"

"I insist."

She opened the case and reached for the stone. Evie watched with rapt fascination as she plucked it off the dust-free shelf and held it out to her. The stone rested in her palm.

Evie hesitated, unable to decide if she should take it or not. Finally, she reached for it. As soon as she took it and the cool stone rested against her palm, a flash went through her mind. She sucked in a breath. She saw the castle and the face of the man—both from her dream. It was a fleeting thing before it disappeared.

The stone was smooth. The edges of the carving were well-worn, as though it were old. Centuries old.

"It looks as though it's broken."

"A piece of another stone, aye. You have the right of it."

"Where is the other piece?"

"Pieces," she corrected with a grin. "Lost. Not yet ready to be found."

Evie looked at her, confusion flickering through her. She didn't understand her cryptic response.

"Where did it come from?"

"The Isle of Skye."

Icy pinpricks trickled through her as a sense of familiarity shuddered over her. Her heart did a wild thump against her chest. She didn't know why. She had never been to the Isle of Skye, but when she heard that, another image burst into her mind.

The castle from her dream. But this time, it was clearer.

Why did she keep seeing it?

The image of the rugged castle was so strong in her mind, it was as though she stood right in front of it. The magnificent structure with its stone walls and imposing turrets was perched on the shores of a loch surrounded by cliffs.

"Let me package it for you."

"Thank you," Evie said.

She tore her gaze away from the stone and handed it back to Moira, who took it and headed to the register at the back of the store. She followed, her mind still in a haze and the image of the castle still burning through it.

She didn't understand.

Behind the register, she noticed a picture hanging on the wall. Gooseflesh erupted along her arms. It was the exact castle she'd seen in her mind.

"What is that place?" she nodded to the picture.

Moira turned to glance at it then said, "Och, that's Dundale Castle. Once the home of Clan MacLeod. It's all but ruins now." Then she gave her a look that pierced through her. "But it doesn't have to be."

She didn't understand. It seemed as though the woman was full of cryptic messages.

"Where is it?"

"The Isle of Skye. You'll visit there soon, in your proper time. Here you go, lass." She handed her a blue velvet drawstring bag.

She didn't know what the woman meant by her proper time and wasn't sure how to ask her. Instead, she said, "I have no plans to visit."

"Och, but you will." She gave her a knowing grin.

It was difficult to stifle the sense of unease throughout her. "Are you sure I can't pay for it?"

"Free of charge, Sinclair. And here. Take my card."

She took the bag and the business card, a numbness skittering through her. So stunned was she by the woman calling her Sinclair, she didn't think to ask how she knew.

The card was simple with gold letters embossed across the front reading *Mystic Treasures*. Below was the line *where the past meets the present* and then her name. Moira. No surname. No phone number. No address.

She placed the bag and card in her pocket and then headed out of the shop. The eerie sensation lingered with her as she headed to meet Chloe and Bruce. It seemed as though seeing the castle and the stone were pieces of a puzzle she needed to put together.

She couldn't wait to examine the stone closer but that would have to wait until she was alone. Now, she headed to meet her sister and her boyfriend for lunch.

CHLOE AND BRUCE kept her busy the rest of the day. She didn't have a chance to look at the stone she carried around in her pocket. Since Chloe's first big gala was that evening, she knew she wouldn't have a chance to look at it then either. She'd brought one cocktail dress to wear for the event—a sleek black number that hit her right above the knees and a scooped neckline that pushed up her bosom, giving her a hint of cleavage. Much to her dismay, she left her matching bolero jacket at home.

Chloe had pulled out all the stops for this event and hired a car to take them to the museum. Bruce had a gig at the pub and was unable to attend, so it would be the two of them. Evie had to admit, she was looking forward to spending some time alone with her sister. Her sister was so excited, she was about to vibrate out of her skin. She chatted nonstop—one of her nervous habits—while Evie was distracted by the stone. She had tucked it in her tiny handbag and found she could not stop thinking about it.

"Are you even listening?" Chloe huffed out a breath.

Evie pulled her thoughts back together and blinked, focusing on her sister's furious face.

"You did it again," she said. "It's like you go somewhere else. You've been doing it all day."

"I'm sorry," she said, the guilt washing through her. "I'm a bit distracted."

"You've been that way since you arrived. What is it?"

How to tell her sister about the erotic dream with the hot guy? She couldn't. Nor could she tell her about the flash of the castle she had in her mind when she talked to the shopkeeper. She bit her lip.

"You used to tell me everything," Chloe said, her voice low as though she might be hurt.

"I still do," she said, trying not to sound defensive. Instead, she came up with an excuse for her off-putting behavior. "This is all a bit overwhelming."

Realization seemed to pass over her features. She scooted closer to her in the backseat of the car and wrapped her arms around her shoulders, giving her a tight squeeze.

"That's my fault. You landed and I immediately dragged you to a pub, then all over Edinburgh today. I should have thought you might want to rest more. I was excited to see you again and I wanted to share this amazing city with you."

She patted her arm and gave her a reassuring smile. "It's all right, Chlo. I know how you feel. I was excited to see you, too. And I'm glad to be here. Truly. I can't wait to see your museum."

Her sister chuckled. "Well, it's not *my* museum."

"It is as far as I'm concerned."

They shared a grin and for a moment, everything was as it should be. The car pulled to a stop outside the museum. The driver got out to open the back door for them. Evie followed Chloe through the gathering crowd to the entrance of the museum where she flashed her badge at security, then told them Evie was her guest. They handed her a visitor badge and waved them through.

As soon as they were past security, Evie watched her sister's eyes light with wonder and excitement. There were no patrons inside yet, and the set-up crew rushed around in a flurry of activity preparing for the evening in the main gallery. Tables of ten were scattered around the room covered in black tablecloths. Workers placed silver chargers at every setting while another group positioned elaborate centerpieces that included pillar candles in glass hurricane candleholders and sparkly floral arrangements. Chloe instantly went into business mode, bustling around the museum to make sure everything was in order.

That left Evie alone for a moment. She found a quiet corner and took the opportunity to open her small handbag and peer inside. The blue velvet drawstring bag rested there along with her ID and her cell phone. The stone called to her, pulling her in a way she could not explain. As she was about to reach for the bag, she heard the clack of her sister's heels.

"There you are! I want you to meet some people."

Chloe hooked her arm in hers and away they went. The stone would have to wait.

CHAPTER FOUR

THE GALA EVENT was amazing and exhausting. Chloe was a social butterfly, which Evie found to be different from the sister she grew up with. But she seemed to be in her element and was so full of life that it made Evie's heart smile.

Still, though, she thought about the stone in her handbag. Thinking about looking at it had nagged her to the point she had to excuse herself from the table to get a moment to herself.

She nudged Chloe, who sat next to her. "I'm going to the ladies' room."

She gave her a nod as Evie rose from her seat and headed away from the event, leaving behind the hum of voices.

All four stalls in the restroom were empty. Thankfully, she was alone. She placed her handbag on the countertop by the sink and opened it, staring down at the blue velvet bag inside with her pulse drumming a fierce tempo.

She had left the business card Moira gave her in her luggage in Chloe's flat. She didn't know why she had even kept it, but she hid it away in case she needed it again.

Why was she so nervous?

"Geeze, Eve, it's a funky little *rock*. Not drugs," she muttered to herself.

She pulled the blue velvet bag from her purse and opened the drawstring, dropping the stone into the palm of her hand. As soon as it hit her skin, it hummed.

Odd.

She placed the velvet bag on the counter next to her purse and stared down at the marking that was worn smooth. She ran the tip of her finger around the jagged edge. She had no doubt that it was part of a bigger piece and that it would fit snugly against it.

But what was the bigger piece? Where and how would she find it?

Evie glanced up at herself in the mirror. She had bags under her eyes and fatigue lining her face. No amount of makeup would hide the exhaustion pounding through her since the moment she had landed in Scotland.

"You look awful," she told her reflection.

Then she leaned closer to inspect her face. Flecks of mascara dotted her skin under her eyes. She brushed them away. Stepping back, she smoothed her free hand over her dress.

The stone continued to hum.

"This is ridiculous," she said.

She was about to replace the stone into its velvet bag when she heard what sounded like gunfire. She spun toward the door, her eyes wide and her heart pounding like mad. What the hell was that?

She kicked off her four-inch heels in case she needed to make a dash for it and tiptoed to the bathroom door. She cracked it and peered out. Though she couldn't see anything, she heard the commotion in the main gallery. Shouts. Screams. More gunfire.

She clutched the humming stone in her hand and slipped out the door, pressing her back against it and listening. The bathrooms were under the staircase, hidden from the main gallery. She crept toward the corner. She had to find her sister and make sure she was all right. She had to get her and get the hell out of the museum.

Six masked men roamed through the tables. All of them held guns. They forced the partygoers onto the floor, face down.

Where was her sister?

There was no way she would be able to sneak out into the gallery. Not with everyone on the ground except for the intruders. What was she going to do?

She had to think. Perhaps she could run around the corner and sprint up the stairs before they caught sight of her. She had no idea what was upstairs. She hadn't explored the museum because she'd stuck by her sister's side the entire night.

With her heart beating a wicked beat, she peered around the corner. The two men closest to her had their backs turned. Now was her chance.

Clutching the stone tight in her hand, she ran around the corner and started up the stairs as fast as her legs would take her. Her thigh muscles burned as she ran. But her tight skirt was keeping her from going as fast as she wanted.

"Stop her!" one of the men shouted.

The thump of boots on the ground alerted her to the fact they were running after her. How many men, she didn't know. She didn't dare turn around. Hope that she made it up the stairs to find a place to hide pressed through her. But then what? Like an idiot, she left her purse and cell phone behind in the bathroom. She wouldn't be able to call for help.

"Evie!" Chloe shouted.

She stumbled, stubbing her big toe on the step, making her fall forward. Unwilling to release the stone, she threw out her right hand to break her fall. Her shins bashed against the edge of the stairs, sending shooting pain through her.

"Run, Evie!"

"I said *shut up.*"

Evie glanced over her shoulder in time to see the masked man shove her sister to the floor, then pointed the gun at her. She sucked in a sharp breath and climbed back to her feet, turning on the step. Sweat trickled down the side of her face. Behind her, two men were coming up the stairs.

But she was focused solely on Chloe. Her sister looked at her, their eyes met, and she understood. She had to keep going.

As she made the decision to start back up the stairs, one of the assailants was on her. She yelped and leapt up to the next step as he reached for her.

"Grab her!" the other man ordered, his voice low and gruff.

As she leapt, the man directly below her wrapped a hand around her ankle. She fell forward again, this time bashing her chin against the stair. She tasted the sudden metallic tang of blood in her mouth and knew she had bitten her tongue.

In an awkward move, she twisted and kicked out with her free foot. Her heel connected with the man's forehead. He grunted.

"Dinnae fight me, lass," he said in a deep voice.

Something familiar about the sound of his voice made her stop. She stared down at him, stunned.

"Bruce?" she whispered.

His steely blue eyes lifted to hers and in them she saw pain and anguish.

"Give me the stone, lass, and I willna hurt ye or yer sister."

Shock rolled through her as her brows drew together. "What?" The word exploded out of her in a roughened whisper.

"The stone in yer hand." He nodded to her hand still closed into a fist.

She didn't understand how he knew she had the stone.

"Och, aye, it calls to us," he said, as if sensing her confusion. "Dinnae ye hear it?"

Fear pounded through her with such a heated rush, she saw black pinpricks behind her eyes. She tried to blink them away.

"I don't know what you're talking about," she said finally. She kicked him again. This time, hard enough to make him loosen his grip on her ankle.

It was all she needed. She bolted up the stairs on her hands and knees. When she was at the top, she crawled across the cool tile floor. Bruce was right behind her and closing in.

She climbed to her feet and ran hard, thankful she had ditched the heels in the bathroom. She ran past the balcony café into an exhibit featuring Asia and Ancient Egypt. She hid behind a statue of a samurai, trying to catch her breath. Her neck, back, and face were coated in a slick sheen of sweat.

And yet she still managed to clutch the stone in her hand. She opened her fingers to look down at it. The jagged edges left deep indentations in her palm where she'd held it tight. The stone still hummed.

Was that the stone calling to him? Is that what he meant?

"Evie?" he called.

She stopped breathing.

"Come on, lassie. Dinnae make this more difficult than it has to be."

She had to do something before he found her. The problem was if she moved, she would be out in the open. He'd see her. Then he would be on her in an instant.

The humming got louder. She glanced down at the stone, wishing it would stop. Then she noticed something odd. The lines of the triquetra had started to glow.

Unbidden, the image of Dundale Castle burst through her mind. An urging pounded through her to touch the stone. To swipe her finger over the marking.

"Found ye." Bruce was next to her, a gun pointed at her. He held his other hand out to her. "Hand it over, lass."

"I don't think so."

Her thumb swiped over the stone and the next thing she knew it was as though the floor dropped out from under her feet and she went tumbling, tumbling, tumbling through the air. Thankfully, she had managed to close her hand around the stone. As she fell, the air was sucked out from her lungs and a burning sensation took up there. She was suffocating, as though she were underwater trying to breathe. Her lungs were being crushed by a weight she did not understand.

Then everything went black.

CHAPTER FIVE

"CALLUM! YE BEST come quickly, lad!"

Callum halted his swing of the sword when his father shouted. Sweat glistened on his upper torso, his breath see-sawing in and out as he paused his training with his brother to turn. His father, Hamish, hurried toward him.

"What is it, Da?" Alarm went through him when he saw the fear etched on his da's aged face.

He paused to catch his breath. "I cannae explain. Ye must come quickly." He waved him to follow.

"Ye best go, brother," Malcolm said, holding his sword against his side.

Callum dropped his weapon where he stood, then reached for his discarded tunic, pulling it on over his head. He followed his da from the courtyard through the castle gates. Hamish hurried ahead of him favoring his left leg. The limp had grown more pronounced over the last few years. An old war wound that never healed properly. Callum saw nothing ahead and wondered if his da had gone daft.

Finally, he halted, peering down at something on the ground. When Callum stopped next to him, he was shocked to see a woman lying unconscious in the grass. Her legs and feet were bare, her arms outstretched, and her face turned to one side.

Something shifted through him as he looked at her. He had seen her before...in a dream. A sense of familiarity was like a crashing wave through him.

But it couldn't be. It didn't seem possible the woman of his dreams was here in the flesh.

"'Tis a lassie," Callum said, a bit dumbfounded.

"Aye. Ye noticed, did ye?"

"Where did she come from?"

Hamish's eyes held a curious gleam. "Och, laddie, did ye no see the flash? The prophecy has come true."

Callum had never believed in the prophecy and snorted derision. He tipped his head to the side as he looked at his da.

"Ye ken I dinnae believe that. 'Tis no but codswallop."

Hamish frowned his annoyance. "I saw it with me own eyes. Like in the tale of the Shattering. While ye were practicing, the flash ripped the sky in two. I watched the lassie as she fell. I thought she was dead. I dinnae ken how she survived the fall. Look there." He pointed to her hand.

"What is it?" Callum kneeled in the grass next to her to get a closer look.

Resting in her palm was a small stone, her flesh red and angry with the imprint of the curved marking. The jagged piece of stone rested against her hand, her fingers open and limp around it. It looked as though she had clutched it so tight, it left deep indentations on her palm as well as the imprint from the stone itself.

Her clothes were odd. The black garment she wore barely covered her arse. Her long legs were smooth and her feet bare. Her skin was the color of the moon. She had a shock of red-and-gold hair splayed out behind her. A fair lovely lass, to be sure.

But the stone was of the most interest to him.

"I think it's the verra keystone we are to protect."

As Callum looked closer, he saw the jagged edges. "But it's no the whole stone."

Hamish shook his head. "Doesna matter. It is the stone foretold to come to us."

"But a piece of the stone?" He shook his head, still unconvinced. "Who is she? Where did she get it?"

"I dinnae ken," Hamish said, sounding as perplexed as he felt. "Do ye believe the prophecy now, laddie?"

"I think the better question is *how* did she get it?" Malcolm said.

He joined them and stood next to his da, his fisted hands on his hips. He'd donned his tunic, which was damp from their workout. He gazed down at the lass with interest.

"A fair question, lad. 'Tis clear she time traveled here," Hamish said. "By the looks of her garment, mayhap from the future."

Callum looked up at his father. "The future? But how?"

"Why else would she be here?" He waved his hand to encompass their land. "She has a piece of the keystone. A piece we were promised we'd have."

Callum shook his head and scoffed. "'Tis a farce."

"I ken ye dinnae believe it, but ye must," his da insisted.

"Mayhap argue about that later. We best no leave her here," Malcolm said.

"No, we cannae leave the wee lassie here," Hamish agreed.

"No, we cannae," Callum agreed.

"What do ye suggest, brother?" Malcolm said.

"Take her to the keep," his da said, as if that were the most obvious thing to do.

Callum rose to his full height, still gazing down at the sleeping lass. "Are ye half mad, Da? If we bring her to the keep, then she becomes our responsibility."

"So, ye mean to leave her here in the field?" he asked. He clucked his tongue.

"Well, brother, if yer no goin' to pick her up and take her to the keep, I will." Malcolm thumbed at his chest. There was a glint of mirth in his brother's eyes as though he were goading him to take her. He started to lean down when Callum grabbed his arm and stopped him.

"I'll do it."

Malcolm chuckled as Callum once again kneeled down. He

took the stone from her hand and placed it in his sporran. He scooped her into his arms, cradling her against his chest. Her head lolled against him. He noticed a gash on her chin. Freckles dotted her nose and cheeks. Her breathing was shallow. Her skin was cold and clammy.

"We best get her inside. She's cold," he said.

The lass was light in his arms as he carried her back to the keep. His da and brother were right behind him.

"I'll put her in my chamber," Callum said. "She'll be safest there. Send for Dougal."

He charged inside and headed up the curved staircase to his bedchamber. He kicked the door closed to keep the others out until the healer arrived. Then he placed her gently on the bed. As he did so, he noticed the bruises along her shins. What had happened to her? He reached for the thick coverlet, pulling it over her. She made not a sound as she slept on.

He stared down at her, wondering where she got a piece of the keystone. It was also called the Chronos Stone, at least according to the Triple Goddess. He wasn't one to believe in that *or* the existence of the Triple Goddess. The idea of an all-powerful stone that had mystical abilities to control time seemed like far too much madness.

Yet here was this mysterious lass holding the piece promised to come to him.

Well, not him personally. His clan—Clan MacLeod.

Or so his da had told them.

What were the words of the prophecy? Something about MacLeod blood guarding the stone. He couldn't recall, though his da touted it whenever he had the chance. He'd heard the story as he grew up and yet he never believed in it.

He pushed away those thoughts, though. It seemed senseless to continue to dwell on them.

Now that he was alone with her, it gave him time to look her over without his brother or da hovering. The bruises and cut along her chin, as well as the contusions blooming color on her shins, made him think she'd run from something…or someone. As though she ran from something or someone and took a tumble. But from who and why? He hoped when she awoke, she'd be able to tell him the answer.

Even looking at her now, that strange sense he had seen her before wafted through him. Unbidden, remnants of a dream flickered through his mind. A dream in which a lass with fiery red hair, golden strands shining in the candlelight, climbed into his lap. It had seemed so real at the time when he awoke, he thought for sure she was in his bed. Disappointment flooded him when he realized he was alone.

Remembering the stone, he removed it from his sporran to get a good look at it. When he first saw it nestled in her hand, he'd noticed the carved engraving. Now that he held it, he was able to get a better look at it and see it was part of a triquetra with the arc of a circle going through the top of it.

He cut her another glance. Was she from the future?

Could this be part of the keystone that represented all of time?

She shifted on the bed with a faint moan.

He pocketed the stone once again as a knock sounded on his door. He pulled it open and welcomed Dougal, the healer and their steward, inside.

"Dougal," he greeted.

"I hear ye have a visitor, Callum." He shot him a grin as he entered the bedchamber, then halted when he saw the sleeping woman on the bed. "Aye, a fair bonnie lass."

Impatience bubbled through him and a sudden sense of possessiveness. "Get to it."

He chuckled as he moved closer to the side of the bed to check her over. As he reached for her, her eyes flew open. She sat up and screamed.

WHEN EVIE OPENED her eyes, the first thing she saw was a scruffy man with long, tangled hair leaning down toward her. Panic surged through her. Before she could think, a yelp tore through her throat as she scrambled back away from him.

It was then she realized she was in an oversized bed with four posts covered in thick velvet curtains. She moved backward on the soft mattress that felt as though it were stuffed with feathers to get away from the intruder.

"Stay back!" she warned.

"Och, lass, I mean ye no harm."

His thick Scottish brogue made her realize she was still in Scotland. She glanced around the room, though she didn't recognize it. The last thing she recalled was being in the museum and hunted by Bruce MacDonald.

A second man shoved the first out of the way. "Move aside, Dougal. Ye scared the poor wee lass."

As soon as she saw him, she sucked in a sharp breath. His sharp blue eyes met hers. A moment of recognition pounded through her. The strange dream she had of the man by the fire flared bright in her mind. She was certain this was the man she saw in her dreams.

He stood at the side of the bed with his hands up as if in surrender. "We're no goin to hurt ye, lass. What's yer name?"

She looked from him to the man he called Dougal and back again. "Evie. Evie Sinclair."

"Well, Evie Sinclair, welcome to Dundale."

Words escaped her as her mind shut down. No, that wasn't possible. She was in Edinburgh at a museum with her sister.

Her sister! Where was Chloe?

She shoved aside the thick blanket that covered her and leapt from the bed on the opposite side of the man.

"Chloe." Her sister's name came out on a choke.

"Take it easy, lass," the man said. "Yer no fit to be walking."

As soon as she took her first step, her leg gave out and she tumbled to the stone flooring. She cried out when she rapped her elbow against the floor. The man was at her side in an instant, kneeling down in front of her with a concerned look in those gorgeous blue eyes.

"Are ye hurt?"

She gripped her elbow. "Who are you?"

"Callum," he said. "Callum MacLeod."

Moira's words came back to her then. Dundale was home to Clan MacLeod. But how did she end up here?

"Ye best let me have a look at her," the other man said.

Callum waved him off. "Give us a minute."

Nodding, Dougal shuffled from the room, closing the door behind him.

Callum turned his attention back to her. "I'm fair worried about ye. Ye took a rough tumble."

"It's not the first time I've fallen out of bed," she said.

The corner of his mouth lifted in a grin. "I no mean that, lass. I mean ye fell from the sky."

Hot pinpricks went over her as she stared at him. "I fell from the sky? How?"

"It doesna seem possible to me, either, lass. But my da insists ye fell from the sky and are from the future."

He sounded as though he didn't believe that she was from the future. But looking at him in his sweat stained tunic and dirty breeches told her she was no longer in her own time. He was unlike any man she had met. Tall, ruggedly handsome, with muscular biceps straining against the material of his shirt.

Her stomach clenched into a tight knot. She didn't want to believe it herself, but then, it was clear she was no longer in the museum. Her mind raced, trying to remember the last thing she did. Everything was a bit fuzzy, though. Running through the museum, trying to escape Bruce. The way he grabbed her by the ankle. She had kicked him and scrambled up the stairs.

She had the stone.

She glanced down at her hand where the dark red imprint was. Had the stone transported her back in time?

She found her voice at last. "I'm in the…past?"

"It seems so, lass," Callum replied, his tone calm and patient.

"What year is it then?" she demanded.

"'Tis the year 1357."

She had no response to that. Upon hearing she had landed in the fourteenth century, she did the only sensible thing. She fainted straightaway.

CHAPTER SIX

"GOD'S TEETH," CALLUM said under his breath.

Mayhap he should not have told her she was from the future. He, himself, wasn't certain about that.

If she was able to get out of the bed, it was clear she had no broken bones. How she fell from the sky and landed all in one piece, he had no idea. She was one lucky little lass. With a sigh, he scooped her off the floor and into his arms once more. He moved to the bed and placed her on it.

Rather than leave her alone in the bed, this time, he climbed in next to her, pulling her to him and holding her shivering body close. Her teeth chattered. Much to his surprise and delight, she snuggled closer. He stroked the length of her hair, watching as the light shone through the red-and-golden strands.

He admired her delicate features. High cheekbones, long lashes brushing the edges of her upper cheeks. Her nose and cheeks were covered in a smattering of freckles, as if she was sun kissed. Heart shaped lips beckoned for attention. A bonnie lass, to be sure, and one who had elicited an immediate reaction, making him wonder what was wrong with him.

Nothing. Nothing was wrong with him. As he held her close and that remembered dream drifted through his mind again, he was certain she was the one.

Evie. She said her name was Evie Sinclair.

Of Clan Sinclair? Despite what his da said, he was unconvinced she fell from the sky and simply appeared. The Sinclairs had a stronghold not far from their own Dundale Castle. But even so, why was she alone? Did she run away from the keep? Was she lost?

Mayhap he would return her to her clan when she was able to travel. The laird of Sinclair would want to know she was safe.

She was soft and delicate. All skin and bones.

Not for the first time, he wondered what had happened to her chin and shins. It was difficult for him to push aside the overwhelming feeling he had seen her before. As though he knew her. As though they were connected.

An odd feeling, that.

A sigh escaped her as she shifted against him. One smooth leg rubbed against his. Though she didn't mean for it to, it sent a sensation of arousal through him.

Och, now was not the time for that.

The right thing to do was release her, get out of the bed, and tuck her under the thick coverlet. When he tried to pry her from his arms, she tightened her grip on him, as though he were a lifeline and her salvation.

"Don't leave me," she whispered.

He continued to stroke her hair as much to soothe her as himself.

"That feels nice," she muttered.

His hand halted.

"Oh, please don't stop."

He swept his hand over her cheek, letting strands of her silken hair sluice through his fingers and fall through like a fiery waterfall.

She moved from him then, lifting herself up to look at him. Their eyes met. His heart drummed a dangerous cadence before settling back down to a normal pace. Aye, he was certain he had seen her face before in a dream not so long ago.

Her eyes were a deep brown. There was a gold fleck near the pupil of her right eye. That was something he hadn't noticed before. Question was deep in her gaze, as well as a longing and vitality he hadn't seen in a lass before. Her hand with long, slender fingers pressed against his chest, her palm cool against the heat of his skin.

"I'm sorry I fainted," she finally said.

"'Tis the second time I've had ye in my arms." He grinned, despite himself. He tried hard to keep his emotions in check. But there was something about her he couldn't resist.

She flushed, her cheeks turning a pale pink before she looked away. She slipped out of his arms, scooting away from him. When she moved, he had an empty feeling.

She held up her palm with the red mark from the stone. She traced the outline with the forefinger on her other hand.

"We found ye in the field. 'Twas the stone that did that," he said.

"I know," she said on a breath. She closed her hand into a fist. "I seem to have lost it."

"Nay." He reached into his sporran and held it out to her.

She stared at it a long moment, her gaze fixed on it with a mixture of anticipation and dread.

"Did that bring me here?" she asked.

"My da thinks it did, aye. But he believes in the myth."

"The myth? About the stone?" Her brows—a deeper shade than her hair—drew together in question.

He took a deep breath, expelled it. How would he be able to explain the truth of it? While his da believed the tale of the Shattering, Callum wasn't so sure. Telling the lassie the tale might make him sound like a madman. Still, the story would have to be told. Would she believe there was one all-powerful stone that controlled both their destinies and all of Time?

Before he answered, he heard the deep growl of her stomach. She flushed, pressing her hand against it and turned her back to him. She slipped to the edge of the bed and made to bolt from it.

"Sorry about that," she muttered.

"Mayhap I find ye some decent clothes and feed ye."

She looked at him over her shoulder. "Decent clothes?"

"Ye cannae be wandering the keep in that." He waved a finger at her black garment.

"Oh," she said on a breath and glanced down.

She smoothed her hands down the length of her body, which did nothing good to him. His blood heated and he was glad she wasn't pressed against him, or she would understand clearly how much she affected him.

"I suppose not."

She raked her hands through her tangled locks. A sense of calm came over her. She seemed to have grasped being here with him with a clear head and resignation. He tucked the stone back into his sporran for safekeeping.

"Well, if I can't be wandering around in this," she gestured to her clothing, "then what do you suggest?"

He pushed himself out of the bed and stood. "I'll find ye something suitable to wear."

His late sister would have something suitable, he was sure. He said nothing more as he headed to the door and left the chamber. He paused a moment, wondering if she would be all right alone. He refused to let his brother in his chamber to sit with her. Not that he didn't trust Malcolm—but he didn't trust Malcolm. He had a good heart, to be sure, but he and Callum always had a fierce competition about everything. Even the bonnie lasses.

Nor could he ask his father for fear he'd tell her all about the prophecy.

That settled it. He would send Roslyn and hurry.

As soon as Callum was gone and she was alone, Evie sprang from the bed and paced the length of the room. Her bare feet were silent on the cold stone flooring as she went back and forth, back and forth, her stomach twisted into a tight knot. Gooseflesh rose on her exposed arms, and she warded off a shiver. It was cold in the chamber. She eyed the hearth, wishing there was a fire in its place.

What had happened to her? Her mind was still foggy. If what he said was true, and she had time traveled, then how did that happen? But even he didn't sound like he was convinced she had come from the future.

She halted and pressed her cold fingertips to her lips. The stone must have sent her here to the past.

The last thing she recalled was sprinting up the stairs in the museum and running for her life into an exhibit, then hiding behind a giant statue of a Chinese samurai. She was still holding the stone, the only thing she managed to keep with her when she fled the bathroom. Then Bruce found her and…

She sucked in a breath.

When Bruce had found her, she had swiped her thumb over the markings on the stone. As she recalled, the markings seemed to glow. When she swiped her thumb over it, the image of Dundale Castle had burst through her mind.

She glanced around the room, looking at her surroundings.

"Oh, God," she whispered.

Was she in Dundale Castle in the fourteenth century?

She rounded the bed and stopped dead in her tracks.

On the far wall was a hearth, devoid of a fire. Next to it, a chair. The memory of her dream of the guy in the chair by the fire burst through her mind. The man in her dream was Callum sitting in that chair by that hearth with a blazing fire. And she had slipped out of the bed.

She looked at the bed, examining it. Her dream was vague when it came to details of that. However, she was *certain* Callum was the one from her dream sitting in the chair. She had moved to stand before him, removed her nightgown, and climbed into his lap.

Heat flooded through her at the memory. She pressed her

cold hands against her cheeks. She had climbed into his lap naked. And then her mind decided to remind her about how good and solid and perfect his chest had felt beneath the palm of her hand. No, no, and no. She had to stop thinking about that.

And yet, she moved toward the chair. Her breath hitched. She reached for it, sliding her hand over the back of it. It was nothing more than a solid, wooden chair with a cushioned back and seat. Well-worn. As though someone sat in it often.

But if she was here in the past, then what happened to her sister in the future? Was she all right?

The other thing bothering her was that Bruce, her sister's boyfriend, had tried to take the stone from her. He said it called to them. It was because of him she bashed her shins and then her chin. She reached up, running her finger over the shallow cut on her chin. It was sore. Likely she'd have a bruise by now. Glancing down at her legs, she noticed the purple and yellow marks forming.

None of that mattered, though. She'd heal. She turned her thoughts back to the stone. It had been humming when she swiped her finger over it. That coupled with the glowing markings must have sent her hurtling through time and space.

But why here? Now? What was the purpose of that?

Was there a purpose?

Perhaps it was merely a coincidence she ended up here in this time with Callum.

But no, that couldn't be right. She played the exchange with the shopkeeper in the antique store—Mystic Treasures?—over and over in her mind. The shopkeeper alluded to something about her returning to her proper time. The woman had called her Sinclair, as though she knew who she was from the moment she had stepped inside the store.

That didn't make sense, did it? She was born in the future. That's where she belonged. Not here in the past.

She made a decision then and there. She had to get the stone back from Callum and find a way to return home. She had to get back. She had to find Chloe.

A sharp knock on the door jarred her out of her thoughts. Startled, she spun to face the door.

"Yes?"

The door opened and an older woman bustled in. She carried an armload of clothes and plopped them down on the bed, then turned to her with fisted hands on her hips. She was tall with salt and pepper hair pulled back into a loose bun. Sprigs of hair sprung out around her head. She had a kind round face and friendly blue eyes.

"Och, Callum said ye were a beauty. He wasn't wrong."

"Who are you?" She didn't bother to hide the suspicion in her voice.

The woman chuckled. "Roslyn. I try to keep the laird and his lads fed. My husband is the steward when they're away. He also has a talent for healing. He came to check on ye earlier. He dinnae mean to frighten ye."

"Oh," was all Evie managed.

The woman went on as though she hadn't spoken. "'Tis a special thing to have them all here under one roof. Well, all except Jamie." She gave a wistful sigh, as though that was something that didn't happen a lot. "He's off traveling the world after his shameful behavior." She sniffed derision at this, as if she was unhappy with the way Jamie had behaved about whatever it was. Then she cut her a sheepish glance. "I shouldna have said a word about that. 'Tis not my place."

Evie cleared her throat and changed the subject. "You mentioned the laird?"

"Aye, lassie. Hamish." She looked her over, eyeing her clothes. "Listen to me prattling on when there is work to be done. Callum said ye needed proper clothing. I see he was right."

"Callum tells you a lot."

She laughed. "Let's get ye dressed and fed."

"I thought Callum was returning with clothes," she said, watching as the older woman sorted through the garments.

"It isna proper for him to be in here when ye dress," she said. "Now, off with…" She paused, eyeing her black dress.

"It's a dress," Evie said.

"It doesna look like any dress I've seen."

Evie wasn't accustomed to being dressed by someone, so she hesitated, shifting from one foot to the other.

"I can dress myself," she said at last.

The woman lifted a silver brow. "Can ye, now? Are ye sure about that?"

One glance at the pile of foreign clothes on the bed was her answer. Finally, she shook her head in defeat.

"Och, let me help ye."

Evie relented. She reached behind her and unzipped her dress, shoving it off her shoulders and letting it fall to the floor at her feet. Her undergarments were a simple cream-colored bra and panties which Roslyn stared at for a good long moment, making her blush.

"It's what we wear where I come from," Evie muttered.

"Do ye now?"

She said nothing more as she reached for the chemise. Evie pulled it on over her head. The soft material was cool against her skin as it fell to the floor. Next, she handed her another gown for over the top of the chemise. She pulled it on. The material was a heavy wool. Next were thick stockings and shoes. One thing was for sure, she would be dressed for warmth here.

Once she was dressed, Roslyn eyed her hair. It made Evie self-conscious. She pushed her fingers through the locks and realized it was full of tangles.

"I suppose you want to take care of my hair next," Evie said.

"Aye."

She grinned and grabbed a brush. Moments later, Evie's hair was brushed and pulled into a thick braid, pulled tight at her temples. Roslyn stood back and admired her handiwork.

"There now." She stood back and gave her a once over. "The dress is a bit long for ye, but I suppose it will do for now. I can hem it up for ye."

Evie glanced down to see that the hem of the gown she wore covered her feet and trailed the floor. Yes, it would definitely need hemming.

The woman waved at her to follow. She clutched the skirt in her hands and lifted it so she wouldn't trip. They exited the chamber, giving Evie her first look at the castle. For a moment, she was struck by how magnificent it was. They headed down the staircase and to the great hall, where there was a long table in the center and chairs on either side. Callum and two other men were already seated there speaking in hushed tones. They stopped talking and got to their feet when the women entered the room.

One man appeared older than Callum. She assumed this was the laird and his father. His aged face was graced by a thick, dark beard with streaks of white. There was a twinkle in his bright blue eyes that were much like Callum's.

The other man was younger. He, too, resembled Callum. His dark hair hung over his shoulders. Unlike Callum, he had a thick, full beard. His eyes were the color of the sea after a storm, a sea-green she had never seen before. Callum gestured to the chair next to him. Aware all eyes were on her, she moved to his side of the table and sat in the chair.

Roslyn bustled out of the room, leaving her alone with the three men. Three strange men.

If she were in her time, it would be an awkward situation. Since it seemed she was in the past, she placed her hands in her lap and waited.

Who was she kidding? This *was* an awkward situation. Her hands broke into a clammy sweat. She glanced at the other two men who continued to stare at her.

"Well, are you going to stare at me or introduce yourselves?" she finally said.

The younger man glanced away, taking up a wooden spoon and digging into the bread bowl in front of him. The older man chuckled.

"She's spirited," he said.

"My da and laird, Hamish," Callum said, gesturing at the older man. "And my younger brother, Malcolm."

Malcolm lifted his head and gave her a nod of greeting. "'Tis a pleasure."

Roslyn returned then and placed a bread bowl in front of her full of thick, hearty stew. She placed a wood tankard full of ale next to that. Evie peered at the brew. She was never a beer drinker, so having the ale in front of her made her cringe.

But the stew smelled delicious.

Callum angled his body so he could face her, his eyes still on her as she picked up her spoon. Annoyance flickered through her.

"While I do love the company," she said, giving him the side eye, "I'd appreciate it if you wouldn't stare at me while I eat."

Hamish chuckled once again. He picked up his tankard and drained it.

But Callum did not turn away. She put down her spoon and met his gaze.

"What?" she demanded.

"Ye will have to forgive my brother," Malcolm said. "He's no seen a lass from the future before."

"I assure you I'm like the women of your time."

"Nay," Callum said. "Yer different."

She lifted a brow. "How is that?"

It was Malcolm who spoke. "Yer from the future. Ye have seen things we no have. He's trying to decide if ye are from the future."

Interesting. She looked at Malcolm and then tilted her head to one side as she thought about what he said. He was astute to think such a thing. It was true he could not understand all the things in her world—like Internet, cell phones, and streaming music and TV. But she found it fascinating that he had the forethought to consider it.

"I assure you I am," she said, mostly to Malcolm but looking at Callum. "I've never been inside a castle such as this before."

She was intrigued by being inside a live working medieval castle, a castle that had been built hundreds of years before she was even born. Life was different here. More difficult. There were no modern conveniences like running water, or—

Oh, God. There was no running water. No plumbing or electricity. No social media. No way to contact her sister.

Her sister. She slumped against the chair thinking of Chloe. Even if she had her phone, it wouldn't work here.

"What's wrong?" Callum asked.

Curse her face. She was never good at masking her emotions. She always wore her heart on her sleeve, making it apparent to the world at large what she was thinking and feeling. She shifted in her chair, unwilling to tell him about Chloe. Yet she had to find a way to get back to her.

"Am I stuck here forever? Where is the stone that brought me here?"

"The stone is in a verra safe place," Callum said. "As for being stuck here—"

"We dinnae ken the power of the stone, lass," Hamish said.

"What does that mean?" she demanded, her gut clenching into a tight knot.

She didn't want to be here forever. She had to get back to her time, to Chloe. She had to make sure Bruce hadn't done anything to hurt her.

"Surely you must know something about it," she said.

Hamish started to reply, but Callum interrupted. "Nay."

Hot tears pricked the backs of her eyes as the realization of her situation pounded through her. "So, I'm stuck here."

Her gaze alighted on the three men around the table.

"With three strangers," she added.

"Yer safe here with us," Malcolm said.

"Am I?" She fisted her hands, trying to keep them from shaking. "I'm in a strange land. I don't even know who you are."

"I told ye," Callum said.

"You said your name was Callum MacLeod but that doesn't

mean much to me. How do I know you're not some murdering Scot?"

Hamish laughed out loud. He took another swig of his ale and then got to his feet, his chair scraping back along the floor. "She no understands where she is, laddie. Best tell her. Come on, Malcolm. Let's give them some peace."

Reluctantly, Malcolm rose and followed his father out of the great hall, leaving her alone with Callum, the big brute of a Scot who sat next to her, staring her down as though she were an oddity. She sighed and unclenched her fists.

"I suppose you think I'm crazy." She pinned her gaze on the bread bowl in front of her, trying her best to keep her composure.

"Nay. I no think ye daft."

"Well, that's a comfort, I suppose."

"How did the stone bring ye here?" he asked.

She glanced down at her hand in her lap, opening her fingers to see the red marks still there from the triquetra. They'd faded but were still evident.

"According to your father, I fell from the sky."

"That's no what I mean. *How*?"

She understood then he wanted her to tell him how, exactly, she fell from the sky and into the past. As in what were the events leading up to that. She sighed.

"It's a long story."

"Ye must tell me," he insisted.

"And if I do, does that mean you'll believe me? For that matter, will you be able to send me back?"

He shook his head. "I dinnae ken."

She studied him for a long moment, admiring his strong jaw. There was intelligence deep in his eyes as he looked at her, intelligence and compassion and a kindness she had never seen before in any of the men of her time. His shoulders were broad. The tunic he wore was smudged with dirt and sweat-stained, signs of a man who worked out. Except this man didn't work out at a gym, which made him far sexier than the men of her time.

His hair was long with two plaits on either side of his face. He leaned his forearm on the table, which was thick with muscle and covered in a dusting of dark hair.

He was handsome.

And she was smitten.

Much to her dismay.

She didn't believe in love at first sight. It wasn't sensible, after all. There was no scientific evidence that it existed. Yet here she was with the literal man of her dreams.

Crap.

She may as well tell him everything. If she did, perhaps she could find her way back to the future, to her sister. She took a deep breath and expelled it.

"I'll tell you what I know," she said at last. "But first, can I finish my stew?"

CHAPTER SEVEN

W HEN SHE HAD finished eating, she sat back in the chair and emitted a sigh of contentment. It was, by far, the best stew she'd ever had in her life. Even if the meat did taste a bit gamey. She even polished off the bread bowl and tankard of ale. Callum had wandered off, leaving her alone in peace while she ate. Now that she was finished, she took in her surroundings.

The great hall was a large room with an enormous fireplace at one end. A fire crackled in it, emitting a warm and inviting glow. She rose from the table and walked the length of the hall, marveling at the fact that she was in a live, working medieval castle.

Massive tapestries hung along the stone walls. Rushes covered the floor, emitting a sweet smell. She had no idea of time much less what day it was. All she knew was that she had traveled back in time to the mid-thirteen hundreds.

She glanced down at the markings still faint on her palm. That strange little stone had brought her here.

Something the shopkeeper said came back to her about the Isle of Skye.

You'll visit there soon in your proper time.

What did she mean she would visit in her "proper time?" That didn't make sense at all.

"Och, lassie, I see ye finished yer evening meal." Callum's voice echoed through the great hall.

She turned to face him as he walked toward her. Her breath caught. He was rugged and handsome in a way that belonged to another time, another era, another world. Untamed. Unrefined. *Irresistible.*

When he left her, his tunic was dirty and well-worn. Now that he'd returned, it appeared he had put on a fresh one that was no longer sweat stained or smeared with dirt. He had a long plaid that wrapped around his waist and torso with a pin holding the ends together over one shoulder. The plaid was a deep green with faint yellow and red stripes.

She was momentarily taken aback by his appearance and wondered if he was trying to impress her. She suppressed a grin. She was impressed.

"Callum, where is this place?"

His brows drew together, question flickering through his gaze. "This place?"

She waved her hands to encompass her surroundings. "This castle."

He tipped his head to one side. "Dundale Castle has been our home for the last several years."

Dundale.

The shopkeeper told her the name of the castle in the picture was Dundale on the Isle of Skye. Where she would visit in her "proper" time.

"And it's…on the Isle of Skye?" she asked.

"Aye."

"How far is it from, say, Edinburgh?"

"Edinburgh is on the other side of Scotland, lass. Several hundred miles southeast." His tone was kind and patient, as if he understood she would have a lot of questions.

Nodding, she did a turn through the room, looking up at the soaring rafters that no modern builder would have built. This was a marvel.

"I think…" she said slowly. "I think I was meant to come here."

"How do ye ken?" he asked.

Evie paused, clutching her elbows as a strange shiver went through her. "I promised I'd tell you the story. I'm not even sure where to begin."

He moved toward her, his steps slow. When he was within arm's length, he reached a hand to her. Her heart did one wild erratic beat before she took it. He wrapped his fingers around hers, then led her to the table where he motioned for her to sit. She did. He took the chair opposite her.

"Tell me, lass."

"I was born in the twenty-first century. By your calendar, I'm several hundred years older than you." The thought made her giggle.

"Aye," he said slowly, one brow raised in amusement.

She grinned at him. He grinned back. Oh, yes, she was definitely smitten.

"My sister got a job in Edinburgh as a director of the history museum. She was throwing her first gala and wanted me to be there. So, I traveled to Edinburgh to see her."

"I dinnae ken most of what ye said, lass." He looked confused.

This must have sounded crazy to him when she thought about the things she said. She picked out the one thing she thought might be throwing him off the most.

"A gala is a fancy party," she said. "Important people with a lot of money were invited to it. That's how the museum got their funding for the year."

His face was still creased with confusion.

"Never mind. Suffice to say, I was visiting my sister in Edinburgh. I found my way into this little antique shop where there were all sorts of interesting things. One of those things was that stone." She gave him a pointed look, hoping he would reveal the location of the stone.

His face remained devoid of all hints.

"I met the shopkeeper who was an interesting woman. She

told me some odd things."

"Like what?"

"She said she knew my face. She knew my last name was Sinclair, even though I never told her my name. She called me Clan Sinclair and that she would know the look of me anywhere, but I had never seen her before in my life. She told me I would visit Dundale in my proper time. She said the stone was part of another piece that had yet to be found and that they weren't ready to be found yet."

She left out the part where the shopkeeper asked about her sisters. And that Dundale Castle was all but ruins in her time.

He stiffened then, his back going ramrod straight. "She said that?"

She nodded.

He rose and paced several feet away, then came back. His face was ashen.

"What is it?" she asked.

"What did this shopkeeper look like?"

Evie thought back to the encounter with the woman in the antique store. "She had bright blue eyes and long pale blonde hair. So blonde it was white. No, that's not right. It was silver. Yes, silver hair. Oh, and a dimple in one cheek. She seemed young but at the same time, there was something in her eyes that told me she wasn't. I thought she had starlight in her eyes. I'm not even sure if that makes sense."

As she glanced back up at Callum, she noticed his face had drained of color. He remained perfectly still as he looked at her, though his gaze was distant. He was someplace else, and she saw his mind working.

"Do you know her?" she asked.

There was a long pause before he finally said, "Nay."

But something told her he wasn't telling her the truth. She let it go. For now.

"Anyway," she continued, "she gave me the stone. She insisted I take it and not pay for it. And then I saw a picture of a castle.

She said it was Dundale on the Isle of Skye. I know this may sound strange, but…it feels like I belong here. Like I've met you before. But I haven't."

Callum reached for her hand, placing his on top of hers. His palm was rough yet warm. "I feel the same. Like I've met ye before. Whatever force brought ye here, mayhap it was for a good reason."

She nodded agreement.

"Then I guess we best find out what that reason is."

"It's tied to the stone, isn't it?" Not for the first time, she wondered if he still had it. And if he did, how could she get it back from him?

"Mayhap."

"There's something more," she said. "Something else I should tell you."

She rose and moved away from the table, that odd shiver returning to dance down her spine. She turned away, gripping her elbows.

"After I got the stone, I carried it with me to the gala that night. It was in my handbag when I excused myself to go to the restroom."

"Restroom?"

Her mind raced, wondering what he would call it in his time. "The privy?" She looked at him over her shoulder. He nodded understanding. "Once I was in there, I sensed the stone. I took it out to look at it. It was humming. I thought it strange but there was something about it that made me want to hold it.

"While I was looking at it, invaders came." She paused again, choosing her words carefully so he would understand. "I left the privy and tried to flee up some stairs, but one of the men caught me."

She turned to face him then, the memory of it crashing through her. The way Bruce grabbed her by the ankle as she tried to climb the stairs was still fresh. She shivered.

"There was a man. He…he tried to take the stone from me. I

realized I knew him. My sister introduced me to him. He was the man she was dating. I managed to get away from him and run up the stairs to hide. But he found me."

"Ye had the stone with ye?" he asked.

"Yes. It was still humming. When I got up the stairs and hid, though, he found me. He said the stone called to him. I assumed it was because of the humming. That's when I realized it was glowing faintly and then I swiped my thumb over it. The world shifted in a strange way. Then I woke up in your bed."

He stared at her with an expression she couldn't read. Slowly, he rose to his full height.

"The man who chased ye. The one who said the stone called to him. What was his name?"

"His name?"

"Aye. It matters, lass."

"His name was Bruce MacDonald."

Chapter Eight

THE BLOOD WHOOSHED out of his head so quickly he returned to the chair. He rubbed his forehead, trying to will away the sudden throbbing pain that took up residence upon hearing the man's name.

MacDonald.

The MacDonald Clan was their sworn enemy. They were determined to gain more power in the region by pushing out the MacLeods. They had a long-standing feud that continued even after they tried brokering peace, peace that was shattered by his youngest brother, Jamie. But something she said made him take note. The man told her the stone called to him. When his da talked of the prophecy—which he still did not believe—he said the stone would call to the one who would come to help them guard and protect it.

"I fear my sister is in danger from him," she said. "I need the stone back to return home."

His gaze flickered to her. Her face was lined with worry and there was a bit of fear in her eyes. As much as he wanted to give her back the stone, he couldn't. Not without knowing more about the MacDonald and the stone itself.

Not only that, but the fact she had come in contact with the one she called the shopkeeper was a clear sign she may belong in the past. He had to find out why, though. What purpose did it serve? And did he believe that as truth?

"Callum," she said, his name a demand. "I need the stone."

"I cannae give it to ye," he said.

"Why not?"

"Ye dinnae understand the power of it," he said. Nor did he, but he intended to find out.

"Yes, I do. It brought me here. It can take me home." There was an insistence in her voice that was unmistakable.

"Nay."

"Not nay." She dropped her arms to her sides, her hands fisted. "It *has* to take me home. I have to get back to my sister to make sure she's all right!"

"I cannae let ye go."

She charged him, the worry morphing into fury. When she flung her small body at him, her fists raised as if to beat him, he caught her. His hands wrapped around her wrists, and he held her steady.

"You have to let me go. Please."

She tipped her head up to his. There were tears pooling in her eyes.

"God's teeth," he swore and released her. He stepped away from her, turning away. He could stand anything but a woman's tears.

"If anything happens to her, I'll never forgive myself," she continued. "We grew up together. She's my best friend and the only real family I have left."

Och, that nearly did him in. He understood the bonds of family, for he was bonded to his two brothers. He closed his eyes for a long moment, taking in a deep breath. While he wanted to help her, wanted to send her back home, he simply could not. He needed answers first. There was one place to get them.

"Do you understand what I'm telling you?" she said, imploring.

Finally, he turned to face her. "I do, lassie. But I cannae give you back the stone."

At least not yet.

Furious, she grabbed her gown in her fists and stomped out of the great hall. He watched as she disappeared through a doorway, her fading footsteps going up the staircase.

Likely she had returned to his chamber. He sighed. He'd send Roslyn to look after her. He had his own tasks to tend.

Malcolm sauntered in then. "That went well."

"Ye heard?"

"Aye."

"How much?"

"All of it." His brother flashed a grin. "She has a temper, brother."

"Aye, she does. But I cannae give her the stone. Not until I ken what the true power of it is."

"Oh, are ye starting to believe what Da has been saying all these years?" When he said nothing, Malcolm continued. "This shopkeeper sounds like—"

"Aye, I ken who she sounds like. It cannae be."

"Ye dinnae believe it, do ye?" There was a ghost of a grin on his face. "Even after all Da has told us."

Callum swiped his hand over his face, his stubble bristling against his callused palm. No, he didn't want to believe it. The stories Da told them growing up he assumed were merely that— stories. But with the arrival of Evie, mayhap there was something more to them.

Also, it was hard to shake the feeling he had seen her before. As though he dreamed of her. He didn't want to believe that she stepped out of his dream. Yet, he could not deny recalling the dream of her walking toward him in a white chemise while he lounged in the chair by his hearth, the fire blazing bright and hot and wild. Like her. She pulled off that chemise and—

He quickly shoved away the memory. Now was not the proper time to think about that.

"I need answers," he said.

"And where do ye think ye'll get them? We already ken the stories of the Shattering and the Night of Shadows." Malcolm plopped down in one of the chairs at the long table, propping his booted feet on the edge.

It didn't do that his brother looked smug, as if he already had all the answers and believed all the stories.

Even the youngest, Jamie, seemed to believe and would likely tell him so when he returned to Dundale in the spring. Currently, he was traveling with their uncle learning to read, write, and fight. He was sent away after the incident with the MacDonald lass. They needed every hand available when and if the MacDonalds decided to invade, something Callum was determined to fight against.

"I'm goin' to see Da," he said as he stomped out of the great hall.

Malcolm said, "He's in the armory."

Callum made his way through the keep to the armory in the south tower which was situated close to the front of the castle to allow quick access to the weapons. The thick door was open as he approached, indicating his da was indeed there. He heard him humming an old Gaelic tune.

Weapons lined one wall, a gleaming arsenal of death and power—swords, battle axes, spears, and dirks. Each one with a whisper of battle long past or yet to come. Opposite that, armor stood proud and imposing—helms, gauntlets, vambraces, and hauberks. Even the padded shirts stacked neatly along the wall held the promise of preparation. Every inch of space exuded readiness, a testament to their resiliency and pursuit of survival. They were well stocked and prepared for anything.

The room stretched wide and long, the flagstone floor beneath his boots cold. The solid stone walls rose up to the soaring ceiling, at the top of the walls, narrow slit windows hinting at the outside world. The air was thick, heavy, trapped behind a thick, reinforced door. Flickering light from the candelabras did their best to chase away the shadows of the imposing room. A massive wooden table dominated the center with chairs scattered around it, one in which his da sat holding his sword in his steady grip as the whetstone scraped along the blade's edge.

"Da," Callum called. "A word?"

"O'course, lad." He waved him over as he finished with one last swipe down the shiny steel.

"We have an apprentice for that, Da."

Hamish replaced his favorite claymore in the holder as he turned to his son. "Aye, but ye ken I like to take care of me own steel."

"I do," he said.

He eyed the weapons lined up along the wall. Though they had never been to battle, Hamish insisted they remain ready in case the MacDonalds or any other warring clan wanted to try to sack the castle. They were lucky to have one of the finest blacksmiths to forge their weapons and armor.

"Ye wanted a word?" Hamish asked, peering up at him. Curiosity lined his face.

Callum pressed his lips together in a thin line. He hated asking him about the Shattering or the Night of Shadows or even the Triple Goddess, for he knew Hamish would be all too happy to regale him once again with the tale and remind him of the prophecy. A tale he had heard his entire life growing up. A tale he refused to believe. A prophecy he never thought would come to fruition.

"Well?" he pressed.

"'Tis about the Shattering," Callum began.

"Och, ye've heard that tale, laddie."

"I have," he said. "But how do we ken the tale is true? And this prophecy—"

"'Tis true," Hamish said as he slowly got to his feet. "*Warrior's heart and maiden's grace will unite to shield All Time.*"

Callum stared at him. His da had mentioned the prophecy and the woman from the future arriving with a keystone before, but never those words. When she arrived, they would be bound to her to keep the piece of the stone safe.

"'Tis true, laddie," Hamish said. "The maiden arrived as was foretold."

As he looked at his da, it occurred to him he didn't know where this prophecy or tale had originated. For all he knew, his da made it up.

"It isna a fiction," his da said, as though he'd read his thoughts.

Mayhap he'd read his expression, for he was never one to keep his emotions in check. "Where did ye learn of this prophecy, Da?"

A small smile tugged at the corners of his mouth. Even through his thick beard, he could see it. "Come with me and I'll show ye."

CHAPTER NINE

EVIE PACED THE length of the bedchamber with a pent-up nervous energy. When she slammed the door behind her, she hoped Callum would follow her, offer his apologies and give her the stone. Then she'd return home and find Chloe.

He, however, did no such thing.

She took to looking through every nook and cranny in the bedchamber in the hopes he had hidden the stone somewhere within the room. She ran her hands under the feather mattress but found nothing. She looked under the bed. She looked under the pillows. She threw all the blankets off the bed.

When all that failed to produce the stone, she turned her attention to the chest at the foot of the bed. Opening it, she pawed through the linens, tossing them out as she searched. She found nothing. She left a mess of cloth in her wake.

Standing, she bit her thumbnail as she paced the length of the room. She came up empty-handed, which meant Callum must have kept the stone. He had it on his person. She had to figure out a way to get that stone from him to return home and make sure Chloe was all right. She didn't trust Bruce one iota.

A light knock sounded on the door.

She halted her rabid pacing and stared at it, her heart leaping to her throat. She doubted Callum would knock on his own door. Likely he would barge in.

"Come in," she finally said.

The door creaked open. Roslyn popped her head in. Relief to see the woman flickered through her and she waved her inside.

"I came to see about ye." She closed the door behind her. She eyed the pile of linens on the floor surrounding the chest. Evie flushed hot. "What happened here?"

"I, uh, was looking for something," Evie said, floundering for an explanation.

"Did ye find it then, lass?"

"No."

Roslyn picked up the discarded blankets and pillows and started making up the bed while Evie folded one of Callum's tunics. It gave her pause. The man was broad-shouldered. She smoothed her hand over the linen.

"This is his." It was an obvious statement, she realized.

"Aye, it is." Roslyn fluffed the pillows. "What were ye looking for?"

"Oh, nothing." Evie placed the tunic inside the chest, the final piece, and closed it.

It seemed silly to try to explain. She didn't know how much the woman knew. What if she knew nothing? Then she would sound like a lunatic. The last thing she needed was to be locked away and branded a crazy person. She needed to find a way out of this situation and fast.

"Och, this room is freezing." Roslyn set about building a fire in the hearth, placing the wood on the log holder.

Standing still, Evie realized she was right. A chill had set in and she hadn't even realized it, likely because of her frenzied search for the stone. Now that she was standing still, she gripped her elbows and tried not to shiver. She glanced at the oversized bed piled with pillows and the thick quilt and resisted the urge to climb underneath and pull the covers to her chin. Perhaps if she did, she'd fall asleep and wake up to find this was nothing more than a terrible nightmare.

When Roslyn finished building the fire and the flames were bright and hot, she rose and surveyed the room.

"There. That's better. Now, lass, tell me true. How are ye?"

Evie shrugged. "I don't know how I should be feeling about anything."

Understanding flashed over her face. "Ye've had a bit of a shock."

"That's an understatement," she muttered.

Roslyn continued to peer at her as she moved to the side of the bed and perched on the edge. She patted the bed next to her.

"Come tell me, lass, what yer doing here and who ye really are."

Her eyes flew wide with surprise as she looked at the woman. "What do you mean?"

"Och, do ye think me daft. I ken ye are of the English, even if Callum and his da dinnae want to admit it."

"I don't mean any harm," she said by way of explanation.

She walked to the bed and sat next to the woman who seemed to want to comfort her even if she was an English stranger. For all she knew, England and Scotland were already at war with each other. She wasn't great with remembering history. Chloe was the history major.

"I dinnae want to see him hurt," Roslyn said, warning in her tone.

"Nor I. But you are right. I'm not from here. I'm—" She cut herself off from telling the woman she was from the future. "I'm not sure what to do now that I'm here."

Roslyn reached for her and grasped her hand, giving it a squeeze. "Dinnae fash. All will be well."

Hot tears sprang to her eyes as she thought about leaving Chloe behind. Her sister was over six hundred years in the future. If Callum wouldn't allow her to use the stone to return home, then she was stuck here and she would never see her again. It cut her deep to the core, especially after they had reunited after a long separation.

"What is it, lass?" She wrapped an arm around her shoulders, pulling her tight, distress on her face.

She sniffed, trying to keep the tears from falling but it was impossible. "My…sister…" She gulped in a breath.

Roslyn slid an arm around her shoulders, giving her the comfort she needed. She gave her a reassuring squeeze.

"Where is yer sister?"

Evie was uncertain how much Roslyn knew about her situation. She didn't know if Callum had shared any information with her, so she erred on the side of caution.

"It's that I miss her so much," Evie said. "We were recently reunited and when I ended up here…" She paused, uncertain.

The older woman's brows drew together in question. "What happened to ye?"

She sniffed back her tears, whisking them away, and took a deep breath. "It's a long story. Where is Callum?"

"I dinnae ken. Shall I fetch him for ye?"

"Oh, no. That's not necessary."

She thought of the big, broad Scotsman. The first time she woke and discovered she was in a strange bed was disconcerting. The second she woke up and realized she was snuggled against him was pleasant. Thinking of it now sent a warming sensation through her. He had stroked her hair to keep her calm. No one had ever done that before. Or held her so close as if she were this precious thing that was dear to him.

She'd had boyfriends and lovers, sure. But none were…Callum, and she knew so little about him.

"What can you tell me about Callum?"

"Och, he's a good lad, to be sure. He'll be laird someday. He's kind and looks after his brothers. Fiercely loyal and protective of the ones he loves. Honest. Valiant."

Her tone suggested she'd known him for a long time and that she was proud of him and the man he was. Something about that made Evie's heart pound hard and fast.

His brothers, she knew, were Malcolm and Jamie. She had yet to meet Jamie but knew there was something about his shameful behavior Roslyn wasn't willing to share with her. As if she thought it might be gossip.

"He seems like a good man," she said. "As does Malcolm."

"Och, Malcolm is a rogue at best. He's had his fair share of bonnie lasses. And, Jamie, well, he's no much better. I do my best to keep the lads in line. Their sister passed on several years back. And their mam…well, she died when wee Jamie was born. All that's left are the lads and their da."

"Oh, I'm sorry to hear that."

She, herself, had lost her parents when she was a teen, so she understood the loss of a parent well. Even when Brianna came to care for them, she and Chloe had clung to each other, forming an unbreakable bond. It was why it hurt so much to lose her again, albeit under strange circumstances.

"He dinnae say how you came to be here with us, though," the woman said, giving her a sideways glance.

She sensed Roslyn was as curious about her as she was about them. She understood. There were many unanswered questions. Like if the stone could take her back home. Why she was here. Evie bit the inside of her lip, wondering how to reply. She decided to tell her as much of the truth as possible.

"I come from far away. I was…being chased by a man who wanted something from me." She glanced down at her hand in her lap to see the fading lines of the stone still on her palm. "Honestly, I'm not sure how I ended up here. All I know is I woke up in this bed."

And recalling that once again made her cheeks warm.

"Because Callum saved ye from him, didn't he?" She grinned, her eyes glinting with pride for the man. "I've known him his entire life. As I said, he's a good lad. He'll take good care of ye now that ye're in his keep. Ye'll see."

Evie believed her. Even when she sat at the table with the three of them, she didn't have any ill feelings. Not like she did when she met Bruce MacDonald. There was something about Callum, his father, and his brother that gave her comfort. And something about Bruce that made her leery of him.

"'Tis getting late. Ye'll want to get some rest. Let me fetch ye a nightgown."

"Oh, I don't think that's necessary—"

When Roslyn gave her the side eye, Evie complied. "All right."

The woman excused herself from the chamber and returned a moment later with a white garment draped across her forearm.

"This was Abigail's," she said. When Evie's brows drew together in question, she said, "His sister."

She had to admit, she was uncomfortable wearing something of his dead sister's, but Roslyn seemed to think nothing of it. She helped her undress and slip the long night gown over her head. Once she was dressed for bed, Roslyn folded the gown over her arm.

"I'll hem this up for ye."

Evie slipped into the bed, pulling the blankets up and over her. As she sat there, she watched the woman walk to the door.

"Roslyn?" She paused, turned back to her. "Thank you."

She gave her a small grin. "Yer welcome. G'night, lass."

And then she was gone.

CHAPTER TEN

Hamish led Callum from the armory through the keep to the west tower, which was used for guests, should they have any. He wasn't sure why they were heading there but he assumed he would learn why soon enough.

His da paused at one of the doors and then turned to him, a glint of concern in his eye. His hand was on the door handle.

"We dinnae use this room much, ye ken," he said.

Callum nodded.

He continued to hesitate. "'Tis something I've shown no one else. Not even yer mam before she passed, may she rest in peace."

The look on his face made him wonder what his da was up to and why he seemed to want to keep the room a secret.

"Aye, I understand."

He pushed open the door to the chamber. The room was dark save for the shaft of light coming from the hallway. From what he could see in the minimal light, the room was devoid of furniture save for a chair by the hearth and the bed which had no linens on it. The walls were covered with large tapestries woven in muted colors. Hamish entered and moments later, a candelabra came to life, illuminating the room in a soft yellow glow.

Six tapestries lined the walls. He had never seen them before. Callum entered the chamber and approached the first one. He stared at it in quiet disbelief as his mind tried to make sense of what his eyes were seeing.

The first image was of a woman with long silvery hair and bright blue eyes standing on a craggy hill with her hand outstretched above her. Something in her hand glowed with streaks of light shooting out from it over her head. It was a nighttime scene, with gloomy shadows pressing all around her and two women flanking her. One had black hair. The other had red hair.

The second tapestry was of a bolt of lightning hitting the ground in front of the three women as they stood on the craggy hill. The ground was lit up in a bright flash.

The third showed the cloudy sky split in two and a woman falling from it toward the ground.

There were three more tapestries after that lining the walls, but they were devoid of an image. He peered at them for a long moment, confusion flickering through him.

"What am I looking at, Da?"

"The prophecy," he said. Hamish moved to the first one and pointed. "The Night of Shadows. They are the Triple Goddess." Then he moved to the second one. "The Shattering. The Triple Goddess did this to protect All Time and to make sure it didna fall into the wrong hands." Then to the third. "The arrival of the lass."

Callum looked closer at the third tapestry. Indeed, it appeared the woman falling from the sky had red hair and wore a black garment like the one Evie arrived in. But how? How could a tapestry be of an event that happened earlier that day?

"Where did ye get these?" Callum asked.

"They came to me with the prophecy. I dreamed it, ye ken, and then this one appeared." He pointed to the one of Evie falling from the sky.

Callum shook his head, still not believing. "Appeared?"

"Aye. It dinnae appear in the tapestry until she arrived."

He continued to stare at the wall hangings as though they were objects he had never seen before. Well, in some ways, that was true. He had never seen these particular tapestries, but something about them were odd.

"Ye still think it's a farce?" Hamish asked. "Do ye eyes no see the truth?"

He did see the truth, but he didn't want to believe it. Even with the arrival of Evie depicted in the third tapestry, which he didn't understand. He also didn't understand why the others were blank. They were merely hangings made of fine woven thread.

"What about those?" He motioned to the ones devoid of an image.

"I dinnae ken. Mayhap for when the other two lasses arrive."

"Other two?" Callum's brows drew together as he turned to look at his father. "What does that mean?"

Hamish clapped him on the shoulder and nudged him in front of the one he called the Shattering. It had the three women with the lightning at their feet.

"The Triple Goddess," Hamish said. "Past, Present, and Future. The ones who protected the Chronos Stone until they could no longer. 'Tis why the Shattering happened."

Callum stared at the hanging with the three women for a long moment. "Ye ken what happened at the Shattering?"

"Aye. It was told to me. The Triple Goddess harnessed their powers to shatter the stone into three pieces. Two ancient bloodlines. One divine destiny," he said.

"Two?"

"MacLeod. Sinclair. Is the lassie a Sinclair?" Hamish asked.

"Aye. She said her name was Evie Sinclair."

A tingling sensation went through him as he stared once again at the tapestry depicting the girl falling from the sky.

"The Chronos Stone was forged by the gods and given to the Triple Goddess for safekeeping. It holds all of Time itself," Hamish said. "But when the Night of Shadows came, there were those who attempted to steal the keystone and to breach the barriers between the mortal realm and the realm of chaos. Driven by desperation to keep the stone out of their hands, the Triple Goddess made the decision to divide and hide the pieces of the stone, sacrificing its unity to preserve the integrity of All Time.

'Tis became known as the Shattering."

Still staring at the pieces, Callum asked, "How do ye ken all this?"

When his da didn't answer, he turned to look at him. Hamish stared at the tapestries, a pensive look on his face.

"It's more than a prophecy, isn't it?" Callum asked.

"It was a dream," he said. "A beautiful dream I strayed into. The woman came to me." He pointed to the woman in the middle, holding the stone in her hand up toward the heavens. The one with long silver hair and bright blue eyes. "She said her name was Moira and she was here to deliver a message. Och, I've told ye this before."

He flattened his hand against the fabric in reverence.

Indeed, his father had told him the story more than once while growing up. While Malcolm and Jamie were enthralled by the tale, Callum never took it as truth. It was nothing more than a fiction. Da had described the woman in great detail from her silvery hair to her brilliant blue eyes touched by starlight. There was even a dimple in her cheek. Exactly how Evie had described her.

"Aye, ye have but tell me the message again, Da," Callum said.

"The secret lies within the MacLeod bloodline," he said. "When the stars align and the shadows of chaos eclipse the sun once again, the time will come to unite a warrior's heart and a maiden's grace. Together, they'll reunite the pieces of the keystone and protect it, to safeguard it for time eternal. Three pieces of stone. Two ancient bloodlines. One divine destiny."

Hamish's gaze drifted from the tapestry to meet Callum's. In them, he saw a distant look as he remembered the dream of which he spoke. If he didn't know his da any better, he would think this nothing more than the ramblings of an old man. As it was, he knew his father was no madman. He knew his father was clearheaded and would never come up with something so farfetched as this story on his own.

Callum glanced back at the images depicted on the woven fabric. In the low candlelight of the room, he thought he saw the fabric shimmer. He thought he saw the images morph and move as if the scene had come alive.

He shook his head to clear it.

"Do ye believe now, laddie?" he asked.

He was silent as he considered this. He didn't know if he believed it or not. He wanted to believe, but the story seemed to be too outlandish to be true.

"Do ye no see with yer own eyes?" Hamish said, a note of frustration in his voice.

"I see, Da."

His shoulders slumped. "But ye no believe, do ye?"

"I—"

"Ye best be believing, laddie. For the time is upon us to become the protectors of the keystone."

"How can we do that when we have one piece?" Callum demanded, thinking of the one piece he had in his sporran.

"The others will come." Hamish sounded as if he knew this for a fact.

He glanced back at the tapestries hanging on the wall. "Ye dinnae say where ye got these."

"I dinnae," Hamish said. "They were given to me. By the goddess herself."

"The goddess?" He lifted one brow in question.

"Aye. The goddess whose name is Moira."

CHAPTER ELEVEN

MOIRA.

That was the name of the woman who gave Evie the stone. The one she said she talked to in the antique store, whatever that was. She said a great many things he didn't understand, using a great many words he didn't know. One thing was clear, though, she was concerned about the safety of her sister. Her sister whom she had left behind in danger from a man named MacDonald.

Moira, the goddess, was immortal and had used her divine machinations to push them together.

Still, he wasn't sure he believed in the prophecy, even after seeing the tapestries and hearing the story from his da. Even after seeing the arrival of the mysterious lass. The lass he was certain belonged to Clan Sinclair and whom he would return at the first opportunity. He hadn't told anyone this yet, for fear he would face resistance from the lass.

"'Tis all coming true, lad," Hamish said, sounding well pleased.

"I want to believe but—"

"Ye must," he insisted. "If I cannae convince ye, then what will?"

"I intend to take her back to her clan," Callum announced, changing the subject. He'd had enough of this nonsense.

Hamish's eyes went wide. "Ye cannae do that. She doesna belong to them."

"She's a Sinclair," he said. "Where else does she belong?"

"Here with us. Here with *ye*, ye daft bastard." There was no mistaking the frustration in his father's voice.

Callum shook his head and turned from the wall hangings, heading out of the room. "Nay, Da. If she's fit to travel in the morn, then I intend to take her back."

"Och, ye always were a stubborn one." Hamish followed him, closing the door to the chamber behind him with a snap. "Taking her to Clan Sinclair is a mistake. They dinnae ken who she is."

"Taking her to Clan Sinclair is the right thing to do," Callum said. "I willna discuss it more."

He didn't wait for his father to reply as he headed through the keep back to his own bedchamber. It occurred to him as he entered that the lassie was still there.

When he pushed open the door, he came to a halt. Her form was curled under the coverlet. A fire burned bright and hot in the hearth. A candelabra near the bed illuminated the room in a soft yellow glow.

Evie slept on.

He paused in the doorway, indecision flashing through him. It wasn't right of him to climb into the bed next to her, even though he longed to feel her against him once more. Instead, he closed the door and stood a moment, watching her sleep.

Her breathing was steady and calm. Her arm was curled under the pillow as she slept on her side. Her face was peaceful, serene.

And beautiful.

He heaved a sigh. Nay. He was not going to climb into the bed with her, as much as he wanted. He turned to the hearth and tossed another log onto the fire to keep it going throughout the night since it was chilly. Then he lowered down into the chair, stretched out his long legs, and crossed his arms over his chest to think. It was a long day. Made longer by the unexpected arrival of the lassie.

Hamish was insistent the prophecy was true and even if it was, what was there to do about it? He had but one piece of the stone. Not all three. He refused to believe there would be two more travelers from the future to show up to put the pieces back together. It was all madness.

Nay, he did not believe in the prophecy.

It was his last thought as he drifted off to sleep.

SOMETIME IN THE night, Evie woke with a start. Her eyes popped open and she sat up, her heart racing as she tried to remember where she was. Her surroundings were not familiar.

Then she saw the fire burning low in the hearth and the candles still flickering in the candelabra by the bed. The horrible truth came flooding back to her once again. She was in Dundale Castle in the bedchamber that belonged to the hot Scot.

Also, she was hundreds of years in the past. Far, far away from her sister.

Evie drew up her knees, encircling them with her arms and dropping her forehead on them. What was happening with Chloe? Was she safe? Was she looking for her? Was she worried? There must be a thousand things going through her mind.

A shiver went through her. She lifted her head and peered at the dying fire. Slipping from the bed, her bare feet hit the cold stone floor. She shuddered from the cold, gooseflesh erupting all over her skin and skittering up her body.

Pausing there, she saw Callum sprawled in the chair with his legs stretched out in front of him. The memory of her dream flashed back to her. The dream where he sat in that same chair by the fire. In her dream, though, he was shirtless and she moved from the bed and stepped to him, curling herself in his lap.

She pressed her cold hands against her warming cheeks as a flush of pleasure erupted through her.

There was no way she was going to do that now. He didn't know her. She didn't know him.

But she wanted to know him.

Her traitorous mind let the words flicker through her thoughts.

Evie understood it was folly to attach herself to him, no matter how good-looking he was. If she had anything to say about it, she was going to get that stone from him and return home.

But that was something to worry about in the morning instead of sitting on the bed shivering in the cold of the room. She spied the pile of logs by the hearth and decided to add a few more to the fire to keep it going.

Here in the medieval world, there was no central heat.

On silent feet, she padded to the fireplace and knelt in front of it, reaching for one of the logs. Carefully, she placed first one and then another, then sat back on her heels and watched as the wood tried to catch.

It didn't occur to her how close she was to Callum's outstretched legs until he twitched.

She jumped, her head snapping to look up at him. He blinked his eyes open and met her gaze. For a moment, there was sleepy confusion in the blue depths. Then he instantly came wide awake and sat up straight.

"What are ye doing?"

"The fire was dying." She motioned to it as she got to her feet and stepped away. "I added a couple of logs, but—"

"Ye need peat."

He rose and moved behind the chair, pushing it aside and reaching for something on the other side of the hearth. When he stood straight, he held a handful of peat. He tossed it into the fire and moments later, the flames rose, emitting a lovely crackling warmth. She moved to stand in front of it, extending her hands to warm them.

"I didn't mean to wake you," she said, her voice soft.

"Ye didn't. I had a..." He paused, gazing down at her with

something akin to contemplation, confusion, and a bit of desire. "A dream."

His gaze searched her face and she suspected what he meant was he had a dream *about her*, though he didn't say it. She warmed at the thought. She was having a hard time forgetting the one about him.

"Ye shouldna be out of the bed. It's too cold." He nodded back to the bed.

"I had a dream, too," she said, ignoring his order to go back to bed. "I need to get back to my sister."

After a long, quiet moment, he nodded. "Aye, then. I mean to take ye to her in the morn."

Hope skipped through her. "You do?"

"I do. Get some rest, lass. We leave at first light."

Evie turned and padded back to the bed, climbing in and pulling the thick covers over her. Callum sat back in the chair, his hands resting on the armrests as the light from the fire flickered over his face.

"Aren't you cold?" she asked from her perched position in the bed.

He cut her a glance, a small smile playing at the corners of his mouth. "Are ye worried about me?"

Evie noticed there were several layers of blankets on the bed. Certainly, she didn't need all of them. Did she? She scooted back off the bed and pulled one of the blankets off with her. Then she walked back to him, holding it out to him.

"I am," she said. "My mother used to say I'd catch my death if I went outside in the cold without a coat. I imagine the same to be true in the cold room without proper covering."

His face softened. He looked completely taken aback by her gesture as he took the blanket from her and spread it across his lap.

"Yer mother said that?"

"She did. She had a lot of things she liked to say to me and my sisters."

"Sisters? So, ye have more than one?"

"I have two sisters. Chloe and Brianna."

His jaw clenched and his brows rose, surprise flickering through his blue depths as if learning she had two sisters was of some significance. "Aye?"

She nodded. "Good night, Callum."

"Good night, lassie."

Evie climbed back into the bed and pulled the blankets to her chin. It wasn't long before she went back to sleep as hope curled in her breast. Hope that she was going home in the morning as he promised.

CHAPTER TWELVE

THE FOLLOWING MORNING, Evie awoke to find she was alone in the chamber. The fire had gone out, leaving the hearth cold and dark. She sat up in the bed, looking at the empty chair, wondering where Callum was and when he had left the room.

Try as she might, she couldn't forget the way he had looked in the firelight. The way his strong jaw had clenched when she told him she had two sisters. She felt that was significant to him, but she didn't understand why.

Before long, Roslyn arrived to help her dress for the day. She brought her newly hemmed gown with her. Evie was aware of the worried expression on her face and the way her lips were pressed together as though there was something bothering the woman. She did her best to pretend everything was fine with her forced sunny disposition.

That concerned Evie. She tried to push that thought away, though, because today was about hope. Today, Callum had promised to return her to her sister. In her mind, that meant she was going to get the mysterious stone and use it to go back to her own time.

Finally, she could stand the woman's silence no longer. "Is everything all right, Roslyn?"

"Och, fine, lassie. Dinnae fash over me sour disposition this morn. I dinnae sleep well, that's all."

She nodded though Evie didn't believe her.

"Come, now, and break yer fast. Callum says he wants to ride out as soon as possible."

"Ride out?" Her brows drew together.

"Aye. To find yer kin."

"I see."

Though she didn't see. Perhaps his idea was to return her to the place they found her in the hopes the stone would work there.

She followed her out of the bedchamber and to the great hall. There was no one about. "Where is Callum?"

"Readying the horses," Roslyn said. "Ye must eat something."

She motioned to the table where a bowl of thick oatmeal sat steaming in front of one of the chairs. Roslyn disappeared out of the great hall, making an excuse that she had things of her own to tend. Evie sat and picked up her spoon, digging in to find it was instead some type of porridge. Next to it, an oat cake which she devoured in a matter of seconds.

When she was finished, she rose from the table, wondering what to do with her dishes when Callum entered.

He was dressed in a long sleeve tunic with a plaid wrapped around his waist and over one shoulder. The plaid was clasped with a silver pin on the shoulder. He wore breeches and boots, a sword strapped to one side.

"I've come to fetch ye," he said.

"Good morning to you, too," she replied, feeling as though something was off. "Where are we going?"

"I told ye. To return ye to yer sister." He waved for her to follow. "Come, now."

"And where would that be?" A wave of unease shifted through her as she followed him through the keep.

He exited and headed across the courtyard toward a building that looked like the stable. This was her first time leaving the keep. The wind whipped through her, cutting her right through her wool gown and stockings. She clutched her elbows and clenched her jaw to keep from shivering. But then she remembered she was in a medieval castle and craned her neck to gape up at the soaring towers. There were three rising up into the morning sky dotted with gray clouds threatening rain.

Standing there, gazing at the structure, a sense of belonging came over her. For the first time in her life, she felt as though she belonged somewhere—strange that it was in Scotland's past.

Roslyn came running out of the keep then, a garment in her hand. Her skirts flapped as she hurried to catch up to her.

"Ye'll need a cloak, my lady," she said, a bit out of breath. "There's a chill in the air."

A chill in the air was an understatement, she thought, as she accepted the cloak. It was more than a chill to Evie. As she pulled it around her, she was grateful for the warmth from the wool garment.

"Thank you, Roslyn."

Roslyn's sharp eyes cut to Callum who waited a fair distance away behind her. Then she reached for Evie, taking her hand in her cold ones and squeezing it. Distress flickered through her eyes, as if the woman was sad to see her go.

"Godspeed to ye, lass."

Evie squeezed her hands back. "Thank you for everything, Roslyn."

Again, a strange feeling flickered through her as she clutched the material of the cloak around her thin frame and turned back to Callum, who waited patiently. When Roslyn returned to the keep, he started toward the stable once more.

Inside the stable, Malcolm waited with two horses. He held the reins of both. One was a large black horse that looked to be a war horse. The other was a smaller gray horse that was likely meant for her. A moment of panic shifted through her.

"Can ye ride, lass?" he asked, glancing down at her.

She eyed the big beast as apprehension shifted through her. It wasn't that she was afraid of horses—she had always been told they were gentle animals—but the sheer size of the horse was intimidating.

"I've never ridden a horse in my life," she said.

Malcolm chuckled. Callum frowned.

"Ye best ride with me, then," Callum said.

He went to the large black horse and stuck his foot in the stirrup. He settled into the saddle as if it was something he did every day and likely it was.

"Help her up, brother." He reached a hand to her.

She stepped forward and placed her hand in his as Malcolm put his hands on her waist. Callum gave her a gentle tug while Malcolm lifted her. In a moment of awkwardness, she was unsure what they meant for her to do.

"One leg over, lass," Callum said.

After fumbling, she managed to settle on the back of the horse behind Callum. Her gown was not fit for riding and hiked up around her legs. She positioned the cloak so it would cover most of her and keep her warm.

"I'll see ye after," Malcolm said as he looked up at his brother.

Callum nodded. "I should be back by nightfall."

And then they were off, trotting out of the stable toward the gatehouse. The portcullis was up to allow them to exit. Evie wrapped her arms around his solid waist, holding onto him to keep from falling off the back of the horse.

She didn't want to notice how muscular he felt. Nor did she want to notice how warm his body was against hers. She was still unsure why they were riding away from the keep when he could merely give her the stone and send her on her way.

But she didn't question his method. She went along with it, assuming he was taking her back to the field where he had found her to give her the stone. Perhaps that was the best place to use the stone's power to send her back to the future.

He was quiet as he galloped across the field, the cold wind whipping through her. She pulled up the hood of her cloak and ducked her head to keep her face out of the wind, pressing it against his back for warmth.

When she did, he grunted.

She took that as a signal he was okay with her huddling close to him. If he wasn't, too bad. She was freezing.

She didn't even have the forethought to take in her surroundings until they were riding for a good bit. Finally, she lifted her head and saw the rugged mountains of the Highlands and realized they were not going to the field where he'd found her.

"Where are we going?" she demanded. It took a good bit of strength to keep her teeth from chattering in the wind.

"I told ye. I'm returning ye to your clan."

Fear punched through her, hot and wild. "My clan? What do you mean, my clan?"

"The Sinclairs. That's where ye belong."

Confusion etched through her. Did he not believe she was from the future? If he was taking her to the Sinclairs, then he must think she was some intruder instead of who she said she was.

"I don't understand."

"Ye said ye wanted to return to yer sister. I'm taking ye back there."

"Where?" Her heart pounded a wild beat as she realized he was taking her some place she most certainly did not want to go.

"To the laird of Sinclair. Their keep is not far."

Oh, God. He *was* taking her some place she didn't want to go. Panic bubbled through her as she clutched him.

"Callum, I don't belong to them," she said, trying to keep the hysteria out of her voice. "My sister won't be there."

"'Tis the place for ye," he said, a stubbornness to his tone that made her want to punch him.

She would have if she wasn't sitting on a horse behind him. "Callum, please don't do this. It's a mistake."

When he said nothing as he continued to ride on, hot tears sprang to her eyes. "You don't believe I'm from the future, do you?"

He tugged on the reins, pulling the horse to a halt. He turned in the saddle to look at her over his shoulder. "My da believes ye are."

A lump formed in her throat, making it difficult to respond. "But *you* don't."

He turned away, facing forward again. "I cannae believe it, no."

How the hell was she going to convince him if he didn't believe it? She had to stop this madness and get him to listen.

"Everything I told you was the truth." When she spoke, her voice wobbled with emotion. "Why would I lie?"

Again, he was silent.

Stubborn man!

"My name is Evangeline Sinclair. I was born in Dallas, Texas. My sister, Chloe, is my twin. My other sister, Brianna, is ten years older than us. Our parents were killed in an accident when we were fifteen. A *car* accident. Do you know what a car is, Callum?"

When he didn't reply, she continued, desperate to make him understand.

"A car is a thing people ride inside with four wheels. Like a carriage except it's powered by an engine instead of horses. My parents were celebrating their wedding anniversary when they were killed by a drunk driver on the wrong side of the road."

When he heard this, he pulled the horse to a halt once again. "I dinnae ken what ye mean, lass, but I'm verra sorry for the loss of yer mam and da."

"A horseless carriage driven by a man who had too much ale murdered my parents with his vehicle. Do you understand?"

He remained silent. Perhaps he didn't understand.

When she said this, she sucked in a breath and released the pent-up emotion she was holding in.

She hadn't thought of the accident that took away her parents' lives in years. Years since she allowed herself to remember what had happened. The raw emotion that took over her and Chloe as they wondered what to do next. Calling Brianna and telling her the news. The silence on the other end of the phone as their sister processed what it meant for her. For all of them.

It changed all their lives forever.

And now here she was in a time that she didn't understand with a man who wouldn't listen to her. A man who was sending her away to a clan she had never met, giving her away to them as if she were nothing more than a piece of discarded clothing.

Brianna had never listened to her or Chloe either. She was merely doing her duty as their legal guardian to make sure they made it to the age of eighteen. She couldn't wait to get back to the Caribbean where she resumed her beach bum lifestyle, leaving her and Chloe to figure things out on their own. Evie had taken charge of most everything, allowing Chloe to focus on college.

"You still don't believe me," she said when she finally got her emotions in check.

"I—"

"It's fine," she snapped, cutting him off. The anger replaced her frustration as it burned through her. "Do as you will."

CHAPTER THIRTEEN

THEY RODE ON in silence. If Evie didn't feel like she was about to take a tumble off the horse, she would have refused to hold on to Callum. As it was, she needed to keep her arms around his waist for security purposes. And warmth. She didn't want to freeze to death.

Her lips were pressed together in a thin line as the fury burned through her. As midday passed, they trotted up a path, approaching a castle that stood like a sentry on the cliff. In the distance, the azure sea. The castle was a strong structure made of weathered stone. The square building was three stories high with rectangular windows and two chimneys rising up on either side. Lazy, gray smoke curled upward from both of them.

The wind continued to whip through her, despite the wool cloak she wore around her shoulders. Her legs were cold. Her face was cold. Everything was cold.

Except her anger. It was scorching hot deep in the pit of her psyche.

She didn't know what was going to happen to her now when Callum turned her over to the people he assumed were her clan. She had given up trying to explain to him. He didn't want to listen.

If he wanted to continue to deny the truth about her, so be it. There was nothing she could do about it.

As they approached the gatehouse, her heart thundered in her chest at the idea of being left here. Not that she had any allegiance to Callum. He was nothing but a cad and a lout for dumping her off on someone else. She would never forgive him.

He pulled the horse to a halt.

"What's yer business here?" the guard asked, peering up at him with a squint. The sun was in his face.

"I'm Callum MacLeod. I've come to see Laird Sinclair."

"For what purpose?" he demanded.

He nodded to her with a jerk of his head. "The lass here is a Sinclair."

The guard leaned over to get a good look at her. She stared down at him with all the animosity she could muster. He flashed a grin when he looked at her.

"Aye, well, then. Come with me. I'll fetch Angus."

Callum dismounted, then turned to her holding up his arms. She had no choice but to swing her leg over and fall into his arms. She hated him even more than she did hours ago as he caught her, his strong hands on her waist. He held her there a long moment as the guard took the reins of the horse and led it inside the bailey.

"Why?" she said. It was the only word she could manage.

"'Tis the right thing to do," he said, still so sure of himself.

He dropped his hands from her waist, then clasped her by the elbow and led her inside. The guard handed over his mount to what she assumed was a stable boy. They followed him into the great hall of the keep.

"Wait here," he said.

They paused there, which gave her enough time to examine the interior room. There was a large hearth on one end that warmed the room with a blazing fire. A dais on the other with a long table and four chairs on one side. In the middle of the room, several long tables and chairs, as though they were expecting a large crowd. Colorful tapestries were along the walls and rushes along the floor to warm the place and give it a sweet-smelling aroma.

The guard returned with a man trailing behind him. He was tall, broad shouldered with a shock of red hair that reminded her of her own fiery locks. His face was covered in a faded red beard with a sprinkling of gray. Eyes the color of a winter morning paused on her. Eyes that reminded her of her sister Brianna's. There were crinkles at the corners of his mouth and eyes. He wore a long tunic, a plaid over one shoulder, breeches and black boots that had seen better days.

He paused in front of them a few feet away, giving Callum first a once over, then peering at her with mild curiosity.

"I'm Angus Sinclair, laird of this castle. And ye are?"

"Callum MacLeod. I've come to return yer..." He paused, turning to her and motioning his hand toward her. "The lass."

Angus Sinclair stepped closer and looked her over, that wintery gaze boring into her. "I dinnae seem to recall missing a lass. 'Tis a beauty, though."

"She's of yer clan," Callum said.

Still peering at her, he said, "What's yer name, lass?"

She shoved off the hood of the cloak and lifted her head higher, jutting out her chin and looking down her nose at the man who was laird of Clan Sinclair.

"Evangeline," she said. And she was proud her voice was strong and sure. Not weak and emotional like she was with Callum on the road here.

He continued to stare at her.

"She's yer kin," Callum said, trying to be helpful.

She wanted to punch him. Her hand balled into a tight fist, but she managed to refrain.

"Is she?" Angus grinned at her, as though she were the best thing that had arrived on his doorstep all day. "A bonnie lass, to be sure, but I dinnae ken who she is. I've no seen her before."

"See?" The word burst from Evie as she glared at Callum.

"She is a Sinclair," Callum insisted.

"And what do ye wish for me to do with her?" Angus asked. He folded his massive forearms over his massive chest. There was a humorous glint in his eyes.

"She belongs here with ye," he insisted.

"I don't," Evie said, her voice high and taut.

They both snapped their gazes at her. Callum's was full of ire. Angus' was full of humor.

"Aye, well, she can stay here if ye wish to be rid of her," Angus said. He reached a hand to her. "My lady?"

"No." Evie took a step back away from both of them. "I'm not staying here and you can't make me."

"She doesna sound like my kin," Angus said, one chestnut brow raised.

"That's because I'm not!" she insisted.

"Evie—" Callum began.

She put a hand up to stop him. "You haven't listened to a word I've said. Now, this man…this *laird*… is telling you I don't belong here and you *still* don't believe. What's it going to take, Callum?"

Angus chuckled. "She's a fiery lass, aye?"

"What is the trouble here?" A woman's voice echoed throughout the great hall as she entered.

She was a beauty with auburn hair in a thick braid hanging over one shoulder. Her gown was a rich crimson, her hands clasped in front of her as she moved with an elegant grace to stand next to Angus.

Evie gaped as she realized the woman looked like Chloe. She had the same facial structure as her sister and the same emerald eyes. She took another glance at Angus and his wintery colored eyes that reminded her of Brianna. Perhaps these *were* her ancestors. Callum may not have been too far off bringing her here, but still, she didn't want to stay. She needed to remain with him no matter the cost to get that stone back and go home.

"Who's this?" she asked as she eyed Evie with her hauntingly familiar eyes.

"MacLeod claims she belongs here. She's a Sinclair," Angus said.

"Well, if she's one of yer kin, then she is welcome here," the woman said. She gave them a congenial grin.

"My lady wife," Angus said, gesturing to her. "Fiona."

"I do *not* belong here," Evie insisted. "But Callum is too thick headed to believe it. I've told him the truth."

Fiona's brows rose and her eyes widened. "And what truth is that, dearie?"

"Er…" Evie lost her nerve, not sure what to say. It seemed odd to tell them she was from the future. If Callum didn't believe her, why would they?

"I'll leave her in yer care, then, and take my leave." Callum turned toward the door.

Evie's heart rammed hard against her chest as she saw her one chance of getting back home walking out the door. She wanted to cry out, tell him to stop, but what was the point? He was going to leave her in the hands of these strangers no matter what.

She cut a glance to the couple watching Callum leave with no intent of stopping him. Fiona Sinclair moved toward her, reaching a hand out to her and grasping her by the elbow.

"Come, and I'll see ye to a guest chamber."

She gave her a gentle tug to move her but Evie refused.

"Callum," she called. "If you walk out that door and leave me here, then you're a coward."

That made him halt. He slowly turned to face her. The color was high in his cheeks, the first hint of anger creasing his face.

"A coward?"

Fiona dropped her hand and took a step back to stand beside her husband, her eyes wide and round.

"That sounds like a challenge," Angus said, humor in his voice.

"Yes, a coward," she said, ignoring him. "You think dumping me here with the Sinclairs is getting rid of your problem. You wash your hands of me. Fine. If that's the way you want to play it. Be that way. But if you leave me here with them, you're hiding from the truth."

"And what truth is that, lass?" he asked.

She lifted her chin higher and chose her words carefully. She did not want the Sinclairs behind her to think she was crazier than she already sounded.

"You know the truth I speak of." Then she held up her hand, palm out, and showed him the fading marks from the stone that brought her here. "This truth."

He peered at her hand for a long moment, his jaw clenched and his teeth grinding. Indecision flashed through his eyes. She dropped her hand back to her side.

"If you mean to leave me here and deny all that you've seen, fine. But I will find a way back to you and the—" She stopped speaking, not wanting to mention the stone in front of Fiona and Angus.

The silence in the great hall was deafening. No one moved or said a word. Finally, Callum stomped toward her, reached for her, and clasped his hand on her upper arm.

"Come, then," he said through clenched teeth as he tugged her toward him. Then his gaze flickered to Angus who still stood behind her. "It appears I bothered ye for no reason."

Angus chuckled. "'Tis no bother." He made a hand motion to the guard. "Bring the MacLeod's horse."

"Thank ye, my lord. We'll take our leave, then." He gave him a quick bow without ever letting go of her arm.

Then he dragged her from the great hall, not caring how she stumbled or tripped over her skirt. The anger emanated off him in waves, reminding her of scorching Texas summers. She decided she'd rather deal with his fury rather than be abandoned with the Sinclairs.

As they entered the bailey, the stable hand waited with the giant black war horse. Callum turned to her, put his hands on her waist and hoisted her up without so much as a warning. She scrambled to get her leg over the horse and settle behind the saddle. Then he snatched the reins from the stable boy and mounted. Reluctantly, she wrapped her arms around his waist as he kicked the horse into a gallop and they were away.

He said nothing. She said nothing. There was a silent standoff between them. Fine by her, as long as he was taking her back to Dundale.

The sun was dipping close to the horizon as they put the Sinclair keep behind them. The wind was still cold. Her legs were still frigid. He was still mad. As the day began to wane, he slowed to a walk.

"I should have left ye there," he said, his words terse.

She stiffened, unsure how to respond to that.

Finally, he came to a halt, twisted to look at her over his shoulder. Fire flashed in his eyes. "Ye did nothing but embarrass me in front of them."

"I wouldn't have embarrassed you if you had listened to me," she shot back. "I told you the truth about who I am and where I came from."

He turned back around. She resisted pinching his side. It would be so satisfying to take a piece of his flesh between her thumb and forefinger and squeeze. Instead, she remained still and mute.

"We will return to Dundale. Then I will decide what to do with ye."

"What to do with me?" she repeated. "You act as if I'm some errant child who has to be dealt with. I am *not* that."

"And what will ye have me do, then, lass?" he demanded.

"Give me back the stone and let me go home. Then I'll be out of your hair and no longer a problem."

He remained still and quiet in the saddle for a long moment, then swung his leg over and jumped down to the ground. He held his arms up to her and she realized he meant for her to get off the horse, too. She reached for him, falling against him in a most ungraceful dismount. He grunted as the full force of her body slammed into him, then stumbled back a step, taking her with him. His strong hands managed to keep her on her feet.

She wanted to delight at the way he felt next to her. Instead, she was still angry and shoved off all those amorous feelings.

He reached into his sporran, then held his hand out to her. The stone rested in his palm. To think, all this time he had had it on him.

"Take it," he said, his voice hard and unforgiving. "Take it and be gone."

The way he said it sent a pang of hurt through her. His dismissal cut her to the bone. She snatched it out of his hand, turning away from him and looking down at the stone. It was not humming. Nor were the lines glowing.

She didn't know a way to reactivate it or if that was even possible. She had to try. She closed her eyes and thought of Chloe. Then she swept her thumb over the smooth surface with the jagged edges.

Nothing happened. She tried to remember what she was thinking and feeling when she initially swiped her thumb over it. She was afraid and trying to run from Bruce. She recalled the fear pounding through her and the deep need to get away from him.

She tried to recreate those feelings about Callum.

The truth was, she didn't want to get away from him. She wanted him to... Well, what did she want from him? She looked over her shoulder at him. He stood with the wind whipping through his long, dark hair and his thick arms folded across his massive chest. She hadn't realized how incredibly big he was until that moment.

"Well?" he demanded.

"It didn't work."

He lifted a dark brow in surprise and question. "Ye dinnae ken how it works, do ye?"

She spun to face him. "Do you?"

Callum looked at the stone in her palm, then lifted his gaze back up to her face. The truth was written all over it. "Nay."

She closed her hand around it. "We can fight each other all day long, but it won't change the reality of the situation."

"And what is that, lass?"

"That I'm trapped here in the past with *you*."

Truthfully, it wasn't the worst thing in the world to be stuck here with him. Despite the fact he tried to pawn her off on someone else and make her their problem. She decided she was all his problem and he needed to deal with her.

He dropped his arms and turned back to the horse, his hand on the reins. He stood there a long moment, quiet as he contemplated what to do next. Or, at least, that was her assumption.

"We'll return to Dundale," he said again with a firm tone that sounded final.

CHAPTER FOURTEEN

HE SOUNDED LIKE she was a problem that needed to be handled. She stomped over to him and nudged him around to face her. When he did, she shoved the stone at him.

"Fine, then. Take this cursed stone back. I never want to see it again."

When he refused to take it from her, she grasped his wrist and pressed it into his hand. He held it, staring down at it for a long moment before slipping it back into his pocket. He took her by the waist and helped her back up on the horse, then settled into the saddle in front of her. Despite all her misgivings, her anger, and her ill feelings about him, she still wrapped her arms around his waist for self-preservation.

They rode on. As they did, the rains came, falling in sheets around them. When the first drops hit her on the top of the head, she pulled up the hood of the cloak to ward them off. It didn't help. Callum remained sitting straight in the saddle as he kicked the horse into a full-on gallop to get back to the keep as quickly as possible.

By the time they arrived at Dundale, it was nightfall and she was soaked to the bone and freezing. The wind and rain were both bone-chilling cold.

He galloped into the bailey, sliding off the horse immediately and handing off the reins to the stable hand. Then he reached up to help her off the back of the horse. She slid into his arms and immediately shoved away from him. Quick as her legs would take her, she hurried to the door and pushed it open, entering the keep's great hall.

A warm and inviting fire blazed in the hearth. Hamish and Malcolm sat at the long table enjoying ale. Evie halted there, unsure what to do next as they both gaped at her. Hamish jumped to his feet, shock registering on his face. The shock was quickly replaced with a smug grin. Malcolm, meanwhile, remained where he was as he sipped his ale.

Callum came in behind her, kicking the door closed with the heel of his boot.

"Well, what are ye staring at? We've returned."

Then he stomped off to the curved stairs and disappeared. The hot tears threatened again as she stood there, her hands in fists, her hair and her clothes dripping all over the floor.

"Och! Mercy me!" Roslyn exclaimed when she saw her standing there. She hurried over. "Ye have returned?"

"Y-yes." Evie's teeth chattered.

"Let's get ye in some dry clothes, lass, before ye catch yer death."

"My m-mother used to say that," she said, wishing her mother was here to take care of her, to soothe her ragged nerves, and give her a hug.

Roslyn put an arm around her shoulders and led her from the great hall. "Say what, lass?"

"That I'll catch my death if I don't put on a coat or shoes or whatever."

She shivered uncontrollably as Roslyn took her through the keep to another wing, away from Callum. She was relieved she didn't try to take her to him because she would have flat out refused. Instead, they ended up winding through a few corridors until they came to a chamber that was large enough for two people. This must be where she spent her evenings. As they passed by two servant girls, Roslyn told them to bring in the copper tub and fill it with steaming water.

"That will fix ye right up," she said.

She merely nodded, trying to control her shivering.

In her chamber, Roslyn sat her in a chair by a blazing fire. Then she bustled about the room to find something suitable for her to change into. By the time she had gathered dry garments, the girls had entered with the tub and filled it with hot water.

Evie was so grateful for that she didn't even complain when the woman helped her out of her soaking clothes and into the tub. She sank down into the steaming water that smelled like lilacs. The warmth of the water pressed through her, warding away the chill. Roslyn even helped to wash her long, tangled hair.

As she lathered up the locks, she said, "When ye left here, I dinnae think to see ye again."

"I didn't think I'd be returning." Evie closed her eyes and relished the feel of the woman's nails on her scalp as she scrubbed away the day's torment.

"Can I ask what happened?" It was a tentative question, one in which Evie was all too happy to answer.

"He intended to dump me off with the Sinclairs," she said. "Am I that much of a problem, Roslyn?"

"Och, nay, lass. Callum can be a wee bit of..." She paused, choosing her words, then, "an arse at times."

Evie giggled at that. "No kidding."

"How did ye convince him to return here with ye?" She sounded genuinely curious.

Evie sighed. She wasn't ready to tell the tale. She wanted to enjoy the bath, the scrubbing of her scalp, and nothing more.

"Ye dinnae have to answer," she said in a whisper. "Whatever ye did to make him bring ye back, I'm glad of it."

Her eyes popped open as she looked up at the woman standing over her. "You are?"

She nodded. "I dinnae think it was the right thing to do, taking ye off to the Sinclairs. I dinnae ken their clan, though I understand them to be decent, honorable folk. But I dinnae think ye should be going to them."

Something about the way she said that made Evie peer up at her with admiration. "You didn't?"

"Nay. Let me rinse yer locks, lass."

She dunked a small pitcher in the water and rinsed the soap from her hair. When she finished, and Evie was perfectly pruney, Roslyn helped her from the bath. She dried off and wrapped herself in a thick blanket. The woman combed out her wet hair and braided it. She handed her a nightdress and robe.

"I'll let ye dress while I finish up in the kitchen."

She excused herself to allow Evie some private time to dress. She was grateful for it. Her modern undergarments were discarded on the floor with her cloak and dress, all still sopping wet. She scooped them up and draped them over the chair to let them dry out.

Roslyn hadn't yet returned. But she had left her some thick stockings for her cold feet. She was grateful for that. Grateful for everything the woman had done for her. In a way, she reminded her of her departed mother. Her mother whom she missed dearly even more so now that she was no longer in the same time zone—hell, the same century—as her sister.

When her feet were covered, she went to the door and pulled it open, peering out into the hall. It was silent and no one was about. She ventured down the hall and found her way to the great hall where Hamish was still sipping his ale.

She hesitated a moment, pulling her robe closer together when he saw her and waved her toward him.

"Come in, lass. Can I offer ye a bit of ale?"

"No, thank you." She smiled despite herself. Though if she were being honest, she was starving and wishing there was some leftover meal on the table.

She moved toward him, pausing to warm herself by the fire.

"I dinnae ken what happened between the two of ye, but I'm glad to see he came to his senses and brought ye back," Hamish said.

"Well..." Did she dare explain to him how she bullied Callum into bringing her back? She bit her lip. "Angus Sinclair seems nice enough, but I wasn't interested in being left there against my will."

He chuckled, a sound low and deep in his throat. "Indeed." He took a sip of his ale, dropping the tankard back onto the table with a thump. "Do ye wish to tell me what happened?"

Did she? No. But she cut the man a glance and saw the curiosity shining in his eyes. Eyes that were so much like Callum's. He sipped his ale and gave her a comfort that made her think he was merely curious, nothing more. He motioned to the chair opposite him which was still near the fire. It didn't seem to bother him that she was dressed in her nightclothes.

She perched on the chair, folding her hands in her lap and peering at the fire. It was warm and wonderful as she replayed the events of the day in her mind.

"Callum intended to leave me there as though I were nothing more than a discarded garment," she said, trying to use words Hamish would understand. But the bottom line was, she felt as though she meant nothing to him. That she was disposable. Like a plastic red cup in her time. Tossed away.

"Aye," Hamish agreed. "But he didn't. Common sense prevailed."

"I don't know if it was common sense or the fact that I embarrassed him in front of Angus Sinclair and his wife," she said.

"Did ye, now? And how is that?" he asked.

"I told him he was a coward," she said, still peering into the fire. Hamish emitted a low chuckle. "I told him if he left me there with them, he was hiding from the truth."

There was a long pause, then he said, "And what truth is that?"

"That I'm from the future and he doesn't want to believe it," she said. Her gaze drifted from the fire to Hamish, who had a pensive look on his aged face. "I know it sounds crazy. It sounds crazy to me, too, but I'm living it. I'm here. Maybe for good. I tried everything to convince him. I didn't realize wounding his pride would be the push he needed. And I didn't want to be abandoned by him and left to the Sinclairs, despite the fact that they seem like lovely people."

"Aye…" He said it slowly as he took another swig of ale.

He continued to regard her with an unreadable look. Did Hamish believe her? Would he toss her out on her ear because he thought she was mad?

"He can be a stubborn thing. He doesna believe in the prophecy."

That got her attention. "Prophecy?"

Hamish set aside his ale and got to his feet. He held his hand out to her. "Come with me, lass. There's something I need to show ye."

CHAPTER FIFTEEN

S HE FOLLOWED HAMISH from the great hall down a narrow corridor, pausing at the first door he came to. He pushed it open to darkness. She waited in the doorway, the light slashing into the room casting long shadows. There was the faint outline of the bed on one wall, but that was all she was able to see. He struck a match and several candles flared to life, illuminating the room in a soft yellow glow.

Evie took a tentative step inside and took in the room. The bed had no linens on it. It was a bare mattress. Across from the bed was a dark hearth that still had ashes in it, as if this room had not been used by anyone in a while. One solitary chair was beside the hearth which looked to be the mate to the one in Callum's room. They had the same pattern on the seat and the back.

But what caught her attention were the tapestries along the wall. These were not the same type of tapestries that hung in the great hall. Right away, she noticed they were special.

The oversized wall hangings seemed to shimmer in the half-light as she stood peering at them. Hamish stood off to one side, his arms crossed over his chest as he watched her with keen interest. She moved toward them, the first one a picture of three women standing on a craggy hill. The woman in the middle had silver hair and held something in her hand which glowed.

A sense of recognition shifted through her. The woman with silvery hair also had bright blue eyes and reminded her of Moira, the shopkeeper.

The next tapestry was of the same three women with swirling clouds behind them and the ground lit in a bright flash of light. She swore she saw it moving. She closed her eyes and shook her head to clear it.

The third one, though, made her breath catch. She stared at it, moved closer, and reached out a hand to it to run her fingers over the fine threads. The third was of the sky split in two and a woman with fiery red hair falling through the air. She glanced down at her palm where the faint image of the stone was still there and ran her thumb over it. There was a slight imprint on her skin where the lines had burned into her palm.

As she continued to peer at the tapestry, the falling girl moved closer to the ground as if in slow motion. She blinked, certain she was seeing things, but no. The image moved again.

"Is this…what trickery is this?" She snapped her head around to Hamish who stood with his arms crossed and his feet shoulder-width apart.

"'Tis the prophecy come to life," he said.

"Is this…me?" Evie leaned closer to the tapestry and watched in fascinated horror as the image of the woman moved closer to the ground.

"Aye, I believe it is."

A breath shuddered out of her as she gaped at it. The material felt like any other woven textile, yet there was something…*more* about it. It was as though she were looking at a living picture.

Then she turned her attention to the other two tapestries. "And these?"

"The first is the Night of Shadows. The second is the Shattering."

She gave him a questioning glance. He moved to stand next to her and pointed to the first one.

"The Night of Shadows is the night everything changed."

He told her of something called the Triple Goddess representing Past, Present, and Future. He called the stone a keystone and that it held all of Time itself. The Night of Shadows was when others tried to steal the keystone and breach the barriers between the mortal realm and the realm of chaos. The three goddesses decided to break the stone into three pieces and hide it to keep it out of their hands. This became known as the Shattering.

"You said others came to steal the keystone. Who are the others?" she asked, still peering at the image of the three women on the craggy hill.

She glanced at him to see his response was a shrug of his shoulders.

So, he didn't know. But she might.

Bruce MacDonald chased her through the museum and told her the stone called to him. It called to her, too. She was certain that was the humming she sensed when she held it. If she were part of that prophecy, then what about her sisters?

Past, Present, Future. That was what the keystone represented.

Were her sisters, too, part of the prophecy?

"What does this prophecy say exactly?" she asked.

"When the stars align and the shadows of chaos eclipse the sun once again, the time will come to unite a warrior's heart and a maiden's grace. Together, they'll reunite the pieces of the keystone and protect it, to safeguard it for time eternal. Three pieces of stone. Two ancient bloodlines. One divine destiny."

The blood drained from her head in a whoosh. She stumbled back a step, pressing cold fingertips to her forehead.

Three pieces of stone. Two ancient bloodlines. One divine destiny.

If that were true, then she was destined to go to Edinburgh just as she was destined to travel back in time. She made her way to the bed and sat on the edge, feeling lightheaded.

"Where are the other two pieces of the stone?" she asked, peering up at Hamish, trying to control her violent shaking.

"I dinnae ken. Only the Triple Goddess does."

"And they didn't share this information with you, I gather."

"They did not."

But if she were part of the prophecy…then did that mean Chloe and Brianna were, too?

Oh, if she could send them a message to ask! Centuries separated them from her. Chloe must be frantic with worry by now. And Brianna…well, Brianna was living a life of leisure in the Caribbean and ignorant of everything she and Chloe had been up to the last few years.

"Thank you for telling me, Hamish," she said. "I do appreciate it."

"Ye believe me and the prophecy?" He gave her a look of hope.

"You believe I'm from the future?"

He grinned. "Aye, I do."

How could she *not* believe the prophecy? She glanced down at the lines in her palm. "Yes, I believe."

"Och, good, lass. Then ye'll have to make Callum believe."

She frowned. It was a task she was not looking forward to. Nor was she interested in spending the night with him in his chamber, even if he did sleep in the chair. She glanced around.

"Perhaps tomorrow I can discuss it with him. Now, I'd like to sleep."

"I'll take ye to him—"

"No," she said, too sharply. "Here."

He gaped at her. "Here? This room is no used."

"Good. Then I won't be disturbed. All I need is a fire and some bed linens."

The room had but one window, darkened from the nighttime gloom. She would sleep peacefully knowing she would be alone the rest of the night without anyone bothering her.

He gave a nod of understanding. "Ye have to make him believe," he said. "Yer the one who can. I'll fetch Roslyn to bring ye some linens then," Hamish said at last.

"Thank you."

His words lingered—that she had to make Callum believe she was from the future and this prophecy was true. No pressure or anything.

When he left the room, the door ajar, she turned once again to the line of tapestries. She noticed, then, there were several blank ones after the one of her falling from the sky. She noticed something she hadn't seen before as she moved closer to one and leaned toward it. An image was starting to form on the blank tapestry next to hers. It was so faint it was hard to see. A woman's face peered back at her.

A woman who looked remarkably like her sister, Chloe.

ROSLYN ARRIVED NOT long after Hamish left and helped her make up the bed with clean linens. She left and returned with an armload of firewood and some peat to get a fire going in the hearth. Evie had to admit it was cold, but she tried her best to ward off the chill that was seeping into her bones by pacing the length of the small room.

She also did her best to ignore the tapestries along the wall that seemed to move at odd intervals, as if the threads depicting the events were alive and moving. She cut a glance at Roslyn, but the woman seemed not to notice the strange wall hangings. She told herself it was merely her overactive imagination.

Still, it was better than sharing a room with Callum, the cad who was willing to pawn her off to some strangers.

"Dinnae fash yerself about him, lass," Roslyn said as she lit the fire. "He's a good lad and tries to do the right thing."

She brushed the dirt from her hands and rose, turning to face her as the fire caught in the hearth, lighting up the room and throwing off some heat. Evie moved to stand next to her, extending her hands to the warmth.

"I know he meant well thinking he was taking me to family, but…"

It was hard for her to voice the mixed emotions she had. Betrayal. Hurt. Like a punch in the gut. Which was ridiculous since she hardly knew Callum. He had no allegiance to her, so why should she feel that way?

Roslyn gave her a sympathetic smile and patted her on the shoulder. "Get some rest, lass."

She headed for the door.

"Roslyn," she called. The woman turned to face her, pausing with her hand on the door. "Thank you for taking care of me."

She gave a nod and then slipped out the door, closing it behind her. Evie sat in the chair, extending her legs and allowing the warmth to press against the bottoms of her feet. She wiggled her toes in the thick stockings, grateful for the warmth. The last person who had cared for her the way Roslyn did was…her mother.

She drew up her legs, propping her heels on the chair and encircling them, resting her chin on her knees. Since her parents died, she had often felt alone, even when she had Chloe. Chloe was an outgoing extrovert. Evie was the introvert wallflower who would rather die than have to stand up in front of a crowd and speak.

Chloe was her best friend and her life preserver in a sea of strangers when they had to face a double funeral for her parents. And though Brianna was their legal guardian, she was less than interested in caring for the two of them. Brianna was distant and angry most of the time because her life was interrupted by their untimely death. Brianna was clearly doing only what she was required to do.

Now that Evie was divided from Chloe, she was once again bereft and alone. Heaving a sigh, she stood from the chair and climbed into the bed, pulling the blankets to her chin, and finally drifting into sleep.

CHAPTER SIXTEEN

C ALLUM LEFT THE great hall without so much as a by-your-leave and stomped to his bedchamber to be alone. When he slammed the door behind him with a satisfying thud, he leaned against it, his heart throbbing with all the fury pounding through him.

The lass was infuriating.

He was no coward simply because he didn't believe in his da's maddening notions of a prophecy. How could he believe in that?

Seeing the fire in his hearth was out, he set about rebuilding it with the mindset that eventually the lass would arrive, and she would want to warm herself by it. Once the fire was going, he sat in the chair and kicked off his boots and brooded, waiting for her.

Regret shifted through him, then. Regret that he told her to take the stone and be gone. He watched, his teeth on edge, as she swiped her thumb over the smooth surface and then waited.

He didn't want to admit how relieved he was she was still there and hadn't disappeared. Why? He didn't know. He didn't understand his feelings for her at all.

The fact she *didn't* disappear told him all he needed to know. That her arrival from the future was a falsehood. It was true Angus Sinclair didn't know who she was, but he was determined to find her clan and return her once and for all, whether she wanted him to or not.

He huffed out a breath as he slumped in the chair, his legs

stretched out in front of him.

He waited and waited but she never came. Finally, when it was in the wee hours and exhaustion pounded through him, he stood and strode from his bedchamber back to the great hall. His da sat alone by the hearth with his feet propped up on the table and a tankard of ale in front of him. Callum paused there a long moment, glancing around the room and wondering where to find the lass. Had she left of her own accord? If she had, then his problem with what to do with her was solved.

"If yer looking for the wee lassie, she's no here," Hamish said at last. Callum opened his mouth to reply when he cut him off. "And dinnae be thinking she's left us for good. She hasna."

"Where is she, then?" he demanded.

"She's staying in guest bedchambers." He paused, then added, "With the tapestries."

A trickle of fear went through Callum as he stared at his da. "Did ye tell her about the prophecy?"

"Aye, I did."

"Da—"

"Dinnae chastise me, boy. Ye werena going to tell her, so I did."

Silence stretched between them. "Does she believe?"

Hamish met his gaze, steady and sure. "Aye."

Callum cut a glance to the other side of the great hall that led to the guest chambers. He made no move to head that way.

"You willna be bothering the lass this night. Give her some peace for a wee bit," his da said. He dropped his feet to the floor and rose. "Ye best start believin' in the prophecy. 'Tis coming true."

He sauntered away, leaving him alone in the great hall.

It occurred to him the lass may not want him anywhere near her. Could he blame her? If what his da said was true—that she believed in the prophecy and she was from the future—then he was nothing more than a bampot for taking her to Angus Sinclair with the intent of leaving her there. In his defense, though, he was convinced they were her clan.

Now he was not so certain.

Another sign was the fact the stone did not transport her back to her time when she tried to use it on the road back to Dundale.

Everything he thought was true wasn't. Everything he assumed about the girl was wrong.

He reached into his sporran and pulled out the small piece of stone, examining it closely. The arched lines were faint, but still there. He recalled the way she had shown her palm to him while standing in the Sinclair's great hall. The lines were still there. He ran his thumb over the lines, recalling the fury, the indignation, in her beautiful face. A bampot, indeed.

His fingers closed around the stone as he held it, the jagged edges piercing his palm. When he opened his hand and glanced down, he saw the imprint from that but not from the symbol.

She had said the stone hummed and the lines glowed, hadn't she?

That meant that whatever the stone was doing was activated at the time and that's how the symbol burned into her skin.

The impulsive side of him wanted to go to the guest bedchamber and bang on the door, demanding to see her hand. But what good would that do? It would make her even more irate with him than she already was.

Callum stuck the stone back into his sporran. All that was left to do was return to his own bedchamber to try to sleep. He headed there, shoving thoughts of her out of his head. In the morn, he would decide what to do about her.

The trouble was, he was uncertain there was anything *to* do about her.

EVIE AWOKE TO a cold room, the faint morning light pressing against her closed eyes. She forgot where she was and it took a moment to reorient herself to her surroundings. Ah, yes. She was in what Hamish called the guest bedchambers. She was still in Dundale Castle. She was still in the fourteenth century. None of that had changed while she slept.

Was she going to feel out of sorts every morning she woke? Or would she eventually get used to the idea of being in the past?

Sometime during the night, the fire had gone out, but she was still snuggly and warm in the bed. She burrowed down under the covers for a few more minutes of drowsy warmth. She lifted her hand and studied the lines in her palm. The faint image of the stone was still there, though somewhat faded. She wondered if it would ever go away.

Thinking of the stone made her think about the prophecy and the tapestries hanging on the wall beside the bed. Did she believe what Hamish told her? She was uncertain. All she was truly certain about was he believed every word of it. She saw the truth of it burning deep in his eyes.

She pushed away the blankets and slid to the side of the bed and stood. Pausing there, she pulled one of the heavier blankets off the bed and wrapped it around her shoulders. When she looked at the tapestries again that morning, she gasped.

The one of her falling through the sky showed she was closer to the ground than she was when she looked at it the night before. Next to that was the one that showed her sister's face and someone else. Another figure behind her was merely a silhouette she could not fully see yet.

The morning light glinting through the windows illuminated the room, making the threads shimmer in the light of day. So, she hadn't imagined that the previous night when Hamish was showing her the wall hangings.

The other curious thing she noticed were more hangings that were devoid of a design. They were nothing more than plain woven wall coverings that might be seen in any number of places. But something told her there was more to them than what she saw. There was something mystical about them.

Mystical.

"Mystic Treasures."

The words burst out of her as her gaze moved back to the first hanging of the woman with the silvery hair billowing in the wind, the light moving around her in a way that indicated there was an object in her hand that glowed.

Evie reached out and ran the tips of her fingers over the threads and watched them glisten.

"I bet your name is Moira," she said, tracing the line of the woman's hair. "And I bet you are the one who gave me that jagged piece of stone."

Hamish mentioned the women were the Triple Goddess. That they were the ones who were the protectors of the keystone.

As she stared at the design, something in the bottom righthand corner caught her eye. It was the tip of a sword emerging, ever so slowly as if in slow motion. She didn't know how long she stood there staring at it without blinking, but her eyes had gone dry. Finally, she shook herself from the hypnotic, trancelike state. When she shook her head to clear it and looked back at the hanging, she saw something that wasn't there before.

Shadowy figures.

An army.

A knock on the door startled her, making her jump. She turned toward the door, her hand at the base of her throat where her pulse was rapidly beating.

"Come in," she called.

The door opened. She expected to see Roslyn coming to help her dress for the day. But no. It was Callum. He paused in the doorway, his big body filling up most of the empty space as he stood there staring at her from the threshold. He wore his breeches, boots, tunic, and the plaid draping over one shoulder.

She stiffened at the sight of him, then clutched the blanket around her shoulders. "What do you want?"

She hadn't meant to sound so abrasive, but she hadn't forgiven him for taking her off to Clan Sinclair.

"Good morrow, lass," he said, his deep timbred voice rumbling in his chest. "Did ye sleep well?"

He ignored her jab and remained in the doorway. She peered at him with some curiosity, wondering why he was here.

"Well enough." After she paused a moment, she asked, "Did you?"

"No. I dinnae sleep a wink."

That got her attention. "No?"

"Can I come in?"

"Oh," she breathed as she moved to sit on the bed. "I suppose."

He came into the room, closing the door behind him, but remained where he was. His gaze drifted from her to the tapestries on the wall. Surprise flickered across his handsome features as he looked at them.

"The...pictures..." he started.

"They've changed," she said, following his gaze. "As though they're moving."

He walked into the room and stood in front of the one she decided was Moira, peering at it intently with his hands clasped behind his back. She stepped next to him, still clutching the blanket around her shoulders. She wished she had thought of grabbing her robe instead of standing there in a blanket, but there was nothing to be done about it now.

"This wasna here before." He pointed to the one with Moira and the images emerging of an army in the corner.

"No, it wasn't," she agreed.

He turned his head and met her gaze, confusion etched in them. "I dinnae understand."

She shrugged one shoulder. "My guess is they're enchanted."

"Enchanted?" he repeated.

"Yes, you know. Magicked. This woman here..." She pointed to the first tapestry. "That's Moira, the shopkeeper. I'm sure of it."

Surprise flickered through his blue depths. He glanced back at the image. "The one who gave ye the stone."

"Yes," she said. "She had silvery hair like that." She pointed to the wall hanging.

As she did, he caught her hand in his, holding it and turning toward her. Her first instinct was to pull away, but something made her stop. She liked his large hand wrapped around hers, holding her. Gently.

But then he turned her hand, pushing her fingers open to expose her palm and the lines burned into her flesh. She tried to tug her hand away, but he held onto her with a firm grip.

"The stone?" he asked, his gaze flickering back to hers.

"Yes," was all she managed.

He traced the lines with the tip of his finger. It sent delicious swirls of desire through her. Then he closed both hands on hers, clutching her hand between his.

"Lassie," he said, his voice low and soft. "I came to tell ye how sorry I am."

"Sorry?" she repeated, stunned to the soles of her bare feet. "About what?"

"About taking ye to Angus Sinclair. I no should have done that."

"Oh." The word came out on a breath. She couldn't tell him it was okay because it wasn't.

"I should have listened to ye," he said.

His thumb traced the back of her hand in a way that made her knees turn to water. He should stop that at once, but she didn't want to tell him to stop because it felt too nice. And…sensual. Oh, God, yes, it was sensual the way his thumb moved over her skin in a slow, sweeping, delicate motion.

"Listened to me?" She sounded dumbfounded as she repeated his words. "About?"

"My da thinks yer from the future," he said. Then he looked at the wall hanging that depicted her falling through the sky. "Ye told me ye were from the future."

Hope filled her as she continued to stand there, watching him look at the wall hangings. Understanding came into his eyes and though he said nothing, she saw his mind working.

"He told me I best start believing in the prophecy," he said.

She swallowed hard, her mouth dry. "And do you?"

"I dinnae ken." He turned to look at her then and his eyes met hers. "But I want to. It seems to be coming true."

She reached up with her free hand and clutched his other one, squeezing it. "I want you to believe, too. But, like you, I'm not sure I believe in prophesies or destinies or anything like that. However, here I am standing with you, holding your hand. I thought this was a dream at first but now I know it's not."

He released her hand and reached up, brushing his knuckles over her cheek. The sensation of his cool skin sent a wicked shiver through her. Then he dropped his hand to his side. He inhaled a deep breath through his nose, then expelled it.

"Give me some time, lass, to get used to the idea." A smile tugged at the corners of his mouth.

"All right," she said at last.

He released her other hand and walked toward the door. He paused there and turned to look at her once more over his shoulder.

"Would ye like to break yer fast with me?"

Her stomach rumbled as if on cue. She pressed a hand against it, hoping to silence it. "Yes, please."

"Good, then. I'll send Roslyn to help ye dress. Join me in the great hall when yer ready."

She nodded. He pulled open the door and was gone.

Her anger with him dissipated. Even she could accept an olive branch when she saw one. With her heart pattering hard in her chest, she found she was looking forward to breaking her fast with Callum.

CHAPTER SEVENTEEN

Roslyn arrived not long after Callum's departure and helped her dress for the day. A long chemise with a wool overdress, thick stockings, and shoes. She joined Callum afterward in the great hall and was relieved to see he was there alone. No Malcolm or Hamish. She didn't question it as she took the seat across from him at the long table.

Roslyn brought thick porridge, oat cakes, ale, and water to the table. When she had it all placed, she scurried out of the room, leaving the two of them alone with their awkward silence. As hungry as she was, she didn't wait for him to dig in. She realized she hadn't eaten a meal the night before and was now ravenous.

He watched her a long moment with a half-grin on his face before he took up his wooden spoon and dug into the bread bowl.

"Would ye like to see the keep and surrounding area?" he asked.

Her hand halted halfway to her mouth as she looked at him from across the table. "You mean like a tour?"

"I do."

"I'd love that."

Her heart skipped a happy beat at the thought of seeing the rest of the keep and the castle grounds. It was especially interesting to her since the closest she had come to a castle was reading about it in a history book. She never imagined she would be living in one.

"We'll go when yer finished."

She broke the oat cake in half. She wondered why he had a sudden change of heart about everything. Why did he accept her as being from the future and wanting to believe in the prophecy? She wondered if it was something Hamish said to him the previous night, though she wasn't certain.

Well, she certainly wasn't going to look a gift horse in the mouth, as her mother used to say. She was going to accept him at his word and hope it wouldn't backfire on her at some point.

When she finished the rest of the oat cake, she brushed the crumbs from her hands. "I think I'd like to take you up on that tour now."

He smiled and got to his feet, holding his hand out to her with a genuine smile that sent a warmth cascading through her. Gosh, he was handsome.

She rose and walked around the end of the table, sliding her hand against his. Her heart was doing a funny pitter-pat, something she had never experienced before, and there was a curious swooping in the pit of her stomach. She liked the way his roughened palm fit against hers. The fact that his hand was calloused indicated to her he was a man of action. Not at all like the men of her time with their soft hands and their even softer egos. She had a sense that Callum would take no shit from anyone.

What had Roslyn said?

Fiercely loyal and protective of the ones he loved.

She cut a shy glance up at him as he walked toward the door to exit the castle. Stubble bristled his cheeks and chin. He had a strong jaw and his skin was tanned as though he had spent a great deal of time outside in the elements. She had no doubt he did. Life in the medieval world involved hard labor, not sitting under fluorescent lights staring at a computer screen twelve hours a day.

"I thought we'd start with the grounds," he said.

He tipped his head to look down at her. His eyes locked with hers, making her breath hitch. A rush of warmth spread through her chest.

"I'd like that," she managed, her cheeks warming.

What the devil was wrong with her?

"'Tis a bit cold. Ye'll need yer cloak. I'll fetch it for ye."

He started off toward the guest chambers.

"It's in my room," she said as though he needed direction. He didn't.

As she paused there, glancing around the great hall, she wondered how long the castle had been in their family. How many generations lived here? Moira had mentioned Dundale was nothing but ruins in her time. How sad to think the keep had fallen into decay and neglect.

Callum returned a moment later holding her cloak. His face was white, as though he'd seen a ghost. She took the cloak from him, looking up at him with concern.

"What is it?"

"The tapestries have changed again."

"Again?"

He nodded and waved for her to follow. She hurried after him back to her bedchamber where she halted next to him, gaping at the wall hangings. Indeed, they had changed. The first one depicted Moira showing the army advancing on her. It had not been there earlier that morning.

The one of her falling showed she had finally landed on the ground. Next to that one, the image of her sister's face had become clearer. There was no doubt that Chloe was the woman in the design with someone standing behind her, though that had not come clear yet.

"What does it mean?" Evie asked, though she thought she knew already.

"It must mean what we both need to believe."

There was fear in his eyes when she looked at him.

"And what is that?" she asked.

"That it's all true."

He sounded as though he believed. And perhaps she should, too. If Chloe was the next image in the wall hanging, did that mean she was the next to time travel? Did that mean she would find another piece of this mystical keystone? And if she did, what of Bruce?

"This woman...this looks like my sister, Chloe." She traced the woman's face with the tip of her finger. "What do you think it means?"

"I couldna say."

"I need to think on this some more," she said, her voice a rough whisper.

"Aye," he agreed. He reached for her hand, taking it in his once again. "Come, lass. Let's carry on with our day."

She nodded agreement as they turned away and exited the bedchamber. He paused to turn to her, slipping the cloak from her hand and wrapping it around her, closing it tight at the throat. Her heart was a wild beat in her chest. He gave her a winsome smile as though proud of his handiwork, then took her hand again and headed out of the keep into the yard.

"But...what about you?" she asked.

"Och, I'm fine, lass."

He didn't even seem to notice the cool wind breezing through the bailey. He showed her the stables and the four horses. She patted each of their noses while they snorted their greeting. One gray mare in particular caught her eye. She stood at the stall, patting her nose and crooning to her in a soft voice she didn't even know she possessed.

"Do ye like the mare?" he asked, a smile in his voice.

"She's beautiful," she said.

"She's a gentle creature. She was my sister's before she passed."

"Oh." Evie pulled her hand away and stepped back, as if she had crossed some type of boundary that shouldn't have been crossed. "I'm sorry. I—"

"Go on," he said in an encouraging tone.

She glanced in his direction to see him give her a nod of approval. The horse nudged her as if to say she wanted more nose pets. Evie giggled and went back to stroking her nose, getting closer. The horse nuzzled her hand.

"She's looking for treats," he said. He produced an apple and handed it to her.

Evie took it and fed it to the mare who seemed to enjoy the sweet treat. "What's her name?"

"Name?"

"You don't name your horses?" she asked. "When I was growing up, I had a friend who was crazy about horses. Her parents had a ranch outside of town. She named them all."

Evie had forgotten about her friend who lived in the small town that was close enough to the big city to allow them to go to school together. She hadn't thought of her in years.

"She doesna have a name."

"Then I should name her," Evie said. "Unless you think that's absurd."

Amusement creased his face. "Aye, then, name her."

Evie turned back to the mare, letting her nuzzle her again and chortle. "She's like the gray mist on a foggy morning. That's what I'll name her. Gray Mist. But Mist for short."

"Would ye like to ride her?"

That stopped her cold. She hadn't any idea how to ride a horse. She shook her head. "Oh, I don't think so."

Callum chuckled. "She's a good mount. If ye wish to ride, I can have her saddled and ready. We can ride out to the place I found ye sleeping when ye fell."

That caught her attention. "Truly?"

"O'course." He waved to the stable hand to get his attention. A moment later, the boy bustled up. "Saddle the horses, lad. We're going riding. This one for the lady."

"Aye, my lord." He scurried off to do his bidding.

"Are you sure I can ride?" she asked, skeptical.

"There's nothing to it. I'll teach you."

Evie wasn't sure about that but she took Callum's word for it and decided to throw caution to the wind and give it a try. The stable hand had the horses saddled in record time and led them into the yard. Callum motioned for her to follow. As apprehension swept through her, she did.

Once the horses were out of the stable—his the giant war horse and hers the smaller gray mare—he showed her how to put her foot in the stirrup while grabbing onto the saddle horn to hoist herself up into the saddle. It took some doing, but she managed to get herself settled into the saddle, holding the reins far too tightly in her hands.

Callum gave her instructions on how to make the horse go and how to steer.

"Ye can do it," he said, sounding far more confident than she felt.

But she took the reins in her hands and gave him a winning smile. He got into the saddle of his horse, holding the reins.

"Ready?" he asked.

"As I'll ever be," she said.

He nudged his horse into a slow walk as he headed toward the portcullis. She did the same, surprised the mare she'd named Mist decided to follow. Evie wasn't sure about any of this but she was happy to be out of the stuffy keep even if it was a bit chilly outside. Mostly, she was happy to be by Callum's side. He took it slow as they headed away from the keep, keeping a good pace which was not too fast or too slow.

He pointed out the tall, thick stone curtain wall connected by towers that circled the keep. In the stone were arrow slits. Several of his men strolled along the walkway to keep a lookout for any invaders. The view of the loch glistened in the late morning light, making the water sparkle. Beyond that, more rolling hills and rough terrain but it was breathtaking and beautiful. As the wind trickled over her, tickling her face, she smiled and closed her eyes.

He steered his horse toward the gatehouse. "I'll take ye to

where we found ye."

"You said I fell from the sky," she said.

"Och, it was Hamish who saw it," Callum said. "He said the sky lit up and was split in two and he saw ye falling to the ground. 'Tis a miracle ye dinnae die."

"Or break any bones," she said.

"Aye," he agreed. "It's there." He pointed ahead.

The place was an open field in the middle of nowhere. Behind them was Dundale Castle and the glittery loch as its backdrop. Ahead of them, the soaring mountains of the Highlands, the Scottish heather, and the purple thistle dotting the landscape. The wind was cool and crisp and bright as she inhaled it.

"It's so beautiful here, Callum," she said.

"Aye," he agreed, smiling and looking proud. As if he had anything to do with the beauty of the land. "I'm glad ye like it. Have you no seen a place like this before, lass?"

"I live in the city." When he gave her a questioning look, she tried to elaborate. "There are tall buildings made of steel and glass. It's noisy with people and traffic. Not calm and quiet like this. Where you hear nothing more than the breeze through the trees. I wish I could show you a picture."

"Do ye like this place better then?"

It was a fair question. She wasn't sure she liked it better. It was merely different.

"It's calmer here," she said at last.

"And ye like that it's calmer?"

It seemed important to him that she like it. She nodded. "I do."

"Good. This is where we found ye." He pointed ahead as he dismounted.

She slid out of the saddle in a most ungraceful movement, landing on the ground next to Mist. The horse seemed unconcerned with her awkward dismount. Evie followed Callum as he walked a few feet away and paused. He stood there, his hands on his hips, as he peered down at the ground.

"I dinnae notice that before."

"What is it?" she asked. He pointed to the flattened grass that was charred. "That's where I landed?"

"Aye. Where I picked ye up and took ye back to the keep."

Her heart fluttered at the idea of that. She knelt, running her hand through the flattened grass. It was as though her body was hot when it landed. Like it was fused with fire. The grass felt brittle.

"Strange, isn't it? To think I landed here without injury."

"Indeed," he agreed.

And though neither of them said it, they both understood there was something that had protected her during her fall. Some form of magic that had kept her alive as she plummeted through time and space and landed here on the ground near Dundale Castle.

"There is something else I didn't tell you," she said.

"What is that?" Concern laced his voice.

She craned her neck to look up at him. "That day when I first met you, I had this unmistakable feeling I knew you already. That we had met somewhere before."

Her cheeks warmed as she thought of the dream she had had before leaving Edinburgh. That he was the man in her dream and she had climbed into his lap. That she had dreamed of the castle not far in the distance.

There seemed to be an understanding that came into his eyes as he looked down at her and then he gave a slow nod.

"I felt the same."

Her brows lifted. "You did?"

"Aye. As though I…" He halted, pressed his lips together and looked away.

"As though you dreamed about me?" she asked, hopeful.

His head snapped back in her direction. His voice was a low whisper. "I did dream of ye."

A breath shuddered out of her. "I dreamed of you, too."

They stared at each other a long, quiet moment. There was

nothing more than the whisper of a breeze across the highlands. She smiled at him, relieved they had finally found some common ground.

"Mayhap there is something to this prophecy, then," he said.

"Mayhap," she agreed.

Beneath her palm, the ground vibrated. She looked out into the distance but saw nothing.

"What was that?" she asked.

His brows drew together as he followed her gaze. "I dinnae see anything."

Then they heard it. The distant thunder. But it was not a storm brewing. It was something else. Hooves.

She rose to her full height which meant she came to the edge of his shoulder. He moved closer to her, wrapping an arm around her shoulders and pulling her close as they both looked out into the distance. Shapes formed on the horizon moving quickly. Shapes that looked like men on horseback.

"Horses?" she asked.

"Aye," he agreed. "I dinnae like the looks of this. We best get back to the keep."

He helped her into the saddle quickly and together they rode back to Dundale. But Evie could not shake the feeling that something was not right.

CHAPTER EIGHTEEN

T HEY HURRIED BACK to Dundale. As they galloped through the portcullis, she spied Malcolm and Hamish in the yard sparring. Callum brought his mount to a quick stop and shouted for the stable hand who ran up to take the reins from him. Before she could dismount, he was at her side, lifting his arms up to her. She slid out of the saddle, grateful for his strength. Taking her by the hand, he rounded the horses and charged toward Hamish and Malcolm.

"Riders approach," he said.

They stopped what they were doing. Hamish turned to look at Callum. "Riders?"

"At least a dozen or so," Callum said.

"Headed here?" Malcolm asked.

"I dinnae like the looks of them," Callum said.

There was a heartbeat of silence, then Hamish shouted, "Close the gates!"

Callum turned to her then, grasping her by the shoulders. "Go inside and find Roslyn. Stay with her until I come for ye. Do ye understand?"

"What's happening?" she asked, trying to squelch the terror that shifted through her.

"I dinnae ken. But I dinnae want ye in harm's way. Go, now, lass."

"But, Callum—"

"Go." He turned her toward the door and gave her a gentle nudge.

Evie did what she was told and hurried into the keep, closing the door behind her. She paused there, wondering what was going to happen to him, his father, and brother. Something told her the riders approaching were not friendly and the three of them intended to face them in whatever capacity they needed.

She hurried through the keep to find Roslyn. She was in the kitchen preparing the evening meal by kneading bread. Flour was smudged across the front of her gown. She glanced up when Evie entered.

"Ah, lass, there ye are. Did ye have a nice ride with Callum?"

Evie rushed over to her. "I did but…Roslyn, something is happening."

Sensing her near panic, she put aside the dough and reached for a kitchen towel, wiping her hands on it. "What is it, lass?"

"There are men approaching on horseback. Callum told me to find you and stay inside the keep." She took several steps toward the woman, reaching for her and grasping her by the arm. "It's something bad, isn't it?"

The woman's face drained of color as she pressed her lips together into a thin line. Then she reached for Evie's hands, squeezing them in hers.

"Everything will be all right, lass. Dougal!"

The man came from a back room. He was the same man Evie had seen when she first woke in Callum's bed. "What is it now, woman?" When he saw the two of them standing together, he halted. "What is it?"

"Riders," Roslyn said. She jerked her head toward the front of the keep. "Best go see."

He said nothing as he hurried by her. Roslyn grasped her by the hand and pulled her deep into the kitchen.

"What's going on?" Evie demanded.

"If it's what I think, they'll be fighting before too long."

"Fighting? Who?" Alarm bells went through her.

Roslyn tugged her toward a set of stairs off the kitchen that led down. They headed toward a room at the bottom where she pushed open a door and led her inside. It was well stocked with sacks of flour, oats, rye, and other grains on one side. On the other, dried beans, peas, and lentils, as well as salted and cured meats. There were oak barrels she assumed contained their favorite ale. She spied large wheels of hard cheese and one area reserved for herbs and spices.

"We'll wait here in the larder," Roslyn said as she closed the door behind her, plunging them into cool darkness.

"Here?" Her voice quivered. She was unsure what to make of that.

She struck a match and lit a couple of candles. It didn't do much to illuminate the room, but at least they weren't in total darkness.

"The men will be fine," she added. "Dougal will come for us when we can leave."

"I don't understand what's happening." Evie clutched her elbows to ward off the impending chill.

Worry flickered through the older woman's eyes. "If the riders are who I think, then it's a long-standing feud between the clans."

Evie didn't like where this was going. "Between which clans?"

"The MacLeods and the MacDonalds." She said it matter-of-factly.

The blood whooshed out of her head, making her see black pinpricks dotting her vision. Her knees gave out. She faltered but leaned against one of the large wooden barrels as she pressed a hand to her head.

"The MacDonalds," she repeated.

An image of Bruce MacDonald chasing her up the stairs exploded in her mind. Were they Bruce's ancestors come to fight Callum and his brother and father? And if so, why?

"Are ye all right, lass? Let me fetch you something to drink." She started for the door.

But Evie stopped her, fear skipping through her. If they were hiding in the larder, it was for a good reason.

"No, I'm fine. I wasn't expecting to hear the name MacDonald." She rubbed her forehead, getting her emotions in check, and lifted her head to look at the woman standing across from her. Candlelight flickered over the other woman's face. "Why are they feuding?"

"Well, 'tis a long story, that," she said. She found her own barrel to lean against. She expelled a sigh. "Ye've no met the younger lad, Jamie MacLeod, have ye?"

She shook her head.

"The boy is a rogue at best." She harumphed as if she were disappointed in the younger MacLeod.

He must have done something to earn the older woman's ire, but Evie couldn't imagine what. She waited while Roslyn collected her thoughts. She heaved another sigh.

"It started over a year ago when wee Jamie was offered the hand of Margaret MacDonald in an attempt to make peace between the two clans," she said. "They were to be handfasted. Do ye ken what that is?"

When Evie shook her head, she continued.

"They were to live together for a year and a day. And if she produced a child from the arrangement, then they would be married forever. But no child was born within the year and a day and Jamie cast her out. He returned her to her kin. Well, that dinnae bode well for the MacLeod boy. It did nothing but fuel the fight between the two clans. It was an insult, ye ken."

"I see," she said, slowly, as dawning came. This must be the scandal Roslyn mentioned her first day here.

"When Margaret was returned, the MacDonald took no kindly to it. It was why wee Jamie was sent away to visit his uncle and travel with him."

"So, you think they've come to continue the fight?" Evie asked.

"I ken they do," she said. "And we are to stay here out of

sight until it's all over."

"Here," Evie said. "In the larder."

"Aye."

They lapsed into silence. There was no sense in asking any more questions. Even though she wanted to ask what happened if all the MacLeod men were killed, she didn't think she would like that answer so she kept her mouth shut and clasped her hands together in her lap. Worry for Callum, his brother and father, gnawed at her. If they didn't win this fight, then what would happen to her? Terrible things came to mind and she wasn't interested in any of them happening to her.

But she also had a difficult time believing that the fight continued over a woman.

Things were different in the fourteenth century. She had to remember that. This was not modern America. This was practically the dark ages.

How much time passed as they waited in near darkness for Dougal to return?

There was a swift knock at the door followed by its opening. Roslyn got to her feet and reached for Evie, taking her hands in hers once again and squeezing. Every muscle in the woman's body was tense. She clung to the woman, too, as fear gripped her. Moments later, Dougal pushed the door wide.

His face was streaked with mud and blood. His hair was a tangled mess. His clothes were soiled with more blood and dirt. Roslyn gasped. Evie gaped.

"There ye are, wife. Bring clean cloth and boil some water. The laird is hurt."

"Hamish?" Evie asked, his name slipping out in a whisper.

Roslyn didn't respond as she sprang into action. Dougal disappeared back up the stairs in a hurry. They followed.

"Is he going to be all right?" It was a silly question. Roslyn would have no idea if he was or not.

And now Evie worried about Callum. And Malcolm, too, but mostly Callum.

"I dinnae ken. Help me, lass." In the kitchen, she took a dish towel and began ripping it into long strips. She shoved the pieces into Evie's hands as she snatched a kettle from the fire. "I already had water boiling."

She hurried out of the kitchen. When Evie didn't follow, she turned to look at her over her shoulder. "Come. We must see to the laird."

But Evie didn't want to. She stood there a long moment, paralyzed by her own fear and the dread coiling through her. When Roslyn waved for her to follow, she made her feet move. But she was not looking forward to seeing a bleeding, injured man.

Chapter Nineteen

Hamish was laid in the laird's chamber, which was down the hall from Callum's. Evie followed with the strips of cloth in her hands and her stomach in knots. As soon as they entered, the metallic tang of blood accosted her. She clenched her jaw to keep from wrinkling her nose. Dougal was already there, pulling away a bloodied rag and tossing it to the floor.

Callum and Malcolm stood on the other side of the bed. Callum's hands were coated in blood. His clothes and face were splattered with it. He looked fierce and terrifying standing there with his blue eyes blazing as he peered down at his father. When they entered, she caught his gaze. He had a worried expression on his face and something inside her told her Hamish wasn't going to make it.

Roslyn poured the hot water into a porcelain basin. She held her hand out for the strips of cloth. Evie handed them over. She dunked first one, then another, turning to hand them to Dougal.

"I ken it looks bad," Hamish said, his voice a harsh whisper. "Stitch me up, Dougal, and I'll be fine."

"'Tis no that easy this time, my lord," he said. He dabbed at the bloodied area of his abdomen.

Hamish sucked in a sharp breath, clearly in a lot of pain. Callum stepped to her, taking her by the arm and leading her out.

"Come, lass. Ye dinnae want to see this."

He closed the door behind him and they paused there in the

drafty hall. Her pulse pounded. A sharp spurt of fear punched through her.

"What happened, Callum?"

"We rode out to meet them," he said, his voice low. She tried to ignore the feral look in his eyes as he began to recount the battle. "It was the MacDonalds coming for another fight."

"Roslyn told me about the long-standing feud between you," she said.

"Och, Jamie and his devilish ways." He clenched his fists, clearly vexed by his younger brother. "If he hadna spurned the MacDonald lass, we wouldna be at war."

"You're at war?" Roslyn hadn't made it sound so dire.

"Aye. Though I understand why he did it. She dinnae bear him a child and so he dinnae see fit to stay with her. All of us understood the MacDonalds were more interested in expanding their clan territory and using their handfasting as a way to get more of ours. When he returned the lass to her da, the laird was unforgiving."

She nodded. Roslyn had already told her as much but now she understood more.

"Da tried to reason with MacDonald, but he wanted to fight again." He turned away from her, his hands clenched.

"So, you fought," she said, filling in the blank.

"He took a sword to the gut," Callum said. He turned back to her then, his face pinched in anguish. "I dinnae expect him to live."

She pressed cold, shaking fingers to her lips. "Callum, I'm so sorry."

A muffled groan full of pain came from behind the closed door. Callum started to reach for it, but she grabbed his sleeve and held him back. When his blazing eyes landed on her, she wanted to back down, but she managed to keep her wits about her.

"There's nothing you can do, Callum. Let's get you cleaned up."

She started for his bedchamber, tugging him along behind her. He reluctantly followed. At the door, she pushed it open, then stood aside and waited for him to enter. She closed it behind her. He slumped in the chair by the hearth that was devoid of a fire.

When she realized there was no water in the pitcher or the basin, she snatched up the pitcher and then headed for the door.

"I'll be back," she said.

"Evie."

The sound of her name on his tongue stopped her. She halted.

"Ye dinnae have to."

He looked and sounded so weary. It tugged at her heart. She softened, giving him a smile. "I don't mind."

Then she was off and headed to the kitchen, wondering where she would find water for the pitcher. She needn't have worried. One of the kitchen maids was there and showed her the well outside. She filled the pitcher with cold water and then asked for some clean linens.

"For Callum," she clarified.

The girl nodded and handed her a small stack of linens. When she returned to his bedchamber, she tried to ignore the wailing moan of pain coming from Hamish's room. As she paused at the door, Roslyn exited, her eyes misty. Evie's heart dropped to her shoes.

"Is he…?" She didn't want to ask, but she had to know.

"Best get Callum, lass. The laird hasna much time."

A lump formed in her throat as she opened the door to Callum's bedchamber. "Callum, your father…"

She didn't have to say anything else as he jumped to his feet and brushed by her, not even looking at her. He hurried down the hall to his father's bedchamber and pushed open the door, disappearing inside and leaving Evie standing in the doorway with a pitcher of water and a stack of clean linens. Roslyn moved to stand next to her, the two of them peering down the hallway at the closed door.

"He's going to die, isn't he?" Evie asked.

"Aye," the woman said, her voice weak. "And then Callum will be laird."

A tremor of surprise went through her. It hadn't occurred to her until Roslyn said so that if Hamish died, Callum would inherit. He would be the laird of Dundale. She gripped the handle of the pitcher so hard, her hand cramped.

Roslyn eyed the items in her hands.

"I was going to help him clean the blood off his hands," she said by way of explanation.

"Och, yer a good lass. Save it for him, aye? He'll need it." She peered inside the room and saw it devoid of a fire. "Come. Let's warm his bedchamber so it will be ready for him when he returns. I'll show ye how."

Evie followed her inside and kicked the door closed with the heel of her foot. She replaced the pitcher next to the bowl and the linens next to that while Roslyn set about adding logs in the hearth. Evie kneeled to help her. They worked in silence until the fire was built and the peat took off. Then Roslyn sat back on her heels, brushing the dirt from her hands. There was a sorrow in her aged face.

"I dinnae ken how the lads will fare with their da gone," she said, as though speaking to herself. "They've lost so much. Their mam, their sister." Tears watered her eyes. Then she pulled herself together, taking a deep breath as she rose. "I best see to the kitchens." She glanced down at her, question in her eyes.

"I'm going to stay here and wait for him." It was a snap decision.

She nodded understanding and then was gone.

Callum shoved inside the room, closing the door behind him.

The heavy odor of blood and death hung in the air and he knew his da's time was upon him. He didn't want to see his da die, but he also understood there was nothing to be done for him. Dougal gave him a nod, acknowledging him, as he passed and exited into the hallway. Malcolm stood on the other side of the bed, his face somber.

"Callum. Come here, lad."

Callum moved to the side of the bed as his da reached a blood-stained hand out to him. He grasped him by the wrist, pulling him down closer.

"Ye must tell me ye believe in the prophecy," he said.

"Da—"

"Tell me. I need to hear it before I pass."

"Nay. Yer going to live."

He emitted a watery laugh that descended into a cough. His other hand was across his middle where his tunic was soaked through with blood. "Promise me."

Callum lifted his gaze to Malcolm, but his brother's face remained impassive with a perfect stony expression. He was the same way when their mam died. He never did show his emotions.

Hamish tightened his hand on his wrist. "Ye must believe. 'Tis up to ye now, lad, to find the other two pieces of the keystone and protect it with yer life."

Callum felt there was nothing to do but agree. "Aye, Da. Ye have my promise."

"And the lassie. Promise me ye will take good care of her."

A flush of heat went through him. "Evie?"

"Aye."

"Of course, Da. She's safe here at Dundale."

His hand tightened again on his wrist, tugging him closer. Callum leaned down and heard his raspy breathing and knew it wasn't long now before death would take him. "The MacDonald." His voice was a rough whisper.

"He will pay for his attack," Callum said, a vehement declaration. "He and his clan."

"There is something else I dinnae tell ye about the Shattering. There was…" He paused to catch his breath, cough. "There was someone else who wanted the stone. Someone who would kill for it."

A sense of horror passed through him. Callum's brows drew together as he waited. "Who, Da?"

Hamish shook his head, the effort nearly too much for him. "Before he sliced me in half…" He paused to catch his breath, changing the subject as if he had to get it all out before it was too late. "He said to me…he kens of the keystone. He kens we have it. And he wants it back." He released his wrist. "Do ye believe now, lad?"

Blood drained from his head as he stared down at his da, making him lightheaded. He recalled Evie telling him the man chasing her before she swiped her thumb over the stone and fell through time was named MacDonald. Could it be true? Had they found a way into the past, or was there another explanation?

After a long pause, Callum nodded slowly. "Aye. I believe, Da."

"Good. Protect it. Protect her."

Those were his last words as Hamish's eyes closed and his hand released his wrist, dropping to the bed. The breath went out of him and then he was gone.

CHAPTER TWENTY

SILENCE DESCENDED IN the room as both Callum and Malcolm remained after the passing of their father. Neither said a word. Malcolm stood straight, unmoving, his hands clenched at his sides and his face stony.

"What did he mean there was someone willing to kill for the stone?" Malcolm said, breaking into the silence. "Someone else?"

Callum shook his head as if to say he didn't know. He thought of the tapestries in Evie's room and how they were changing, how the images were morphing as though showing the past history of the fabled keystone as well as the present with her falling from the sky.

He had no other explanation for that other than there were mystical forces at work. Mystical forces he had long denied.

He could no longer deny their existence, for Evie was here with him in the past.

Malcolm's gaze was still on their father. "I will kill Rory MacDonald for what he's done."

"Aye, he will pay," Callum agreed.

Malcolm charged toward the door. Seeing the look of fierce determination on his brother's face, Callum stepped up to grab him by the arm and stop him.

"Where do ye think yer goin'?"

"To war, brother. I will rally the rest of the clan and pay MacDonald a visit." Fire sparked in his brother's eye. The same fire he, himself, felt.

"Nay, brother. We cannae attack." When Malcolm started to protest, he said, "No the now. We must wait, lay Da to rest, and then rally the rest of the clansmen."

He stared at him a long moment, and then seemed to relax his stance, releasing his clenched fists. His shoulders slumped as he gave him a stiff nod. "Aye, then. Yer laird now. I willna go against ye, brother. But Ian MacLeod needs to hear of this."

He tugged his arm free and stomped from the room, slamming the door behind him. Ian MacLeod was leader of Clan MacLeod and resided on the far reaches of the isle. His brother was right in that their clan leader would need to know, and he would in time. For now, he would find Dougal and ask him to prepare his da for burial.

He didn't need to search for the man. When he opened the door to the bedchamber, he waited outside in the hallway, apprehension pinching his face.

"He's gone, then?" the man asked.

Callum nodded, his jaw clenched as a sense of melancholy settled over him.

"Dinnae fash, my lord. I will take care of him."

He patted Dougal on the shoulder. "Aye, ye have my thanks."

"Yer lady waits for ye in yer chamber," Dougal added.

He thought of Evie and her fiery red hair and flashing eyes. Eyes that had mesmerized him from the first moment he looked into them. How she had fretted over him, determined to clean the blood from his hands. He glanced down and saw his skin was still stained with it, the grit and gore still under his fingernails.

Dougal didn't wait for a reply as he entered the bedchamber that already smelled of death. It turned his stomach. He headed down the hallway to his own bedchamber and pushed open the door. Evie sprang to her feet from the chair by the fire, worry creasing her pretty features. She clasped her hands in front of her, waiting for him to tell her.

But he didn't. She knew by the look of him.

"Oh, Callum. I'm so sorry," she said, her breath but a whisper.

The was a fire blazing in the hearth. With a weariness, he settled into the chair next to it, stretching his long legs out in front of him. He heard water splashing in the basin and then she brought it over with clean linens. She kneeled at his feet, dipping a cloth in the water. He watched her with interest as she began to clean the dried blood from his hands.

"So much…" she whispered as the linen turned pink with every swipe. "Are you hurt?"

She glanced up at him, meeting his gaze. Firelight reflected in her deep brown eyes. The one gold fleck in her right eye seemed to wink back at him. Concern creased her face—concern for him. He shook his head to indicate he wasn't hurt at all.

No, it was his da who had taken the great axe to the gut. His da who had shoved him out of the way when MacDonald charged toward him. His da who died to make sure he lived.

She went back to cleaning his hand, doing the best she could. When she had his right hand mostly cleaned, she dumped the water in the chamber pot and replaced it with fresh from the pitcher. Then she returned with a clean linen and started on his left hand.

"Ye dinnae need to do that," he said, his voice gruff.

He wanted to pull away, to tell her to go back to her own room, but his voice faltered and his hands remained still. He was reluctant to make her leave. Her touch was gentle, her hands soothing as she carefully cleaned his. The soft cloth moved over his skin, her movements unhurried and full of care. The warmth of her closeness and the care in her touch made him hesitate, lingering in the comfort she unknowingly offered.

"I know, but I want to."

Surprise flickered through him. She wanted to? He watched her as she dipped the cloth into the water, then held his hand in her small one while she dragged the cloth over his knuckles, revealing redness there. Ah, yes. He had punched one of the

MacDonald lads in the nose. A young lad, too, by the looks of him. Young and green and not well versed in the ways of war or battle. Callum had knocked the sword out of his hand and when he charged, thinking to fight him hand to hand, it had taken nothing more than one punch to lay him flat on the ground.

Silence hung between them, soft and heavy, like a comforting blanket. The gentle trickle of water echoed through the quiet room, mingling with the steady crackle of the fire as flames flickered and danced in the hearth. The warmth from the fire washed over him, a soothing contrast to the cool air. As she continued to tend to him, her touch careful and reassuring, a deep sense of peace settled in his chest. The gratitude swelled inside him, warming him more than the fire—grateful for her presence, grateful he didn't have to face this moment alone.

He dared not speak of his da yet. He wasn't ready to discuss it with her or anyone else. While Malcolm channeled his grief through fighting and war, Callum was a different sort. He preferred to brood in silence alone.

And yet, he wasn't alone.

He had spent the long days after his mother's and sister's deaths quiet and alone, preferring the company of his horse to anyone.

All of this could have been avoided had Jamie not been such a lascivious knave. Why couldn't he marry the girl to keep the peace?

When Evie finished her task, she sat back on her heels and looked up at him. "There. Not perfect but better." A faint smile fluttered over her pretty face.

There was still blood under his nails. Still, he appreciated her.

She rose and dumped the bloody water into the chamber pot as she did before. Then she picked up the soiled linens, tucking them under her arm. She picked up the bowl and the pitcher.

"I'll leave you be, now," she said, heading for the door.

"Ye dinnae have to," he heard himself say.

This stopped her in her tracks as she came even with his

chair. She tipped her head down to look at him, curiosity and question in her eyes.

"I should let you rest and…be with your thoughts. Besides, I need to clean these."

"It isna necessary now, lass."

He wasn't sure what he was thinking. Perhaps his mind was too mottled with grief and despair to think about it. But he rose from the chair and turned to her, taking the items out of her hands and placing them on the floor at their feet. Then he tugged away the linens, dropping them too.

It was easy to see how her chest rose and fell with each quickened breath. Her cheeks were pink as she looked up at him and he thought he saw her hands shaking.

"Did you…want me to stay?"

He wasn't sure what he wanted. On the other side of the room was another chair. He went to it, dragging it toward the hearth and placing it across from the one he had vacated. He motioned her to it. Without a word, she sat, smoothing her skirt under her as she did so. She crossed her feet at the ankles, perching on the edge, and placing her hands in her lap. An expectant look crossed her face.

He sat across from her, frowning and staring into the fire, which was starting to die. He reached for a small brick of peat and tossed it on, watching the flames reignite. She remained silent, waiting for him to say something. Anything.

But he didn't know what to say.

"When Hamish is laid to rest," he said finally, "I will ride out to speak with the clan leader." He cut her a glance, meeting her gaze. "Will ye come with me?"

Her face remained impassive for a long moment until she finally nodded. "If that's what you wish." Then she gave him a ghost of a smile. "It will give me a chance to practice my riding skills."

He turned back to the fire, his hands resting on the arms of the chair to keep from reaching for her. All he wanted to do was run his fingers through those fiery locks, letting the strands fall through his fingers like the day when she arrived and he had held her close.

"Callum," she said, her voice soft. "Is there anything I can do?"

He gave her a questioning look.

She spread her hands. "To help."

His initial thought was to say no, but when he looked at her, her expression one of concern and care, he changed his mind. "Stay with me here."

She nodded, though he saw the apprehension in her face. He wasn't sure why. Mayhap she worried staying would bother him in some way. Or that being in the same room with him would not be wise. He was aware of the fact she didn't return to his room the night before. That she had stayed in the guest bed-chamber with the tapestries.

The truth was, though, he was comforted by her presence. He needed her there with him.

To put her at ease, he said, "Hamish…his last words were of ye."

Her eyes flew wide with surprise. "Me?"

"He asked me if I believed in the prophecy." He curled his fingers around the end of the chair arm, peering into the fire to avoid looking into her eyes.

"And do you?" she asked finally.

"I think I have to," he said. "Then he told me to protect the stone and protect ye, too. And…" He turned to look at her, at last meeting her lovely gaze. "That ye would do the same for me."

CALLUM'S WORDS MADE her heart thud hard in her chest. "Hamish said that?"

"Aye, he did."

He looked as though something else was on his mind by the way he pressed his lips together. There was contemplation in his eyes. Something had shifted in him to accept her for who and what she was, though she was uncertain what that something was. Had Hamish said something to him on his deathbed that had made Callum change his mind about her, the stone, and the prophecy?

There was also the matter of him asking her to visit the clan leader with him. Why he wanted her with him, she had no idea. She could barely sit a horse, much less ride. When they saw the men riding toward Dundale earlier that day, it had taken everything she had to keep the mare under control while they galloped back to the keep.

"There is more," he said at last.

She took that as a sign that he wanted her to stay. He needed someone to talk to who had a different perspective. Someone who was not of his family. She was definitely an outsider.

She relaxed in the chair, resting her hands on the arms and waiting while he collected his thoughts. And for a brief moment, sitting there with Callum seemed so right, so perfect. As if she had done it before. As if she had always been a part of his world and would forever be.

That thought terrified her. Despite being out of her element with no running water, no electricity, and certainly no toilet paper, there was something comforting about being here with him in Dundale in the past.

"What is it?" she finally asked when it seemed as though he wouldn't continue.

"Something Da said before he passed haunts me."

That got her attention. She sat straighter in the chair and leaned toward him, reaching her hand to him. "Whatever it is, you can tell me."

He took her hand in his, his fingers curling around hers with a firm yet careful grip. His roughened palm was against hers. She liked the way his hand felt against hers—warm and grounding.

His thumb traced a leisurely line across the back of her hand. Slow, soft, sensual. It sent a ripple of delight through her. Though they were from two different worlds, when they were alone, together, it didn't seem to matter.

"He said there was something else about the Shattering." He paused, meeting her gaze. "Ye understand what that is?"

She nodded. "Hamish told me the story, yes."

"He said there was someone else who wanted the stone. Someone who would kill for it."

The blood drained from her head. She gripped his hand tight as the thought skittered through her mind. That someone else was Bruce MacDonald. She was sure of it.

"MacDonald?" she asked, her voice wavering on a whisper.

His eyes held hers, those blue depths so full of pain and angst with the underlying hint of questions and disbelief.

"Ye told me his name when ye first arrived," he said.

"I did," she said. "You said it mattered."

"It did. It does. But I dinnae want to believe the MacDonald clan was interested in the keystone."

"This feud between your clans...it started because of your brother, Jamie?"

"It started because of him, aye," Callum said. "But I wonder if it continues because of something else."

"The keystone," she guessed. "Do you suppose Bruce Mac-Donald from my time has anything to do with what's happening here and now?"

"I dinnae ken," he admitted. "It doesna make sense to me."

She dropped her hand from his and thought of the tapestries hanging in her room. The one that was changing and morphing with Moira and the army in the lower corner. Then the other one that looked much like her sister with a shadowy figure behind her. She got to her feet. He gave her a questioning look.

"I think we should go look at the tapestries," she said.

He gave her a look as though she'd gone mad. "Why?"

"Because I think we need to see if the images have changed again."

Slowly, he got to his feet and motioned her toward the door without a word. She nodded and pulled it open. He followed her from his bedchamber through the great hall to the other side of the keep where she shoved open the door to the guest bedchamber. The hearth was devoid of a fire and it was chilly in the room. Likewise, there were no candles lit. Light slashed from the hallway in an odd angle, illuminating the wall hangings.

The first one depicted Moira and the other two women, the light all around them. In the corner the army had grown, nearly covering the lower half. Evie stared at it in abject horror. Callum walked over to it, pausing in front of it. His hands clenched into fists. She joined him and peered up at him. Anger lined his face.

"Someone who would kill for it," he muttered.

"Someone like Clan MacDonald?" she asked.

"Aye."

He reached a hand out, tracing the lines of the finely woven fibers that seemed to shift and change as if the events were happening in real time. His finger traced the lines of a weapon that was clearly held aloft by the leader of the army. Light glinted off the blade.

"Do ye see this, lass?"

She eyed where his finger was and nodded. "It looks like some type of weapon."

"'Tis a great axe. I've seen this weapon before. It belongs to Rory MacDonald. The man who killed my father."

CHAPTER TWENTY-ONE

EVIE PERCHED ON the bed. Her insides twisted into a tight knot. She didn't know Hamish that well, but the idea that he was gone was like a knife to her heart.

"Callum, what happened out there?"

His expression was stony as he continued to stare at the wall hangings. He dropped his hand to his side and clenched his jaw, the muscles working there as he decided how to answer.

"We rode out to meet them. There were a dozen of them."

She quickly did the math. Callum, his father, and his brother were sorely outnumbered and yet they battled them anyway.

"Da with his claymore," he added. "And Malcolm, too."

His eyes took on a faraway look as he remembered. She glanced at his hand, saw the blood and mud still caked there under his nails and warded off a shudder. Her imagination ran wild with images of him swinging his sword. She hadn't any idea what a claymore looked like, but she assumed it was a big-ass sword.

"And you, too?" she asked.

"Aye. We dinnae expect to use them." He paused, swallowed hard. "We dinnae even have time to dismount before they were on us, swinging their swords and trying to kill us."

She shivered as a chill crawled through her. She couldn't bear the thought of Callum dying.

"Da is—was—skilled with a sword. He killed three of them

straightaway. And Malcolm, too. He's good with a sword."

He paused a moment and then continued on with his story. They were outnumbered, sure, but they held their own. When Rory MacDonald swung his great axe, it connected with his father's gut, nearly slicing him in two.

"He said that was a warning," Callum said, turning to look at her. "That he would be back to wipe out the rest of us in time."

Fire blazed in his bright blue eyes. Fire and anger and hatred. There was a lot of hate between the two clans.

"That great axe is what killed my da."

She had no reason to disbelieve him, but she did have a question. "How could the great axe of Rory MacDonald be in this image?"

"Mayhap it was passed down to him from his ancestor. The way Da talked, the Shattering happened long ago."

"How long ago?"

"Centuries. During the dark times."

She stared at the tapestry. The one of her sister's image was clearer. She walked to that one, standing close to get a better look at it. Behind her, Callum lit the candles in the room to give it more illumination. He stood behind her, peering over the top of her head at the image.

"Yer sister?" he asked.

"Yes," she said.

The shadowy figure was behind her and still had not become clear.

"This wasna here before," he said.

"No," she agreed. She glanced to the wall hanging next to the one of her sister. It was still devoid of an image as were the remaining hangings. "The images are moving and changing as time goes by. Do you think this is showing what will happen next?" She pointed to the one of Chloe and the shadowy figure.

He said nothing but a *hmm* deep in his throat. She felt the rumble of his chest behind her. It sent a delicious little shiver through her. It made all her parts stand up and take notice. As much as she wanted to turn and fall against him, she forced herself to remain in place. She craned her neck to look up at him. Though she had stood next to him before, she was still amazed at how tall and broad he was.

His gaze was fixed on the wall hangings as he looked at each and every one of them. She wondered then if he still didn't believe in the prophecy or what he saw there. His hand slipped into his sporran and then he froze.

"The keystone…" His face drained of color. There was an unmistakable panic in his voice. "It was in my sporran when I rode out to face the MacDonalds."

Hot pinpricks of fear pounded through her. His gaze met hers and she saw the alarm deep in them. Alarm that she also felt within her, shuddering through to the marrow of her bones.

"'Tis gone."

She kept the foul swear word she wanted to say bottled up. Instead, she bit her bottom lip and sucked in a deep breath through her nose, then expelled it, trying to remain calm.

"It must have fallen out while you were fighting. We need to look for it."

She darted around him and headed for the door, but he caught her by the hand and pulled her to a stop. She turned to face him, the fear pounding hard and fast within her now. That stone was her lifeline to the future—how she was able to return home to see her sister again. If MacDonald had it, then she was screwed.

"'Tis no use, lass. It's dark now. We'll never see it without daylight."

"But what if—"

"I ken what yer going to say. And I agree. What if they found it? Even if they do have it, there is naught to be done about it now."

She clenched her jaw to keep from lashing out at him. It wasn't his fault he lost it. Well, it was, but she didn't want to blame him. She shoved aside those negative feelings and merely nodded.

"In the morn, we will look for it," he said, then headed for the door.

"And if we don't find it, then what? We'll go after it, won't we?" she asked. She tried hard to hide the sheer terror that arose in her voice.

He paused to look at her over his shoulder. He said nothing. But the grim expression on his face told her everything she needed to know. If the MacDonalds had it, there was no way to retrieve it.

"We will search in the morn," he said again, as if that was the final word on the matter.

There was nothing for her to do but watch him go. Frustration edged through her. She wanted answers *now* but she wasn't going to get them. She turned back to the tapestries, clutching her elbows and peering at her sister's face. If that keystone was lost, then what was to become of her? Would she ever get home again?

Heaving a sigh, she climbed onto the bed, curling into a ball, and squeezing her eyes shut. Before long, she was asleep.

SOMETIME DURING THE night, she awoke. Her stomach rumbled from the pain of hunger. She shoved off the blankets, her feet on the cold stone floor. There was no fire to warm the chamber and gooseflesh blossomed on her legs and arms. She realized she was still fully dressed. Roslyn hadn't come to help her into her nightclothes and at some point, she must have kicked off her shoes. Thick stockings kept her feet from turning into ice cubes.

A candle blazed in a candleholder near the bed. She picked it up and headed out of the chamber in her stocking feet, wondering if there was any food to be had. She found her way to the kitchen. No one was about. She spied a half-eaten loaf of bread wrapped in a cloth. Then she recalled the larder and headed down there to grab the wheel of cheese. When she returned to the kitchen, she placed the cheese and the candleholder on the work table, then rummaged around until she found a knife.

When she was alone, after Chloe had deserted her for her job in Edinburgh, Evie often had late night snacks that consisted of cheese and crackers and sometimes wine. She was trying to drown her sorrows in snacks and wine. She didn't see any wine, although she didn't need to be drinking in this strange place.

As she cut slices of bread and then cheese, Callum entered the kitchen looking half asleep and rumpled and so handsome she nearly swooned. He was wearing clean clothes and looked as though he had had a bath to finally wash away the blood and grit of the earlier battle. Their eyes met and for a moment, they merely stared at each other in silence.

She told herself there was no sense in bringing up the location of the keystone. Now was not the time and she didn't want to fight about it. She wanted peace and quiet and snacks.

"Och, I dinnae ken ye were here, lass."

"I was looking for a midnight snack." She waved toward the bread and cheese. "Want some?"

He ran a hand over his face, his skin bristling against the growth of beard on his cheeks and chin. "Aye."

She sliced more bread and cheese, portioning it to split between the two of them. He disappeared for a moment and returned with a flask of something that looked like wine. So much for not drinking. He poured two cups full and handed her one while she slid his serving of bread and cheese toward him. They stood there, in the medieval kitchen at the work table, munching on their midnight snacks and drinking wine and saying nothing. But that was all right with her. It was a comfortable silence. Not every second had to be filled with someone talking.

Chloe would hate it. She hated prolonged silence. Thinking of her sent a pang of homesickness through her.

"What are ye thinking, lass?" he asked.

She glanced up at him. "How do you know I'm thinking anything?"

"I see it in yer face."

She flushed hot. There it was. She was never any good at hiding her emotions. She dragged her lower lip through her teeth as hesitation skipped through her.

"I dinnae mean to pry."

"You didn't," she said quickly. "I was thinking of my sister. She's a chatterbox. I was thinking how much she would dislike the silence and try to come up with something to talk about to fill it."

"Chatterbox?" He tilted his head to one side in question.

"You know. Someone who likes to talk a lot." She waved a piece of cheese in the air as if that would explain it.

"Ah," he said, giving a nod of understanding. There was a long pause, then he said, "I dinnae thank ye."

"Thank me? For what?"

"For taking care of me before."

She wasn't certain, but she thought a bit of pink colored his cheeks, as though he had never had a woman care for him the way she did. She didn't do much, if anything.

"You mean cleaning your hands?"

"Aye."

Now it was her turn to flush. She didn't know why she did it but something inside her made her want to do it. When he returned to the chamber with that look of grief on his face, she was compelled to do something. A small kindness that would ease the pain of his loss, though she knew from experience nothing would ever ease the pain of losing a parent to an untimely brutal death.

She fiddled with a piece of bread. "Oh, that wasn't anything special. I wanted to help."

"It meant a lot to me." His gaze pinpointed her with a smoldering look that made her want to squirm.

But she didn't. She remained standing still, her heart doing a weird thud in her chest she had never experienced before. She reached for the cup of wine and drained it, then ate more cheese and bread to keep from getting totally drunk.

"I'm glad I helped," she said around a mouthful.

He moved from his side of the table toward her. Heat washed over her as he neared. She was unsure what he meant to do, so she remained perfectly still as he approached her. He reached for her hand, taking it in his once again. Something he was doing more and more and something she was starting to like more and more.

"Ye did more than help."

"I did?" She blinked up at him, her pulse racing at rapid speed. She was sure he was able to see it pounding.

"Aye, lass. Ye dinnae ask questions or make demands of me. Ye were there for me when I needed ye to be."

"Well, I…" Her words trailed off. She paused, swallowed hard. "I wanted to be there for you."

His other hand reached for her, resting on the side of her neck. His skin was warm and wonderful against hers. Her head tipped back as she looked up at him. He towered over her by several inches. She never thought she would like to have a man so much taller than her. Until now. A breath shuddered out of her as she licked her lips. His gaze landed there, then back up to hers as he leaned in. Closer. Closer still.

Her eyes fluttered closed as he kissed her. Soft, sweet, short. Way too short. It was nothing more than the brush of lips against hers. But enough to let her know she wanted more of that. She resisted pulling him to her and mashing her mouth against his because that wasn't the ladylike thing to do. She realized that in the medieval world things were different. So, she allowed the brush of his mouth against hers.

Then he released her and walked away. Leaving her standing there, alone, in the kitchen with her heart racing and her blood pumping and desire flooding her.

"Bloody hell," she murmured. She snatched up the remaining cheese and bread and decided to head back to bed.

CHAPTER TWENTY-TWO

After her midnight excursion with Callum, Evie headed back to bed, climbed under the covers and pulled them to her chin. She was cold but she was too tired and too lazy to get up and make a fire in the hearth. Instead, she burrowed deeper under the blankets and curled into a tight ball. She had no idea when she finally dozed off.

She awoke at the sound of a light knock on the door, followed by the scraping of it as it opened. Faint morning light pressed against the windowpanes, not yet slashing into the room. The sun wasn't high enough.

"Och, lass, ye let yer fire go out."

Sleepy-eyed, she yawned as she sat up, still fully buried under blankets. Roslyn set about building a fire in the hearth.

"You don't have to do that," she muttered, her voice thick with sleep.

"I do if ye wish to bathe," she said without turning around.

A hot bath did sound nice. She slid from the bed, her feet hitting the floor, as she began to unplait her messy braid. When Roslyn turned to her, she frowned and propped her hands on her hips.

"Ye slept in yer clothes, I see. I should hae woke ye last night."

"You were in here last night?" She finished unplaiting her hair and ran her fingers through the wavy, tangled locks.

"Aye. And ye were fast asleep. I let ye go since it was a trying day for all of us."

"Yes," Evie agreed. Though she didn't say anything more, she thought of Hamish. She didn't know him well, but there was a pang of sorrow that went through her for him now that he was gone.

Roslyn spied the hangings on the wall by the bed and peered at them a long moment, her hands still on her hips. Confusion followed by curiosity flickered over her face. Evie was fascinated by her reaction to the tapestries and followed her gaze to them. They hadn't changed since the last time she looked at them.

"The tapestries," Evie heard herself say. "Have you seen them before?"

The woman shook her head. "Where did they come from?"

"I don't know," Evie admitted. "Hamish brought me here and showed them to me. He was convinced they were part of the prophecy."

The moment the words left her lips, she clamped her mouth shut and cut a glance to the woman. She wasn't sure what Roslyn knew and didn't know. Nor was she sure if the woman had heard of the Shattering or the keystone or even the Triple Goddess.

"The laird was convinced there was one," she said at last. Her gaze drifted from the wall hangings to her, lingering on her face. "I ken ye aren't from here, but I dinnae ask questions as it isna my place."

Evie blew out a breath. "He told you about it? The prophecy, I mean."

"Aye, he talked of it before. He said a woman would come from the future."

Her gaze never left Evie's face as she said it. Realization came over her as she realized the woman had not once questioned her sudden appearance or even her strange dialect, for surely, she had noticed Evie's accent was far different from hers, from all of theirs, in the keep.

"Do you think I'm from the future?" Evie asked.

One brow lifted as a ghost of a smile crossed her face. "Are you?"

"If I was, what would you think?" Sometimes, evasion was the best way to answer a question one did not want to answer.

"I would think Hamish was right about everything." She dropped her arms and headed for the door. "I'll be back with yer bath."

And then she was gone, leaving Evie to wonder what she meant by that.

ROSLYN DID IN fact return with the tub and pails of warmed water. She helped her bathe and dressed her in a clean gown and then combed out her long, wet hair, getting all the snarls out. She braided it while it was still wet. Then it was time to break her fast. Evie followed her to the great hall where Callum was already enjoying a bowl of porridge and some oat cakes.

There was a place setting waiting for her across from him. She dropped down into the chair and did her best to avoid his gaze while she broke the oat cake in half and popped it into her mouth. What she wouldn't give for a strong cup of coffee and some of her favorite creamer. Chloe always made fun of how she drank her coffee—creamer with a few drops of coffee. There was a dull headache behind her eyes and at the base of her skull but she decided that was caffeine withdrawal and sleep deprivation.

"Good morrow," he said, his voice deep and gruff and terribly sexy.

She told herself to stop feeling all swoony when he did the smallest things.

"Morning," she muttered around her mouthful of oat cake.

"When yer done, grab yer cloak and we will see if we can find the stone."

"All right," she said.

He finished his morning meal, brushed the crumbs from his hands, and pushed back from the table. His chair scraped along the floor followed by the thump of his boots as he headed out the door.

She heaved a sigh and sat back in the chair, staring down at the porridge that was growing cold. How was she ever going to look him in the eye after last night? She was not a love at first sight girl. She wasn't even a love at any sight girl. She was picky beyond belief about the men she dated, though Callum was definitely not like any man she'd ever dated. She didn't want to get too attached to him because she was determined to go home. She had to get back to Chloe. She had to get back to her life.

What was her life? She thought about that for a moment. If she returned, she would spend a few days with Chloe in Edinburgh, then pack up her suitcase, get on a plane to go home. A home that was empty and lonely. A job that was a dead-end with nothing but long hours and demanding bosses who wanted her to do their bidding. Not that she had to fetch coffee, but she was responsible for making sure their days ran smoothly and their calendars were up to date and—

She shoved all those thoughts aside. All of that seemed so trivial. Life there was nothing compared to life here. Life here was fragile. Where one swing of a great axe to the gut could kill you in an instant.

Evie shoved back from the table and went back to her chamber. She snatched her cloak off the back of the chair by the hearth, which was nothing more than bright red and orange embers, and wrapped it around her shoulders.

With renewed determination, she was going to face Callum.

Hopefully, he would kiss her again.

She exited the great hall and found him in the yard holding the reins of two horses. His and her little gray mare she had named Mist. He stood there in a slash of early morning sunshine. Her breath caught as she looked at him. He wore his boots, his trousers, a tunic, and his plaid across his torso and tied on one shoulder. His long hair was dark brown but, in the sunlight, she saw a few gleaming golden strands. His eyes—so sharp and blue—were nothing short of spectacular.

Gosh, he was handsome.

"We're going to ride?" she asked, a shiver of nerves shuddering through her.

"Aye," was all he said as he handed her the reins to her mare.

She eyed the saddle with a sweep of apprehension. She had had one lesson and hadn't yet built up enough confidence.

"Do ye need help?" The corner of his mouth lifted in a half smile as he watched her, bemused.

"I can do it," she said with more determination than she felt.

He waited patiently as she stuck her foot in the stirrup, grabbing onto the saddle and hoisting herself up. She was proud of herself for getting it right on the first try and not falling to the other side. With a wide grin, she took up the reins and glanced at him. Her smile faded when she saw the smirk on his face.

"Are ye ready now, lass?"

"Stop looking at me like that and let's go."

He nudged his horse and started to walk toward the gate. She did the same and was relieved when her mare followed her orders. Still, she gripped the reins so tightly, her hands cramped. And then she prayed their ride would not take them far.

She managed to get her horse next to his and they rode side by side. Silence stretched between them as they put the keep behind them.

"Ye seem to be doing better," he said, giving her a sideways glance.

Still, she had a death grip on the reins but had to admit she was more comfortable than she was when they first started out. "Do I?"

"Aye," he said. "The mare is a gentle one. Ye named her Mist. She's perfect for ye."

Mist huffed as if in agreement. It made them both laugh. Evie released her tight grip on the reins and tried to force herself to relax. It wasn't long after that Callum came to a halt. He leaned on the saddle horn, his keen eyes looking out toward the horizon, as if remembering what had happened the day before.

He swung his leg over and jumped down. She watched him as he took several steps away from the horses, then kneeled down in the grass, his hand flat on the ground.

It must have been here where the three of them fought the MacDonalds. Here, where his father was mortally wounded. She thought she spied dark splotches of dried blood on the grass.

She dismounted and joined him, remaining silent.

"Here," he said. "It would be here or nearby."

She nodded and started to do her search. She knew it was nearly impossible to find the jagged little stone on the ground. Likely it would look like all the other stones.

Callum remained where he was, his hands on his hips as he peered down at the ground. She glanced his way to see his mind working. There was a depth of memory in his eyes. His gaze darted about, as though he were re-enacting the battle in his mind. And perhaps he was.

He squatted down, running his hand over the ground and looking around him. She continued her own search but was having no luck.

Then she thought she spotted something nestled beneath the heather. The morning sun glinted off it and she wondered if that was their missing keystone. With her heart ramming hard in her chest, she crawled on her hands toward it, daring not to hope.

She was wrong. It wasn't the morning sun glinting off the stone. It was the stone itself. The lines on the stone were pulsing brightly.

"I found it," she said on a gasp.

He hurried over and joined her on the ground. He peered at it, watching as the lines grew bright then faded, then grew bright, then faded.

"What's it doing?" he asked.

She shook her head. "I have no idea."

She reached for it, but his hand clamped around her wrist. Her head snapped up as she looked at him, confused.

"Let me," he said, then released her wrist.

He reached for the stone, plucking it off the ground and placing it in his palm. As soon as he did, the light faded. It stopped glowing.

"That's odd," she said. "It's as though it *wanted* us to find it. Like it was a homing beacon or something."

He stared at it resting against his palm, as if it were a foreign object. When he continued to stare at it and not move, she placed a hand on his arm.

"Callum? What is it?"

"Something Da said to me," he said. "The secret lies within the MacLeod bloodline."

He whispered it when he said it and it sent a cold shiver through her. She peered down at the stone, now dormant.

"What secret?" she asked.

He shook his head as if to say he didn't know. She certainly didn't either.

"Two ancient bloodlines. One divine destiny," she said, remembering what Hamish had told her. "MacLeod and Sinclair?"

He nodded. "Aye, lass. Ye have the right of it. Da said this to me, too."

She considered this as she looked down at the stone, silent in his hand. "Well, then, what if it was a homing beacon? And the MacDonalds couldn't see it. Or we got damn lucky."

"Aye, lass. I think we were *verra* lucky." He rose and stuck the stone into his sporran once again.

She eyed the place he kept it and wondered if she had picked it up, would she have been able to use it to return home since it was glowing?

"Ye wanted to take it, didn't ye?" he asked.

"Yes," she said. There was no reason to lie.

"Because ye think it can send ye home," he added.

She nodded. "Yes."

"We tried that already."

"Yes, but it wasn't glowing then," she said. She lifted her gaze to his. "But it was when we found it."

He reached into his sporran and pulled it out once again, extending it to her. "Do ye wish to try again, then?"

Her heart throbbed at a wicked pace. She eyed the stone in his hand, but it was not glowing. She decided this was a test of faith. He was testing her to see if she would take it once again and try to use it to return home, even though they both saw it was not glowing nor was it humming. He was giving her the chance to leave this place. To leave him and this nightmare behind.

But was it truly a nightmare? He was nothing but kind to her. He'd even kissed her. As she chewed on her lower lip, she tapped into her gut feeling. What did her gut tell her?

Every time she hadn't listened to her gut, she had regretted it. Now, it was telling her not to reach for the stone. Not to return home. She had to stay. There was something here she had to do before going home and it was all tied to this prophecy or her destiny or whatever. She didn't know.

All she *did* know was that she had to stay. She clenched her fists at her sides, lifted her gaze to meet his dead on. She saw there the apprehension, the question, and even a bit of fear she might leave him.

"No, Callum," she said finally. "I do not."

He pocketed the stone once more. "Aye, then. Let's get back to the keep."

He took her by her elbow and led her to their waiting mounts. He even waited and helped her into her saddle. When he was settled in his saddle, they headed back to the castle.

And Evie was certain she had made the right decision, even if that meant she was still divided by centuries from her sister.

❧ ——— • ——— ❧

CHAPTER TWENTY-THREE

SOMETHING HAD SHIFTED between them. Evie wasn't certain what that was. Perhaps because she didn't take the stone from him again when he offered it to her to try to return home. Perhaps it was some other predestined reason.

She never believed in fate or destiny or any of that mumbo-jumbo. She believed what you saw was what you got. She believed love took time to develop and it had to stem from an inherent liking for one another. Friends first. Lovers second.

But what if that was wrong?

She snuck a glance at Callum who rode tall and sure in the saddle, the reins gripped lightly in his hands. Handsome, yes, but was that why she was drawn to him?

No, she didn't think so. She thought it was something more. Something deeper. And for the first time in her life, she *could* believe in love at first sight and destiny.

They arrived at the keep, trotting through the gate. In the yard, the stable hand came to take their horses and care for them. Callum paused as though contemplating something. He reached for her hand, taking it in his and tugging her closer. She was confused a moment until he reached into his sporran and brought out the stone.

He placed it in her hand, closing her fingers around it.

"Ye best keep this on ye, lass."

Her brows drew together. "You're giving me the stone?"

"For safekeeping," he said, a smile tugging at the corner of his mouth.

This was certainly a turn of events. "But, why?"

"If there is a clan war," he said, "I dinnae want to chance losing it."

He released her hand and walked toward the keep, leaving her standing there in stunned silence. She was shocked that he trusted her to keep the stone safe. How did he know she wasn't going to try to use it to return home?

She hurried to catch up to him. "I don't understand. You trust me with this?"

"Aye," was all he said as he entered the keep.

"But...why?"

He stopped and turned to her, gripping her by the shoulders. "I told ye why. If something happens to me, ye need to have it."

Icy fear trickled over her. "Do you think something is going to happen to you?"

His expression softened as if he realized he had scared her. He brushed her cheek with the back of his hand. It sent tendrils of excitement through her.

"Nay, lass."

Then he walked away. He left her standing there in the great hall with the stone in her hand and a million questions running through her mind. She was flabbergasted that he trusted her with the stone. Glancing down, she opened her fingers to look at it. It was not glowing or humming as it nestled against her palm. She lifted her other hand up to see the imprint of the lines still there. As if it were a permanent sunburn.

"Lassie? Are ye all right?" Malcolm's voice echoed through the great hall.

He stood near her, question on his face as he peered at her. His gaze flickered down to her hand and back up again.

"I...I'm not sure."

He walked closer, pausing next to her. He saw she held the stone. "Callum gave ye the keystone?"

"Yes," she said, the word an icy whisper between her lips. "He…he lost it during the battle with the MacDonalds. We rode out this morning to find it. It was glowing when we found it."

Malcolm was silent as he stared at her, an unreadable expression on his face. He looked a great deal like Callum with a hint of Hamish in his face. There were gold strands in his hair and full beard. Chloe wouldn't like a full beard.

It was an odd thought to cross her mind.

"And he gave it to ye?"

"Yes, for safekeeping, he said. In case something happens to him." She lifted her gaze to his.

Malcolm gave a low whistle. "Well, then, lass. Callum has decided to trust ye."

He patted her shoulder as he walked by her. She spun to face him.

"Malcolm, is something going to happen to Callum?"

He paused, turned to look at her over his shoulder. "Dinnae fash yerself about him, lass. He gave ye the stone because he trusts ye, now. 'Tis all."

Malcolm went on his way, leaving Evie alone in the great hall. She slipped the stone into the pocket of her dress. She walked to the table and sat as she contemplated everything that had happened. It was hard to shake the feeling that she was supposed to be here with Callum. Lately, it was difficult for her to get the dream she had of him out of her mind. The way he had sat by the hearth and she had moved from the bed to climb into his lap.

She wondered what those strong arms would feel like wrapping around her as she kissed him.

Heat flooded her cheeks. She pressed her cold hands against them and then rose from the table. She was starting to believe in love at first sight, just as Callum was starting to believe in the prophecy.

Or she hoped.

She stood a long moment in the great hall, alone, wondering

what to do with herself now that he had left her. She didn't want to bother him since the loss of his father was still so new and raw. He might want some time alone. She understood that more than anyone.

She wandered her way from the great hall into the kitchen where she found Roslyn hard at work kneading bread. She, herself, wasn't much of a cook so watching her do something that was nothing more than an ordinary task fascinated her.

"Back so soon from yer ride, lass?" she asked.

"Yes, I…well, that is to stay…" She didn't want to talk to Roslyn about the keystone and standing there stammering was ridiculous. She pressed her lips together. Finally, she said, "Can I help you do anything?"

The woman paused and looked at her, a curious glint in her eye. "Ye want to help me?"

"If you need help, that is." Evie twisted her hands together to keep them still so she wouldn't fidget. "I know you're busy so I don't want to intrude."

"Aye, I can give ye some tasks to do if ye want to help me." She paused her kneading and reached for a towel to wipe her hands. "I've got to get the pottage on but ye can help me gather some of the ingredients I need."

She had no idea what pottage was, so she merely nodded. Roslyn reached for a basket near the back door of the kitchen and handed it to her.

"Fetch me some eggs, lass. I need three or four, but best to bring them all in, aye? And then I need some parsley, sage, and mint from the garden. A handful of each. Can ye do that?"

Evie took the basket on her arm and nodded. Roslyn ushered her to the back door and set her on her way to the chicken coop as well as pointing out the herb garden. The door closed with a snap behind her, leaving her standing there in the cool late morning breeze with questions lingering in her mind.

She was no cook—parsley, sage, and mint were found in the spice aisle of the grocery store. However, she did know how they smelled, so she was going to have to rely on her nose to find them. She decided to tackle that second.

First, it was on to the chicken coop where she was faced with a few hens pecking the ground and one rooster who eyed her suspiciously as she approached. She had never in her life collected eggs from a hen. She was a city girl to the core. How in the world did she think she was going to gather eggs?

She approached the coop, keeping an eye on the rooster who walked with slow, methodical steps as if he were ready to fly into attack mode.

"I'm here for the eggs," she told him, not that it mattered.

When she stepped into the coop, she was relieved to see it was devoid of hens and nothing more than a few nests. She spied several in the first nest and reached for one, picking it up as if it were made of glass. She placed it gently into the basket. Then she gathered the second and the third. By the time she got around the coop, she had solid confidence about gathering eggs. This was easy. She could do this.

Then on to the herb garden. As she headed away from the coop, the rooster still eyed her as though she were an intruder. She kept one eye on him as she left and headed for the herb garden, which was nothing more than a patch of greenery outside the kitchen's back door.

She placed the basket on the ground out of the way and then proceeded to kneel on the ground and inhale the scent of the greenery in front of her. She recognized several familiar smells— rosemary for one. But Roslyn didn't ask for rosemary. She recognized the needle-like leaves on the stalks. Moving down, she spotted a plant with oval, velvety leaves that looked somewhat familiar. She plucked a piece of it, rubbing one of the leaves between her thumb and forefinger and then inhaling the scent.

She got a sudden burst of Granny's cornbread dressing in her mind and was immediately transported back to her childhood on Thanksgiving. Her mother pulling a large, roasted bird from the oven and Granny fussing over the way the dressing still wasn't brown enough on top. She recalled Grandpa telling Granny the dressing "needed more sage" and her shooing him out of the kitchen. She and Chloe would sneak into the kitchen while their mother and Granny were cooking their dinner, looking for snacks and hoping to swipe something to quiet their growling stomachs. They always got caught and were ordered out.

Evie rocked back on her heels and smiled, remembering those moments of her life that were now long gone and far in the past. Or was that in the future? It was all so confusing.

She plucked a few more stems, then moved down to an area with lush green plants with flat leaves that she recognized immediately. Parsley. She didn't have to smell it to know what it was. She added a few stems of parsley to her bouquet. Then it was on to find the mint.

She smelled the aromatic leaves immediately. She grabbed a few of the square stems, smiling and proud of herself as she rose. She placed all of this in her basket along with the eggs and then headed back into the kitchen.

Roslyn was no longer kneading the bread. It was set aside while she worked to place large bits of meat into a pot and cover it with water. When Evie returned, she grinned and took the basket from her.

"Thank ye, lass. This will do verra nicely."

Evie watched as Roslyn placed the fresh herbs aside and then began to chop them.

"What is pottage anyway?" Evie asked.

Roslyn stopped a moment to gape at her. "Ye never had it?"

She shrugged, unsure how she should answer.

"Och, it's a meat soup with herbs and spices." She motioned her to follow her to the other side of the kitchen where she had small containers with pre-measured spices. She lifted one up to Evie's nose. "Smell."

She did and immediately coughed. The scent was sharp and peppery and sweet. "What is that?"

"Mace," she said with a smile. Then she held up a second one.

"And this."

Evie had learned her lesson and took a small intake of breath. This one she recognized as warm and spicy, reminding her of apple cobbler. She closed her eyes and savored it for a moment, smiling.

"Cloves?" she asked.

"Aye," Roslyn said, as if she were proud of her student. She held up a third one.

Evie took another breath and knew this one, too. Slightly sweet and pungent. "Ginger?"

"Aye! Good. And this?"

This one was dark red in color and had a distinctive smell that was both bittersweet and earthy as well as spicy and leathery. She knew that smell, but couldn't place it.

"I don't know this one."

"Saffron," Roslyn said with a smile.

Evie blinked in surprise. In her world, saffron was known as the most expensive spice and sometimes referred to as red gold.

It was clear to her that Roslyn was an accomplished cook. Evie had never learned how to cook anything that wasn't out of a box. She loved watching the woman bustle around the kitchen. Once the pot was boiling, she stirred as it simmered, then turned her attention back to her dough. She proclaimed it ready for the oven.

Something inside Evie came alive and an impulse pounded through her. Her mother had died before she could teach her anything about cooking or baking.

"Roslyn?"

The woman blew a wayward lock of hair off her forehead as she worked to make another loaf of bread. "Aye?"

"Could you teach me to cook?"

She froze for a moment as she looked up at her, their eyes meeting. She had a look of curious wonder as if she didn't understand why she wanted to learn. But then Roslyn smiled, a glint of joy sparking in her eyes. "Aye, lass. I can."

CHAPTER TWENTY-FOUR

CALLUM WAS UP early the next morning thinking about Evie. Relief swept through him when she refused to take the keystone. Relief that deep down she decided to stay. He wanted her to stay. He wanted her with him. That was why he had given her the stone for safekeeping. Because of the trust that had formed between them.

Guilt washed over him with her as his first thought. He should be thinking about his da and worrying about the continued strife with the MacDonalds. Not thinking about the bonnie lass.

He had a difficult time not thinking about kissing her, even though the kiss had been nothing more than the brush of his lips against hers. He couldn't forget the way her pulse had thrummed in her neck or the way she had shivered against him when he had done it.

He still did not know why he had done it. But the impulse had been too great to resist.

It did not satisfy his needy curiosity, either. It served to make him want to kiss her more.

He decided to look for her and offer to take her out for another riding lesson. Mayhap that would keep his mind off the lump of grief in the middle of his chest. When she wasn't in her bedchamber, he found her helping Roslyn in the kitchen. He was surprised to see Roslyn showing the lass how to knead bread and stood in the doorway a moment to observe.

"Aye, like that, lassie. Ye got it!" Roslyn said.

Evie giggled and smiled brightly as she pushed her hands through the dough. For the first time, he noticed the faint dimple in each cheek. She blew a piece of wayward hair that had come loose from her braid as it dangled in front of her face. He clenched his hands into fists, squelching the sudden urge to rush over to her and tuck it behind her perfect round ear.

"Och, Callum! I dinnae see ye there."

Roslyn's voice shook him from his staring. He straightened and cleared his throat, pulling his gaze away from Evie as he stepped into the kitchen. Evie's head snapped up, her eyes wide and round in surprise.

"Goodness me, I've forgotten to gather the eggs this morning," the woman exclaimed.

"I'll help you, Roslyn."

Evie handed the dough off to the woman and then reached for a towel to wipe her hands clean. Her gaze flickered over to him and she gave him a shy smile. It made his stomach drop to the soles of his boots and a tingling sensation prickle over every inch of his exposed skin.

"I was looking for Evie," he said, finally finding his voice. Much to his dismay, it was rough and ragged. He swallowed hard.

Evie's eyes widened again as she looked at him. Those big, brown eyes were so bright and deep he could get lost in them.

"You were?"

"Aye. To see if ye'd be interested in a riding lesson today."

"Oh." The word shuddered out of her on a breath.

Roslyn had a knowing glint in her eye as she busied herself in the kitchen gathering the morning meal to take to the great hall.

"After ye finish here in the kitchen, that is," he added.

"Go on, lass," Roslyn put in. "I dinnae need any more help this morn." She winked as she said it.

Evie flushed. Her lashes fluttered as she nodded, turning back to Callum. "I'd like that."

"I'll make ready the horses."

He turned from the kitchen and fled, his stomach in a tight knot. He chastised himself for that reaction. He had seen bonnie lasses before. But none of them had caused such an uproar of emotions as Evie. He decided he had to calm himself to get through this riding lesson and not act a fool.

At the stable, he ordered his war horse and her mare to be saddled and ready to go. The stable hand was quick and able to get the horses ready by the time Evie exited the keep. She clutched her cloak tight around her small frame, the wind whipping it around her ankles. Sprigs of her fiery red hair came loose from her braid. She tucked a tendril behind her ear. The same one he itched to do.

Her face exploded in a wide grin as she approached, seeing the small gray mare next to him. When she reached the horse, she patted her nose. The mare nuzzled her, looking for a treat.

"She's a sweet horse, isn't she?" Evie asked.

"Aye, she is."

She brushed her neck in a tender, reverent way. "I used to be scared of horses."

"But no the now?" he asked.

She shook her head. "No. Not anymore." She leaned over to eye his large war horse. "Though I have to say your horse is a bit intimidating."

As if in response, his horse stomped a hoof. She laughed, the sound lovely and sweet to his ears.

"Well, then, shall we?" He swung up into his saddle. She followed. "I want to be back before the midday meal."

She settled into the saddle, holding onto the reins with confident hands. "Where are we going?"

He motioned toward the gate. "Yer choice, my lady."

Though he said it in jest, he saw the color rise in her cheeks. She nudged the gray mare into a slow walk and headed for the gate. Smiling, he followed.

When they returned to Dundale after their riding lesson—truly the lass was getting better—Callum was surprised to see his youngest brother, Jamie, had returned from his travels with their uncle. Jamie, along with Malcolm, and Uncle Argyle, were in the great hall seated at the long table. Upon seeing him, Jamie granted him a wide smile.

"Ah, there ye are, brother," Jamie said. "And yer bonnie lass. Malcolm was telling us of her surprising arrival."

Evie cast him an uncertain glance as they paused in the great hall. Callum stepped in front of her to shield her from his brother's piercing gaze full of wonder and curiosity. As though he had never seen a lass before.

"Was he now?" Callum's stern gaze landed on Malcolm, whose face remained impassive.

Callum folded his arms over his chest as he sized up his younger brother. He looked as though he had aged over these last several months while traveling. His face no longer held that youthful glow he once had. Now it was tanned as though he was a man of the world. And mayhap he was.

Argyle was their father's brother. When he saw Callum, he rose to his imposing height, which seemed to tower over all of them. His hair was long and white peppered with gray, his beard full and thick and the same. He had one good eye, which was a pale blue, and the other he had lost in battle some years ago. He kept his blind eye covered by a black patch. His weathered face was lined with age and wisdom.

"Callum," he greeted, tipping his head. He glanced at Evie, looking her over from head to toe then back at him. "I was sorry to hear about yer father. The MacDonalds, was it?"

"Aye," Callum replied as he looked at Malcolm. "We bury him on the morrow. I dinnae expect ye or wee Jamie."

"I cut our travels short. It was a wise decision seeing as how yer da has passed."

There was some underlying meaning there in his terse words and the tone of his voice. Another glance at Jamie revealed nothing, though. Callum had to wonder if there was something the lad had done to warrant a swift return to Dundale.

Argyle made no mention of the fact that Hamish was his older brother, nor did he show any signs of grief or sorrow. But then, that, too, was like his uncle. He was not a man of great emotion. Callum often thought Malcolm was much like him as well.

Jamie rose from the table and ambled over with his normal cad-like swagger. His gaze was firmly fixed on Evie.

"Are ye going to introduce us to the lass?" There was a broad grin on his face Callum didn't like.

Behind him, he sensed Evie edge closer to him. She slipped her small hand into the crook of his folded arms, as though making everyone in the room aware of her status. She belonged to him.

"Evie, this is my brother, Jamie, and my Uncle Argyle."

Jamie bowed with a flourish. Argyle merely regarded her with cool indifference.

"'Tis good to meet the lass who fell from the sky," Jamie said, eyeing her and edging closer. "Since her mention, I couldna wait to see who holds my brother's attention so well."

Callum stiffened, ready to do battle with his brother if he stepped one inch closer. Her hand tightened on his arm but otherwise she remained where she stood. She lifted her chin higher in defiance which made him admire her all the more.

"Is that so?" Evie said, her voice calm and cool. "Funny, Callum hasn't mentioned you at all."

Jamie looked stricken as his gaze met Callum's. Behind them, Malcolm snickered. Callum managed to stuff down the bark of a laugh he wanted to emit. He knew Evie was familiar with his younger brother and the reason for the feud between them and the MacDonalds.

"Ye haven't?" Then he pressed a hand against his chest as if he were mortally wounded. "How that pains me, brother."

"I'm sure you'll recover," she said, with that same exterior coolness.

Jamie's gaze flitted back to her as his eyes widened.

"A sharp-tongued lass, to be sure." Argyle grinned. "I like her."

Callum dropped his arms and turned to her, taking her small hands in his and giving them a gentle squeeze. "Mayhap see if Roslyn needs help in the kitchen."

For a moment, annoyance flashed in those deep brown eyes. It was quickly followed by understanding but even so, she couldn't resist one last barb.

"Right. So you men can talk without me being around. I get it."

Then she did something that completely shocked him. She stood on tiptoe and kissed him on the cheek. When she stepped back, there was a warm smile on her face. A smile that said she understood far too well what was about to happen. She walked away with the swing of her small hips. He watched her go, his cheek still tingling where she'd kissed him.

Aye, he wanted to speak to his younger brother without her in the room. There were things left unsaid between them when Argyle swooped in and took the lad away.

Jamie gave a low whistle. "A bonnie lass, indeed."

"And ye'll stay away from her," Callum nearly barked.

Jamie blinked innocently. "Why so cross, brother? I mean her no harm."

"Yer a cad and ye ken it."

"Aye," Argyle said, then, his face pinched with the fury he had masked before. "Tis why we returned. The lad and his errant roguish ways have caused me enough trouble."

"So, that's the right of it, then," Callum said. "Yer return is because of him."

"I did nothing," Jamie said, sounding cross.

"Would ye like to explain yer behavior in France, then?" Argyle snapped. Fire flashed in his one good eye.

"I would not." Jamie ambled back to the table and sat, propping his boots on the edge. "I did nothing wrong."

"Ye did everything wrong," Argyle said.

Jamie pulled out the dagger at his side and picked at the dirt under his nails, ignoring them both. Malcolm glanced from his younger brother to his older brother, a look of bemusement on his face.

"We can discuss that later," Callum said. "What we need to discuss is the consequences of ye spurning the MacDonald lass."

Jamie rolled his eyes. "That again?"

"Ye dinnae understand the conflict that was set into motion with yer behavior," Malcolm snapped. "Da is dead because of *you*."

"I dinnae kill Da," Jamie said, glaring at Malcolm. "I wasna even here."

"Ye did," Malcolm insisted.

Callum held up his hands for silence. "What Malcolm means is that the MacDonalds were angered by breaking the handfasting."

"She dinnae produce a bairn," Jamie said, as if that was all that mattered.

But if he knew his youngest brother—and he did—there was likely more to the story than what Jamie was letting on. The ire of the MacDonalds was why Jamie was whisked off to travel with their uncle and even that appeared to have failed to tame the little knave.

"Aye. Likely because ye dinnae tup her properly," Malcolm said. Then added with a sneer, "Or at all."

Jamie took offense to that and jumped to his feet, his fists clenched tight and his face red with rage. "Ye ken nothing of that, brother."

Malcolm rose to his feet, his hands also fisted at his side. Callum realized he had to step in between them before they came to blows. Thankfully, he was bigger and taller than the both of them and shoved himself between them, pushing them apart.

"'Tis enough, both of ye," he said, his tone low and warning. "Fighting between us will no get us anywhere. We must find a way to broker peace with Rory MacDonald."

"There is no way to broker peace." Malcolm moved away from them and sat on the other side of the table, putting distance between him and Jamie, which was probably for the best.

"We must find a way." Callum eyed Jamie, who shoved away from him and returned to his seat at the end of the table.

"What do ye want from me, brother?" Jamie asked. "I cannae take the lass back."

"Nay," he agreed. "But ye can go with me to meet with the laird and offer yer apologies."

Jamie snorted. "I will do no such thing."

"Och, yer a hard-headed lad," Argyle said, speaking up. "Callum is yer laird now. If he wants ye to apologize, 'tis what ye'll do."

"And take back the lass if that's what it will take for peace," Callum added.

Jamie's face turned red with fury. "I will no take the lass back and I will no apologize."

Then he jumped to his feet and stormed off. Callum heaved a weary sigh. Argyle shook his head in dismay.

"Ye'll no get him to do either of those things, ye ken," Malcolm said.

"Then he leaves me no choice," Callum said.

"And what is that, lad?" Argyle asked.

"I go to the chieftain to ask for help settling our feud."

◦ ——— • ——— ◦

CHAPTER TWENTY-FIVE

THE FOLLOWING DAY, the group of them rode out to the abbey not far from the keep where Hamish would be laid to rest next to his wife and daughter in the churchyard cemetery. The plot was an area thick with trees. It was a somber affair with the local bishop conducting the ceremony which he spoke in Latin. Evie didn't understand a word of it but caught the sentiment. Tears welled in her eyes as she watched them place his shrouded body in the grave.

Callum had given her the option to remain behind in the keep but she decided she didn't want to miss it. Her mother often told her funerals were not for the dead, but for the living left behind. Even though she didn't belong in this world, she wanted to make sure she was there for Callum.

Evie stood off to the side, her hands clasped in front of her as she tried to huddle into the warmth of the cloak. The wind was brisk and cold, the weather like every other day in the Highlands which was a marked difference from what she was used to—fiery hot summers and moderate winters.

She eyed Callum, who stood tall and silent next to the bishop, his face blank. Malcolm stood next to him with fists clenched at his side, devoid of all expression. Jamie was on his other side, his hands clasped in front of him, and his head bowed in reverence. Dougal comforted Roslyn with his arm around her shoulders while she wiped her eyes with a handkerchief, her grief apparent.

Their uncle, Argyle, was also in attendance. His face was impassive as he stood with his hands clasped in front of him.

When it was all over, and Hamish was deep in the ground, the bishop said something low and quiet to each of the brothers and then walked back to the church. Roslyn and Dougal slowly filed away to head back to their mounts and return to the keep. Evie hesitated, wanting to stay for Callum and yet at the same time flee. She told herself she should follow Roslyn and Dougal and ride back with them, but she couldn't make her feet move. Malcolm turned to his brother before he walked away. Lines of anger were etched on his face.

"He will be avenged," he said to Callum.

Callum's face remained impassive as his gaze flickered to his brother. "You willna do anything rash." It was not a question, but more of a warning. His tone was hard and unforgiving.

Though Malcolm said nothing, he stalked away with Jamie on his heels.

Evie shifted from one foot to the other, wishing she had left with the others and not witnessed the exchange between the two brothers.

Argyle stood next to Callum, watching the younger men stalk away.

"The lad is grieving same as ye are," Argyle said to Callum.

"Aye, but we cannae have more fighting between our clans. It serves no purpose." Callum's eyes were still pinned on his brothers' retreating backs.

"'Tis up to ye to as laird now to keep them in check." He clasped his nephew on the shoulder. "And 'tis time for me to take my leave."

Callum's head snapped toward his uncle. "Yer leaving us?"

"Aye. I left unfinished business behind. I ken ye'll be a good laird. Take care of the lads."

They shook hands and bid each other goodbye. Argyle walked across the churchyard to say farewell to the others. Callum started to turn from the grave when he spotted her. She stiffened as their eyes met and she worried he would be angry with her for lingering behind.

He wasn't, though. His face softened as he looked at her. She moved closer to him, pausing next to him to peer down at the other two graves next to the fresh one. His mother and sister.

"You didna have to come," he said, his voice soft and low.

She merely gave a nod, managing a faint smile. "I didn't want to miss it."

They stood there in awkward silence, the wind whipping around them as she decided what to say next.

"I ken ye heard Malcolm—"

"You don't have to explain," she said, placing a comforting hand on his arm.

He glanced down at her hand and then did something that surprised her. He placed his over hers, gave a light squeeze, then released her. She dropped her hand to her side, her heart doing a funny thud in her chest.

"He's angry," she said into the silence, both peering down at the graves.

"Aye," he said.

"And so are you," she added.

He cut her a glance, his head tipping down to meet her gaze. There was a moment between them where he seemed to want to object, but then gave a quick nod in agreement.

"Aye," he whispered.

"I wish there was something I could do."

"Ye have done it, lass." He smiled down at her, lighting a fire deep inside her. "Yer here, are ye no?"

"I am." And she wouldn't have it any other way. She turned her attention to the grave. One freshly dug. The other two mounds covered in grass. No headstone marking them.

"I'm sorry about your mother and sister, too," she said.

"My mam died birthing Jamie," he said. "Abigail died last winter, succumbing to her sickness."

A pang of sorrow went through her, but she said nothing. She had never lost a sibling to death, but she imagined it would be as horrible a losing her parents.

"Ye told me once yer parents passed," he said, surprising her. She merely nodded. "I'm sorry for yer loss, too, lass."

Their eyes met, and in that silent exchange, an unspoken understanding flowed between them. She felt the weight of it, like a tangible presence in the air. Her heart swelled, a mixture of love and sorrow tightening her chest, making it hard to breathe. The room seemed to fall away, leaving the two of them standing there, shrouded in their shared grief—his sadness reflected in the deep lines of his face, hers a quiet ache beneath her skin.

"It was a long time ago, but thank you," she finally said. She was proud her voice didn't wobble with the unshed tears stinging the backs of her eyes.

His gaze lifted, bright blue eyes sweeping over the landscape as if drinking it in. The churchyard lay eerily still, the silence so heavy it pressed against her ears. The soft swish of the wind stirred the air, cool and faintly carrying the scent of damp earth and weathered stone. In the distance, the abbey loomed, its towering gothic arches standing in solemn defiance against the sky. Shadows stretched long and dark across the cemetery, their edges sharp, like the touch of old memories too close for comfort. The place felt ancient, as if it had seen more than either of them ever could.

"Will you walk with me?" he asked, surprising her.

Despite her coldness, she nodded, not wanting to pass up a moment to be with him, especially since it seemed to please him.

They started down the well-worn path, their footsteps soft against the packed earth. The ground felt uneven beneath her shoes, each step in sync with his. She sensed the quiet longing in his posture, the way his shoulders were slightly slumped, as if he craved the comfort of another presence but not the weight of conversation. So, she stayed silent, letting the air between them hum with unspoken understanding.

As they passed rows of graves, she glanced at the headstones—some weathered and cracked, names barely visible, others left unmarked, swallowed by time. The faint scent of damp moss and old flowers lingered in the cool breeze, and for a moment, it felt as though the past was walking alongside them.

"My brother thinks we should take action against them. That we should retaliate," he said, as if more to himself than her.

"And what do you think?"

He tipped his head down to look at her. "Retaliation will cause more strife."

"And you wish to avoid that," she said.

He nodded.

She didn't know much about what was going on between the two clans, but she wanted to show him she empathized. She understood he did not want to cause more strife between the two clans with an ongoing war.

"On the morrow, I will ride out to meet with Ian MacLeod," he said, his gaze fixed on some distant object.

"The clan chieftain?" she asked.

"Aye."

"And you still wish me to ride with you?"

He stopped walking, turning to her and taking her cold hands in his. Her heart skipped a beat at the warmth coursing through her. She marveled at that, wondering how he managed to have so much body heat against the treacherous wind. He wore his plaid wrapped around his shoulders. How was he not freezing like she was?

"I should tell ye what I mean to do."

Oh, she didn't like where this was going. She forced herself to remain still and allow him to hold her hands despite her impulse to want to jerk them out of his grasp.

"What is that?"

"I mean to ask him for help in this fight with the MacDonalds in the hopes we can settle it once and for all."

"Peace," she said. "You want peace from them."

"Aye, lass, ye have the right of it. And I mean to see to that."

"Do you think he'll help?" She tried hard to keep her teeth from chattering.

"I dinnae ken." He pulled her closer, perhaps sensing her shivering. His body heat radiated outward from him, sending delicious tendrils through her. "There is something else I wish to tell him."

The hot pulse of fear flashed through her. She blinked up at him. "And what is that?"

"I intend to tell him about the prophecy."

She stared at him for a long moment in silence. "To what end? What will that accomplish?"

"He's MacLeod. He will tell me if he's heard of it."

And thus, confirming in Callum's mind the prophecy was real. Standing in front of him as a flesh and blood woman didn't seem to count. She understood and she wanted to bite out a retort, but she held her tongue. It wouldn't do to fight with him on the day his father was buried.

"I see," was all she said and nothing more. She tugged her hands free of his grasp and clutched her elbows. "Thanks for the walk but I think I'll be heading back now to the keep. I'm freezing."

He seemed to understand and fell in step beside her. The silence was heavy between them and she was unsure what to say or how to feel. Hamish had told her she was the one who could convince him the truth of their situation. She felt, deep within her bones, that telling the clan chieftain of the prophecy was a mistake.

Or was it?

What was it Hamish had said? Something about the secret being within the MacLeod bloodline and then something else about a warrior's heart and a maiden's grace. Perhaps the chieftain of MacLeod would have words of wisdom to add to the prophecy.

Evie couldn't understand why he was having such a difficult time believing. She had to come up with some way to convince him before they left in the morning.

"I should warn ye, lass, 'tis a two day ride," he said, breaking the silence.

Her head snapped up at him. "Two days?"

She had barely mastered the saddle. How was she supposed to ride for two days straight?

"I ken I ask much of ye," he said, his voice low and soft. "But I need ye with me."

The way he said it made her heart skip a beat. It sounded like a heartfelt sentiment.

"There's an inn on the road we can stop at for the night."

Heat washed over her despite the chill in the air. All she imagined was spending a night alone with him at an inn. Her mouth went dry at the thought.

"Is that…proper?" she asked.

"Proper?"

"For us to travel together. Alone."

He gave her an odd look as if he didn't understand what she meant.

She hadn't a clue what was proper in these times, but she suspected by the way he was looking at her that she needn't worry.

"Aye," he said slowly.

As they returned to their horses outside the churchyard, she merely nodded. But her hands were shaking when she took the reins and hoisted herself into the saddle. How would she survive two days on the road, alone, with Callum? It was going to be a long trip, indeed.

CHAPTER TWENTY-SIX

T HE KEEP WAS silent that night. After the evening meal, the men scattered. Jamie skulked to his own bedchamber. Malcolm announced he was going to the armory to sharpen his sword. Callum stomped outside, banging the door to the great hall behind him and disappearing into the gloaming.

With nothing else to do, Evie offered to help Roslyn clean up in the kitchen.

"Och, that's no necessary, lass. Go rest, for the day has been trying."

It was the last thing she wanted to do, though she knew she should since she had a day of hard riding ahead of her. She meandered to her bedchamber, pausing in front of the enchanted tapestries. It was a relief to see they had not changed in the last twenty-four hours. The army was still marching toward Moira. Chloe's face had not yet become clear, yet the lines of her visage were apparent.

Her hearth was cold. With a sigh, she placed logs onto the log holder, then sat back on her heels, brushing the dirt from her hands. She wasn't ready to go to bed yet. She wasn't ready to face the next day alone with Callum.

She got to her feet and reached for her cloak, pulling it tightly about her and heading for the door. She decided to head outside to the stables to see the little gray mare who had captured her heart.

Much to her surprise, Callum was in the stable tending to his black war horse. She paused in the doorway as she watched him brush the long neck of the steed with a careful and gentle hand. He spoke in low murmurs to the horse. The horse snorted in response.

He turned as he put down the brush and caught her standing there staring at him. Surprise followed by question flickered through his eyes. She immediately tore her gaze away, her face flushing hot as she moved deeper into the stable.

"I-I didn't mean to intrude." She immediately kicked herself for her stammer but he'd caught her off guard. "I came to see about Mist."

When the mare heard her voice, she popped her head out of the stall.

"She appears to like ye," Callum said, a smile in his voice.

Evie moved to stand in front of her to pet her long nose. She had never been so attached to an animal before. She knew it was because they were never allowed to have pets growing up. Evie had longed for a house cat or a dog.

She sensed Callum next to her. He held an apple in his hand. "Give her this and she'll follow you everywhere."

Evie took the apple from his palm, their eyes meeting, and her heart jumping in a wild thump. Her hand brushed his, sending a zing of excitement through her. She turned back to Mist and fed her the apple. The horse chomped down on it without wasting a moment, making Evie smile.

"She's a beauty," she said.

"Aye, she is," he agreed. "And she's yers from now on."

She snapped her head up. "What? No. I couldn't—"

"The mare belonged to my sister, God rest her." He reached over to pat the animal's neck. "She'd want someone to care for her as ye do."

She started to object, to tell him that she refused to accept such a gift. Because she planned to return to the future. Which made her think of the stone in her pocket. She slipped her hand into the folds of her gown to make certain it was still there. She wrapped the stone in a handkerchief and tied the ends together to keep it secure. Satisfied the stone was still safe, she removed her hand and then went back to patting the horse's nose.

"Thank you," she said, her voice a rough whisper. Then she dropped her hand. "I should go. I don't want to interrupt your time here."

She turned but he caught her hand in his, pulling her to a stop. She looked at him over her shoulder.

"Yer no interrupting," he said. "I'm glad yer here."

Her heart lurched at those words. "Are you?"

"Aye."

He continued to hold her hand, his roughened palm against hers. Then he tugged her closer. She turned to face him as he pushed her fingers open and gazed down at the lines still imprinted on her palm. With a gentle touch, he ran the tip of his finger over them, outlining the strange brand the stone had left behind. He had done this once before, but this time seemed more sensual, more reverent.

"I thought the lines would go away by now," she mused, watching and loving the way his finger traced them with such a faint touch it sent her senses reeling.

Her gaze lifted to his and she found he was looking at her with an intensity she had never seen before. His blue eyes flickered, a sensuous flame passing between them. It was something she had sensed once before when they first met and then when he'd kissed her. Now, she was certain it was there, a strong pulse of emotion that shimmered in the air around them. As if they were meant for each other.

She could not stop thinking about the dream she had had when she was still in Edinburgh. She could not stop thinking about the way the firelight had flickered over his hard, chiseled features. Or the way his hands had curled around the end of the chair arms when she approached him.

That dream, she knew, would become reality.

A breath shuddered out of her.

"I...feel as though we have always known each other," she said, her voice but a whisper.

"I feel the same," he replied. "'Tis a strange feeling, and yet not."

She nodded understanding and dropped her gaze to their entwined hands. She had never felt so comfortable with a man before. She'd dated plenty, of course, but none of them had made her feel as though she were safe and secure. None of them had made her stomach flutter with anticipation and need.

"Callum, I...I can't help but think we were meant for each other."

He lifted his hand, placing it along the side of her neck, his thumb tracing the outline of her jaw. Then he tipped her head upward so their eyes met once again. His eyes reflected the glimmers of light surrounding them and she saw the tenderness in his gaze. It took her breath away.

He was going to kiss her. She knew this as sure as she felt the wild beat of her heart. He had kissed her once before, of course, in the kitchen over midnight snacks but that was nothing more than the brush of his lips. She wanted more. She wanted intense. She wanted fiery passion.

She wanted him.

She tipped her head to the side, ready and waiting and willing. Her eyes fluttered closed to savor the moment. She wanted to memorize everything about it. He smelled of horse and leather and an underlying sweet scent she didn't know. His calloused hand was rough against her skin and she relished it.

Then it happened.

His lips pressed against hers. Gentle at first. She slid her arms around his neck and leaned into him, letting the warmth of his body cascade over and through her. Letting the power of him press into her and relishing in it. His lips sent spirals of desire and wondrous need through her. She had never felt that before with anyone else. She never wanted to feel it with anyone else but him.

She kissed him back with a sudden need and a hunger that nearly consumed her. His arms encircled her waist, pulling her closer to him. She was enveloped in his steady warmth. She was certain she felt the pounding of his heart against hers.

When he pulled away, it took everything in her to squelch the whimper that wanted to escape for the loss of his mouth against hers.

"Aye, lass, I feel the same."

A moment of confusion went over her as she stared up at him, wondering how in the world she had gotten to this point in her life. How had she managed to fall through time and become instantly besotted with a man she had never met? A man from medieval Scotland who had walked through her dreams? Was it predestined? Or was there some other force at work?

It was too easy to fall in love with him. Too easy to want him to be her protector and her lover for the rest of her life.

"What do we do now?" she heard herself say, unable to hide her puzzlement.

A smile tipped the corner of his mouth as he peered down at her, still holding her in his arms.

"I think I'll be kissing ye again."

Before she could take a breath, he did. His mouth slid over hers, making her melt against him with such longing she thought she might come undone.

A snort in her ear startled her. They broke apart. Evie stumbled back a step in her hazy stupor to see the gray mare had moved closer to her and snorted in her ear. She laughed as the horse nuzzled her. Callum emitted a chuckle that rumbled deep in his chest. He stepped away from her and then returned a moment later with another apple in his hand.

Grinning, she took it from him and fed it to the mare who seemed all too happy to interrupt their romantic interlude for the treat.

"'Tis getting late," he said, then. "We have a day of riding on the morrow."

"Yes," she agreed. When Mist nibbled the rest of the apple, she turned to him. "I should get some sleep."

He nodded. "We leave at first light."

"Good night, Callum."

"G'night, lass."

She left him in the stable. As she did, it was impossible to shake the incredible feeling that things were different between them. She had a whole lot of unanswered questions. Questions she didn't know how or when or if she would be able to answer.

CHAPTER TWENTY-SEVEN

C ALLUM WATCHED HER walk away, leaving him alone in the stable. His stomach was in a knot. Much as he wanted to resist, he was unable to stop himself from kissing her. That first brush of their lips in the kitchen nearly did him in and all he could think about from that moment was how she would feel in his arms.

Now he knew.

He would never be the same.

When Evie started to leave, he had to stop her. He had to touch her. He had to hold her soft hand in his. He had to trace the lines of the keystone still branded in her palm. As he did, his da's words came rushing back to him.

One divine destiny.

It was impossible to deny that she was from the future, that she had come to help him protect the keystone. Hell, she'd brought it with her.

But what he had trouble puzzling out was how she had gotten it in the first place. Oh, she said she got it from the woman named Moira. The woman—the goddess—in the tapestries hanging in her bedchamber.

If that were true—and he suspected it was—where, then, did Moira get it?

"It was created to protect all of Time."

The lilting female voice startled him. He spun to see the

woman standing in the doorway of the stable, her silvery hair hanging in long waves over her shoulders. She had bright blue eyes—eyes that sparkled with starlight—and wore a silvery gown that shimmered in the half-light of the stable. He glanced around but no one else was about. The stable boys had retired for the night.

"Who are ye? Where did ye come from?"

Though she seemed to pose no threat, he still planted his feet shoulder-width apart as he stared her down. She gave him a pleasant smile.

"Ye know who I am, Callum of Clan MacLeod."

He clenched his fists.

It couldn't be her.

"Aye, it is."

"Do ye read minds now, then?" he demanded.

"No." She continued to smile. "I see the emotions on your face. The confusion and the disbelief. You look much like your father. He had a similar reaction when I came to him. Now, you are laird."

"Moira?" he whispered.

"Aye." She moved into the stable, the shimmering of her gown glinting in the candlelight.

"So, 'tis true then. The Night of Shadows and the Shattering."

"It is." She gave one nod of her head as she clasped her hands in front of her. "I'm sure your father, may God rest and keep him, told you the story."

She knew his da was dead. Was that why she had appeared to him, then?

"He told me."

"He told you, but you did not believe." It was not a question, merely a statement of fact. When she said nothing, she continued. "Even when the Sinclair lass arrived, you still did not believe. Will no amount of proof make you trust what your eyes see? That is why I'm here."

"I thought it nothing more than a fanciful story." He sounded defensive even to his own ears.

"It is no fanciful story. She holds part of the keystone. I know, because I gave it to her."

He peered at her. "How? She is from another time in the future."

She took a deep breath and expelled it as if prepared to answer the question with a long answer. "Time is not linear for me as it is for you or her. It is always in motion. It moves quickly as though it were nothing more than the blink of an eye. I live in the past, the present, and the future as do my sisters."

He thought of the three women in the tapestry. The ones standing on the hill with Moira with the lightning all around them, and the army approaching them, and the man wielding the great axe that looked much like MacDonald's.

"Aye, you know of them, don't you? I see the truth of it in your eyes."

"The tapestries—" He cut himself off, not wanting to mention those to her. But she smiled.

"My sisters, Bridget and Athea, were there with me on that hill the night of the Shattering. You've seen them. Did your da tell you what happened that night?"

"The stone was broken into three pieces."

"Aye," she agreed. "And more. War," she said as though it were a simple explanation.

He thought again of the tapestries. "MacDonald?"

"Aye," she said. "They know of the stone. The Chronos Stone as it was called then. It is why my sisters and I split it. We sent the pieces off throughout time for safekeeping, but the MacDonalds know it exists. They want its power."

"Why?"

"Because he who holds the Chronos Stone controls all of Time."

He understood what that meant. If the MacDonalds got all three pieces of the stone, it would give them the power to conquer and take what lands they wanted.

"There is more to this clan feud than the spurning of the MacDonald lass, isn't there?"

"There is." She said it matter-of-factly. "The story has been passed down for generations. They have been watching and waiting for the arrival of Evangeline. They know she's here. They know she brings with her the stone. They will not stop until they have her and the stone."

A cold fear slipped through him as he thought of his clan rivals stealing her away from him. He would never let that happen.

"It is why you must protect her and the stone with your life."

"Why me—us? Why MacLeod?"

"During the Night of Shadows, there were two clans who came to our aid. They tried to help us, to save us from destroying the stone." She gave him a pointed look.

Understanding crept through his mind. The Night of Shadows was not merely about the MacDonalds trying to seize power. It was something more. A war, then. And a war that was fought between the three clans. War in which his ancestors and Evie's were trying to protect the three goddesses.

"After the Shattering, the chieftains made a promise to us to protect the stone when the time came. The time is now. The MacLeods and the Sinclairs will make one final stand to protect all they hold dear—time eternal."

She paused there, her starry eyes piercing him. One silvery brow lifted in question as she peered at him.

"Do you believe now, MacLeod?"

There was no denying the truth anymore. The evidence hung in the bedchamber where Evie slept. The evidence was standing before him in her shimmering gown, staring at him with her starry eyes.

"There is no need to visit your chieftain," she continued. "He cannot help you win this fight. You and your brothers can. Once the pieces of the stone are reunited..." She paused, her words trailing off.

"What? What happens then?"

"The MacDonalds will come to claim it."

It was a cryptic answer, but he understood. War would come. There would be a mighty battle between the MacLeods and the MacDonalds. He had to be ready. They all had to be ready. He thought of Evie and glanced toward the keep, wondering if she was sleeping by now. He thought of the sister she missed so much and wondered then if she would end up here, back in time with Evie. He thought of his brothers and how Malcolm was determined to avenge their da.

"Go to her. Love her. Protect her. And she will do the same for you."

When he looked back to where Moira stood, she was gone.

Callum stood alone in the empty stable for a long moment. There was no sound other than the soft whicker of one of the horses, the quiet snore of another. One of the cats who lived in the stable sidled by and brushed against his leg, leaving behind orange fur. It was as if to remind him she was one of the best mousers around and deserved a treat if he was going to stand there all night.

He reached down and patted her head. She responded with a loud purr and more headbutts against his shin.

"All right, then, wee lassie. Let's get ye a treat. I'm sure Roslyn has some scraps to give ye."

The cat trotted behind him, following him to the back door leading into the kitchen, as though she understood fully what he said. And mayhap she did. She spent her days lazing in the stable with the horses and her nights hunting for rodents.

In the kitchen, he found scraps of their leftover meal and tossed them out to the cat. She gobbled them up, purring the entire time. He paused there in the deepening twilight of night, sitting on the stoop and petting her behind the ears. While he spoke with Moira, the sun had plummeted beneath the horizon.

The goddess told him there was no need to visit Ian Mac-Leod, for he would not be able to help him end the feud with the

MacDonalds. It would continue until they had what they wanted—the keystone. He wondered, then, if that was why they had attacked the keep—because they knew Evie was there and had the first piece of the stone.

Love her. Protect her.

But would she do the same?

If her kisses were any indication, she would reciprocate. There was one way to find out.

CHAPTER TWENTY-EIGHT

EVIE HURRIED BACK to the keep as fast as her legs would take her. Her lips still tingled in the aftermath of Callum's kisses.

They were everything she had imagined them to be and more. Her heart pounded hard and fast. Her legs burned with the exertion. But she didn't stop until she made her way to her bedchamber and burst through the door. She slammed it, leaning against it, trying to catch her breath.

Telling him she felt as though they were meant for each other was as though she had told him she was in love with him. What the devil was she thinking? She wasn't in love with Callum.

Was she?

Yet, his reply was not one of dispute. He *agreed* with her.

She closed her eyes, pressing the tips of her fingers against her lips, remembering how magical his felt against hers. How the heat of his body washed over her. How the hard lines of his chest pressed against her. How she bent her head back and allowed him to kiss her thoroughly.

She needed to be kissed *more* thoroughly, though. To make sure her feelings were correct.

A chill skittered up her spine. When she opened her eyes, she saw the abandoned hearth. The logs were still stacked neatly in the holder. She kneeled by the hearth, threw on several bricks of peat as Roslyn had shown her and then lit it. A moment later, the flame sputtered to life, emitting warmth. The flickering brilliance lit up the room.

Heaving a sigh, she decided it was time for her to retire for the night. If they were to ride for two days to meet his clan chieftain, she needed to get some rest. She lit the candle by the bed, then removed the stone from her pocket, pausing a moment to run her finger over the jagged edges beneath the cloth. She placed it on the bedside table by the candelabra.

She tugged the tie off the end of her hair to remove the braid, letting the strands fall loose about her shoulders. It felt good to run her fingers through the tangled locks and over her scalp. She wasn't used to wearing her hair up so much and her head was tender from the constant tension of her braid. She would have to find a new way to wear her hair.

She slipped out of her overdress, remaining in her shift as she pulled back the thick blankets from the bed. She left her thick stockings on since her feet were still cold.

As she climbed into bed, pulling the covers to her chin, she wished she had a book to read to occupy her mind. She was bored, and with nothing to do, it allowed her mind to run amok with things she should not be thinking.

Things like Callum's lips. The way he kissed her. The way his eyes sparkled in the half-light with something akin to adoration. She *wanted* to believe he adored her, but who was she kidding? He was a sexy medieval Highlander and she was…

Well, she was nothing but a plain girl with freckles on her face and boring brown eyes. All that was going for her was her red hair.

A swift knock on her door startled her. She sat up, staring at it while clutching the bed covers to her chest, wondering if she should answer. Wondering who could be at her door this time of night.

Another faint knock.

"Who is it?" she called.

A pause, then, "Callum."

"Oh, my God," she whispered. Her hands started shaking.

What was he doing at her door? Had he changed his mind about her going with him tomorrow?

She slid out of the bed, grabbing a blanket and wrapping it around her shoulders before padding to the door. She pulled it open a crack. He stood on the other side of the door, his eyes wide as his gaze went over her face then the length of her hair hanging in waves about her shoulders. She shifted from one foot to the other. She was not uncomfortable—she could never be with Callum—but his gaze was so *intense* it was unnerving. As though he were seeing her for the first time.

"Yes?" she said, peering up at him.

His face softened and something about the way he looked at her made her want to fling open the door and fall into his arms. She remained where she was, holding the door so tightly, her fingers cramped.

"Och, lass, I came to tell ye…" He paused, took a step back and raked a hand through his hair. He seemed nervous, which was unlike him.

"Tell me what?" she asked.

Her voice was even and cool like she wasn't expecting bad news. Like she was hoping for something else. Perhaps not a declaration of love, but…what? What did she want from him? Frustration edged through her. What was she even thinking? He was not interested in her like that. He kissed her because…well, she didn't know why he kissed her.

He swallowed hard, his throat moving. "We willna be going to see the chieftain on the morrow."

Shock rolled through her. Something had changed. But what? "We won't?"

"Nay." He didn't elaborate.

"Why?" she asked, confused.

"Mayhap I could come in and tell ye what I've learned," he suggested.

Her brows rose. "You want to come in?"

"God's teeth," he swore under his breath. "I ken the hour is late but I came here to tell ye…" He paused again and shifted from one foot to the other. He blew out a breath and met her gaze. "I saw Moira."

Her blood turned to ice as her body stiffened with surprise. "Moira? The shopkeeper?"

"Aye."

She stared at him a long, hard moment as her heart thudded and the blood whooshed in her ears. She pushed open the door wide for him to enter and stepped aside.

"I hope you have whiskey with you for this story."

His handsome face broke into a grin. "Should I get some ale, then?"

A laugh bubbled up her throat as she waved him inside. "I was kidding."

He stepped through the door. She closed it behind him, then wasted no time pulling the chair over from the other side of the room in front of the hearth. She offered it to him while she perched on the foot of the bed, pulling the blanket tighter around her shoulders. He eased down into the chair, which was much like the one in his chamber.

She had a vision—a reminder of her all too erotic dream. Immediately, she pushed it aside. Now was not the time for that.

"So, you saw Moira?" She did her best to sound casual, as though it did not affect her.

"She came to me in the stable after ye left," he said.

"She came to you? Like in the flesh?"

He nodded.

Her skin prickled with gooseflesh. She clutched her elbows. "You sound surprised by that."

In truth, she was surprised by that. How was Moira able to travel through time without the keystone to see Callum? Who exactly was this mysterious shopkeeper? She watched his face as the firelight flickered over it. There was acceptance in his expression.

"Aye," he said slowly. He glanced toward the tapestries behind the bed. "I understand now."

Evie tipped her head to one side. "Understand? Does that mean you believe in the prophecy? You believe I'm from the future?"

"I do," he said.

She thought she would feel some relief over hearing that admission come from him but she didn't. Now that he believed her, now that he knew, what did that mean for her? She fought the urge to look at the stone on the table beside the bed and instead focused on him. There was more he hadn't shared with her.

"What else?" she heard herself ask. Though she had tried to remain strong, her words wobbled.

"She said war is coming." His gaze flickered to the tapestries. As if on impulse, he rose and walked toward them. She turned and watched as he pointed to the one with the three women. "These are the three goddesses: Moira, Bridget, and Athea. They are the Triple Goddess."

Ah, so this Moira was a time goddess.

"And this." He pointed to the army moving toward Moira standing on the hilltop. "The MacDonald clan. They want the Chronos Stone."

"The Chronos Stone?" She moved from the bed and joined him, soaking up the warmth from his body as she stood next to him. She folded her arms, clutching the edges of the blanket.

"Aye," he said, his voice low and slow. "That's what she said they called it. They broke it into three pieces—the night of the Shattering—to keep it from the MacDonald." He turned to her then. "She said the MacLeods and the Sinclairs were there that night. They pledged a vow to her—that the clans would forever protect the stone and keep it safe."

She stared at him a long moment as her mouth went bone dry. She recalled something Hamish had said to her. "One divine destiny."

"Aye."

They stared at each other, the only sound that of the flickering fire. The truth pounded through her. Her destiny was forged in the promise of an ancient clan she had never known existed—until now.

"I was meant to come here," she said then.

Nodding, he said, "I believe ye were."

Her heart thumped a wild beat as she lifted her gaze and met his eyes. The truth flickered deep within those blue depths. The truth he had finally acknowledged.

"And I was meant to find you." Her voice was but a whisper.

Again, he nodded.

It was a deep understanding that pounded through her, too. If she was meant to come here and meant to find Callum, then she was meant to stay here. The thought of returning home faded from her mind in that instant.

"Together we have to protect the stone." She looked at the piece wrapped in the handkerchief on the bedside table. "But what about the other pieces?"

"I cannae say," he said, "but it seems to me they'll arrive here in the past."

Her head snapped up. A wild spurt of hope shot through her. "Then that would mean my sisters…"

Her words drifted away. It was definitely too much to hope her sisters were meant to travel back in time, too. That meant at some point she would be reunited with them.

"Aye, and my brothers."

She lifted a brow in question. "The six of us?" she asked, thinking of her and her two sisters.

"We are the ones destined to put the pieces back together and protect the stone."

A coldness settled over her as she stood there watching the firelight flicker over the hard chiseled features of his face. If that were true, then her sisters—both Chloe and Brianna—would likely arrive in the past. She did not understand why she and her sisters had to travel back in time to help the MacLeod brothers.

Where were the Sinclairs of this time? Why were they unable to help? It was a question she was burning to ask Moira. She wished she had been with Callum when he saw her.

If her sisters came into the past, then what? How would she explain it all to them? Would they believe? Callum was a tough customer. It had taken a visit from the goddess herself to make him believe in the prophecy.

Chloe would adapt with ease after the initial shock wore off. But Brianna? She wanted to laugh out loud to think of her beach bum sister in the rough and rugged Highlands. She would dislike the weather. She would dislike not having the comfort of modern conveniences. Most of all, she would dislike having to be with her and Chloe.

And then something else occurred to her. Bruce MacDonald had told her it had called to her. Was there some mystical silent echo the stone emitted to call them to their destiny?

"That's why MacDonald came here, isn't it? They think the stone is here."

"Aye, they ken the stone is here, and they will be wanting it."

Fear skipped through her, making her nerves jangle. "They'll come for it again, won't they?"

"Aye." He gave her a pointed look. "I will protect ye with my life."

Her knees nearly buckled. Roslyn had said Callum was fiercely loyal.

"Callum, I—"

"There is nothing left to say, lass," he said, as though expecting her to object to the idea she needed protecting. "There is…one more thing Moira said."

Her heart skipped. "What is that?"

He didn't respond as he reached up. His hands smoothed over the sides of her face, cupping her chin, tipping it back as he took one more step toward her, closing the gap between them. Her heart pounded so hard, she thought it might beat right out of her chest.

"She said ye would do the same for me. Protect me."

She blinked. She was unsure how she would be able to accomplish something like that. How would she protect a man like Callum? She was certainly no warrior goddess. She didn't know how but she nodded.

"I will do what I need to do to protect you and the keystone."

"Aye, lass, I dinnae doubt that." A smile lifted the corner of his mouth.

Before she had a chance to respond, he kissed her. She melted into him, allowing him to wrap her in his arms and push her back toward the bed. The backs of her knees hit the mattress. Oh, she understood where this was going and she wasn't going to stop it. She was going to allow herself to enjoy the moment and to fall into bed with the sexy Highlander.

She lifted her arms to wrap around him. As she did, the blanket fell from her shoulders. She tugged him closer until their bodies meshed with nothing more than a breath of linen between them. A moan escaped her throat as he continued to kiss her. Then his lips moved from hers and made a trail down the side of her neck. One hand tangled in the length of her hair, gently tugging her head back to give him more access.

She froze there, the sensation too much for her to handle.

"Callum?"

"Hmm?" His chest rumbled in a delicious vibration against her.

"I…" She didn't know what she wanted to say and instead pressed her lips together.

Well, she did know but she was too shy and chicken to say it out loud. She was never the kind of girl to ask for what she wanted.

He pulled back, his gaze meeting hers. His blue gaze was so intense and so incredible that she never wanted to look away. She loved the depths of his eyes. She could fall into them as though they were the deep blue ocean.

"Do ye wish for me to stop?"

"No," she said slowly.

"Something else, then?"

"You seem…different."

He cupped her face in his hands. She relished the roughness of his palms. He pressed his forehead against hers.

"Mayhap I move too quickly, then," he said.

"No!" she said on a breath. "No, you didn't. I…I don't know what my problem is."

There was a long pause as he continued to hold her face. "I dinnae want to believe ye were who you said ye were. I dinnae want to believe anything my da said about destiny and prophecy was true. But the moment I picked ye up from the ground and held ye in my arms changed everything."

A breath shuddered out of her. "The moment I landed here in the past changed everything for me, too."

He pulled back, still cupping her face and looking deep into her eyes. "If ye were meant to be here as Moira said, then I dinnae think ye can return home, lass. But I can promise ye I will make sure ye are well cared for here. With me."

Well, now. How could she possibly refuse that? She slid her hands up his chest, feeling the curves of the strong muscles there. She encircled his neck, pulling him closer to her. Her mouth was a breath away from his.

"I believe that," she said on a whisper. Then she demanded something she had never demanded of any man. It was a risk, she knew, but she wanted to say it because she felt she had nothing left to lose. "Now, take me to bed, you handsome Scot."

He grinned. "As my lady commands."

CHAPTER TWENTY-NINE

C ALLUM SHED THE tartan he was wearing and tossed it on the chair by the hearth. Then he removed his boots and breeches, kicking them aside. He remained standing in front of her in a long linen tunic. Her heart was pounding so hard she was sure he heard.

Unsure of his expectations, she did the first thing that came to mind. She lifted one leg, knee bent, and reached under to untie the strip of material that held up her stockings. Before she could finish, he moved toward her, sliding his hand under the bend of her knee.

Her hands froze as he slid up and over one knee to the edge of her wool stocking. Then he tugged, ever so gently, as he pulled it down over her knee and the length of her leg. His roughened palm sent deep shivers of desire through her as he pulled away the stocking, dropping it to the floor.

Swallowing hard, she lifted her other leg to allow him to perform the same task. It was as though he were a master at untying the little piece of cloth at the top of her thigh without looking. Then he slid the stocking down over her leg and off.

That was probably the most erotic thing that had ever happened to her. Should she confess she still wore her modern day undergarments? What would he think of that?

She didn't wait for him to move. She gathered the shift in her hands and pulled it off over her head, tossing it away. That deep blue-eyed gaze traveled over her cloth-covered breasts and hips with question and curiosity.

"It's what the ladies wear underneath where I come from," she said. Her voice wobbled with her nerves.

A dark brow lifted in bemusement. With shaking hands, she reached behind her and unclasped her bra, then let the material slide down the length of her arms to the floor. Despite the warmth of the fire blazing brightly in the hearth, there was a chill in the air.

Callum's appreciative gaze was on her as he reached for her. His hands were in her hair, his fingers running through the long length and then letting the strands slide between his fingers in a fiery red waterfall.

"Och, I've wanted to do this since I first saw ye."

Gooseflesh erupted along every inch of her as her nipples hardened with an aching need when they brushed against the linen of his shirt. He bent to kiss her neck, his lips warm and soft. Flames of desire pounded through her.

With a tentative touch, she slipped her hands under his long tunic and was delighted to land on the roundness of his buttocks. A deep guttural groan of appreciation rumbled through his chest. She grinned as she moved upward. His skin was hot and smooth as her fingers traveled over the curve of his back.

He was perfection.

And she was impatient. She pushed the linen up in a move that indicated she wanted it off him. He complied, pulling the material over his head and tossing it to the floor with her shift. He was naked before her in all his glory.

There was a sprinkling of dark hair across his broad, muscular chest. His shoulders and biceps were thick and strong. Her hands landed on his upper arms, feeling the power there as he tensed.

His hand landed on the material between her legs as though testing her. She shivered against him.

"Should I remove that?" she asked. She glanced up at him, looking at him through her lashes and feeling a shyness she hadn't felt before.

"I will."

He flashed a wicked grin as he dropped to his knees, pulling down the material with him. She stepped out of it and kicked it aside, self-conscious and aware of the cool air brushing her bare skin. She crossed her arms over her breasts to conceal them. When he saw her do it, he reached for her, his hands landing on her wrists and tugging them away.

"Dinnae cover yerself, lass."

"But, I—"

He pressed a finger against her lips. "Nay."

He slipped his hands over the swell of her breasts, making the throbbing between her legs increase tenfold. God, if he didn't hurry, she was going to explode.

Wrapping her arms around his waist, she tugged him closer as she backed toward the bed once more and then melted against the feather mattress, taking him with her. He grunted once as he caught himself before landing on top of her—much to her dismay.

But then he tucked his shoulders under the bend of her legs and leaned down to taste her. She sucked in a sharp breath as soon as his mouth was on her, teasing that sensitive swollen nub that held all her secrets. He coaxed her to climax immediately. She clenched her jaw tight to keep from crying out with the pleasure. She clutched the linen bedsheets in her fists as he continued the onslaught.

When she thought she might die of sheer pleasure, he kissed his way upward from navel to neck and then slid his heated, hard body on top of her, pushing her upward onto the bed with a leverage she hadn't known he'd had.

Before she could react, his hardened length slid deep inside her, catching her off guard. A shuddering breath escaped through her lips as she clung to him while he moved, filling her until she cried out again.

She wrapped her arms around him as every muscle tensed

tight as a bowstring while he moved against her. Her legs tightened around his waist, the sharpness of his hipbones biting into the tender flesh of her thighs. Everything about him seemed perfect and right. She allowed the climax to overcome her. It shuddered through her from head to toe. Her nails dug into his back, making him groan in pleasure. That deep rumble vibrated through his chest as they kissed.

Then he pulled out as his own pleasure eclipsed him. Before she could protest, he gathered her close, pulling her into his arms. Though they laid across the bed, she didn't want to suggest they move because she was limp and sated with a joy she had not felt in her entire life.

And before any other thoughts flickered through her mind, her eyes closed and she was fast asleep.

EVIE AWOKE THE following morning. The first thing she noticed was the man sleeping next to her, snoring softly. The second thing she noticed was that the fire had gone out. But that didn't matter too much as she snuggled closer to Callum. His body heat was enough to keep them both warm.

The dream she had of him did not happen the way she expected. No, it was a thousand times better. She knew without a shadow of a doubt she was in love with him. And though she missed her sister and wondered what Chloe was doing, she didn't want to return and be parted from Callum forever.

He may not know how to send her home, but he sure knew how to make her feel things she had never felt with anyone else before. No man would ever come close to Callum.

She remained still as she examined his profile. He slept on his back. His face was quiet and in repose, though he did snore. Perhaps in time she would dislike it and make him roll to his side, but for now it was endearing and proved to her he was flesh and blood and she hadn't dreamed everything that had happened between them.

Thinking of it made her cheeks flush hot.

At some point, she had woken up to find she was snuggled against him in the bed, buried under the thick covers. He had managed to right them so they were no longer across the mattress. Then she had drifted back to sleep with her head on his chest and his hands in her hair. Now that she was awake again and the faint morning light pressed against the window, she admired how fine a man he was.

Her fingers trailed along his muscular chest, the coarse hair springing back as she dragged the tips of her fingers through it. Then she flattened her palm and moved it down the downy softness over his abdomen, enjoying the feel of the sprinkling of hair across his stomach.

The men she had dated before were not big and brawny like Callum. She realized what she had been missing in her romantic life all this time, and it was a man like him.

On impulse, she moved her hand lower and was mildly surprised by the hardened length against her palm. Grinning, she shifted so that she straddled him and yet was able to keep her body close to his.

He never opened his eyes as his hands landed on her hips.

"God's teeth, I hope this isna a dream." His voice was thick with sleep.

She leaned closer to him, her lips brushing his, and whispered, "It isn't."

Settling her hips over his, he eased inside her. The heat pounded through her, making her flush hot and wild as she moved against him. His big hands helped her along, rocking her back and forth as they found their rhythm.

A lazy grin creased his mouth as his eyes opened slowly, revealing those enchanting blue depths that gazed back up at her. Her hair fell down over her shoulders like a curtain, the tips brushing his chest. An appreciative noise rumbled through him, emboldening her as she rocked to and fro, increasing the speed.

With a gasp, she sat upright, bending back enough to get the feeling she wanted out of him. His fingers tightened on her hips, digging into her flesh more as the pleasure pounded through her. She tossed her head back as the climax overtook her, a sigh of bliss escaping through her lips. And then it was all over as quickly as it had begun.

Evie remained where she was as she tipped her head back down to look at him. There was a spark of desire still there deep in the ocean of his eyes, sending her senses reeling. He was, quite simply, the most beautiful man she'd ever been with. She didn't deserve him, but she was certainly glad she was with him.

That lazy grin lit his face again. "Och, lass, yer full of spirit and spark."

She tipped her head to the side. "And that's good?"

He chuckled as he rose up to meet her, his lips landing on hers in an unexpected kiss of fervent passion. Her arms went around him, allowing herself to fall into the blissful moment. When he pulled away, his eyes were flickering with desire and need.

"Oh, aye, 'tis a *verra* good thing."

She knew the morning was waning, but she didn't want their private time together to end. She wanted to keep him all to herself all day in this bed. Naked.

Callum must have sensed her thoughts for he tipped his head to one side. He reached up with one hand and twined a bit of her hair around a finger, then clutched a fistful. With a gentle tug, he pulled her head back. His fiery lips landed on the long column of her throat.

"Ohh," she breathed.

He kissed his way up to her earlobe and then gave it a nip. It ignited a fire between her legs once again and making her realize he was still there, buried deep inside her.

"Oh," she said again.

"I mean to have ye again, lass."

She tightened her arms around him, letting her fingers dive into the length of his hair. Another thing—she had never been with a man who had hair longer than hers. She liked it more than she wanted to admit.

"I mean to let you." The words came out a roughened whisper.

Grasping her in his arms, he flipped her on her back so that she looked up at him. He had managed not to break their intimate connection. That was probably the second most erotic thing that had ever happened to her.

He peered down at her, his gaze flickering over her face. She was self-conscious of all the freckles dotting her cheeks and nose and she flushed hot. She wanted to look away, but there was no place else to look except right at him.

"Why are you looking at me like that?" She forced herself not to squirm against him, but all she wanted was for him to stop that scrutinizing gaze.

"Ye have a gold fleck in yer right eye. Did ye ken that?"

Surprise flickered through her as she stared back at him. "No," she said slowly. "Do I?"

"Oh, aye." He brushed hair from her forehead in a soothing way that made her heart trip.

"And you…like this?"

He gave her half a grin. "Och…aye, lass."

"I always thought my eyes were boring brown. Like the color of a mud puddle." She didn't mean to say it, but the words tumbled out before she was able to stop them.

"Yer eyes are beautiful."

Waves of contentment rippled through her, making her feelings for him intensify. As much as she wanted to push away those feelings, they were all consuming. She was a goner.

"And these freckles on yer cheeks and nose." His finger traced a line along her face from one side to the other, leaving a tingling sensation in his wake.

Again, she flushed hot, the heat pounding through her

cheeks. "I've always hated them."

He kissed the tip of her nose, whispering his love for each part of her face. "Dinnae do that, lass. N'er do that."

God, but she loved his accent. Her eyes fluttered closed as he continued to place long, slow, soft kisses along her face. How had she ever lived before without him? She didn't know.

"I was…" Her words came out a breathy whisper. "People made fun of me because of them."

With his lips still against her cheek, he muttered, "I will kill any who do such a thing."

How endearing was that? She swooned right there in the bed under his big, massive body. And she knew at that moment she was forever and always his.

CHAPTER THIRTY

A N ERRATIC POUNDING on the chamber door startled them out of their happy love cocoon.

"Callum? Are ye in there, lad?"

It was Dougal calling through the door. Callum swore under his breath a vile oath he hoped Evie didn't hear. She clutched him, trying to keep him from moving away from her.

"Ignore him. Maybe he'll go away," she whispered.

Another knock. "Callum, I ken yer there. Ye were no in yer own bedchamber."

"God's teeth." He kissed her quickly. "I'll see what he wants and shoo him away."

Because he had a naked, bonnie lass in his bed—well, her bed—he intended to keep her there as long as possible. He slid from the bed, leaving the warmth of her arms. As he strode to the door, he snatched up his plaid and wrapped it around his hips. At the door, he cracked it open to shield her from Dougal's eyesight.

"What do ye want?" he growled.

Dougal gave him a grin, humor and a knowing glint in his eyes. "Ah, sorry to interrupt, my lord. But there is news ye needed to hear. Best to come from me than yer brother."

He stiffened, his hand tightening on the door. "What has Jamie done this time?"

"It was no Jamie." Dougal shifted from one foot to the other as discomfort flickered through him. "'Twas Malcolm."

Alarm sounded through Callum as he stood there staring in disbelief at his steward. "Malcolm?"

Dougal, looking ashen, continued. "Aye. The village under MacDonald's care was set ablaze."

Hot, wild anger shot through him.

"By God's blood, how do ye ken this?" he demanded, unable to stifle the fury in his voice.

"He went during the night since he thought ye were gone with the lass to see the chieftain. We had word early this morning about what happened. When I questioned the stable hand, he admitted he saw Malcolm riding out under the cover of darkness."

"And Jamie?" For Callum knew he looked up to his other brother and was often an accomplice to his misdeeds.

"As far as I can tell, the lad is innocent."

"Hell's bells." He pressed his lips together in a thin line as the anger pounded his temples. "Where is Malcolm now?"

"Confined to his room," he said.

"Bring him to the great hall. And Dougal…" He paused, a sick feeling in the pit of his stomach. "Bring my claymore."

The steward's face paled but he nodded. "Aye, my lord."

Callum closed the door and turned to face Evie who sat up in the bed clutching the blankets to her chest, showing off her pale, slim shoulders. Fear sparkled in her eyes.

"What's happened?" she asked.

"Malcolm took it upon himself to attack one of the MacDonald villages. He burned it."

She swallowed hard. "Were there…people killed?"

"I dinnae ken, but I intend to find out." He gathered his clothes and started to dress. "Dougal is bringing him to the great hall."

"Why would Malcolm do such a thing?"

Callum paused in his frantic dressing to look at her. For the first time, he saw her for who she was—a woman who didn't understand their ways.

"Retribution for killing Da," he said.

Evie slid to the edge of the bed. "I'm sorry, Callum."

"Aye, so am I. For now, as laird, I have to punish him."

When he finished dressing, he turned to her. She still sat in the bed, holding the blankets to her chest.

"What are you going to do?" she asked.

"What I have to." He leaned in for a kiss. "Stay here, lass. I'll be back when I can."

He didn't want to leave her, nor did he want for her to stay behind, but he knew it was the right thing to do. He didn't want her to see him punish his brother—nor did he want to do that—but if he didn't, then it would send the wrong message that Callum condoned his actions, which he didn't.

As the door closed, he heaved a sigh and headed for the great hall.

EVIE WATCHED HIM close the door behind him. She hated seeing the anger coupled with disappointment on his face. The moment he was gone, she slid out of the bed and did a frantic search for her undergarments. By the time she tugged her shift over her head, there was a knock on the door.

"Yes?" she called.

Roslyn poked her head in, her brow creased with worry. Evie waved her inside.

"Help me dress," Evie said. "I'm going to—"

"Nay, lass. The laird sent me to look after ye."

Evie shook her head. "No, I need to be there. I need to—"

"There's no arguing with me," she said, her tone stern. For a moment, the woman reminded Evie of her own mother. "I cannae disobey him. Neither can ye."

She wanted to object with some tart reply that he wasn't the boss of her, but that didn't seem like the adult thing to do. It sounded childish. Instead, she sagged against the mattress with her hands in her lap. A tight knot of fear was in the pit of her stomach.

"What's he going to do? I heard him tell Dougal to bring his claymore."

"Aye," was all Roslyn said with no elaboration.

She busied herself at the hearth, rebuilding the fire to get it started once again. Evie clutched her elbows as gooseflesh tickled over her arms and legs. She had a horrible idea of what Callum intended to do with that claymore and perhaps it was right that she stayed in the bedchamber with Roslyn. She didn't want to see a man murdered in the great hall—a man that was the laird's own brother.

She spied her stockings on the floor where Callum had left them—a heated flush pulsed to her cheeks—and snatched them up. There had to be some way to convince the woman to let her out of this bedchamber.

As she tugged on the first stocking, she paused there as the thought crossed her mind. What did she think to do? She had no power here. Callum was in charge as laird and Malcolm was his younger brother. Still, though, the thought of him wielding the claymore against his brother made a cold shiver of fear run through her.

When Roslyn got the fire going, she pushed up from the floor, brushing the dirt from her hands.

"Was what Dougal said true?" Evie asked. When Roslyn gave her a questioning look, she added, "About what he did."

Worry followed by sorrow crossed her aged face as she sank into the chair by the fire. She clasped her hands in front of her and held them still in her lap, as if she were determined not to fidget.

"Aye," she said, her voice low.

"Did people die?" Evie asked.

Roslyn cut her a glance. There was pain in her eyes which gave Evie her answer. A sickening feeling crept through her as her hands shook. It was hard for her to believe that Malcolm would attack innocent people and burn down their village. All in the name of vengeance. It seemed barbaric.

"So…what do we do now?" Evie asked.

"Stay here until the laird comes for us." Her voice was low and wobbled with a bit of emotion as she spoke.

Evie understood then there was nothing for her to do but wait. But she was never good at sitting around and waiting. She got to her feet and turned her attention to the tapestries along the wall. They hadn't changed much in the last twenty-four hours but something did catch her eye.

The one next to Chloe began to show a new image. The outline of Dundale Castle was clearly there. In front of it, the outline of a mob heading right for the keep. The leader held aloft a great axe. She sucked in a breath and looked back at the one with Moira on the hill and the army approaching. The same great axe was wielded in that tapestry. The light glinted off the blade.

"Oh, God," she whispered, pressing her cold, shaking fingers against her lips.

She glanced back at the hanging with the newly formed image of the castle and *knew* without a shadow of a doubt who was leading that army.

MacDonald.

"Roslyn, I need to see Callum immediately." She spun to face the woman as she spoke.

Her head snapped up as if she was sleeping with her chin on her chest. "Och, lassie, I cannae take ye to him."

In a fit of frustration, she jerked the tapestry from the wall. It fell in a heap to the floor. She knelt and quickly rolled it up, scooping it off the floor in a bundle. The material was heavier than it looked hanging on the wall.

"I need to show him this."

Roslyn's brows drew together in confusion as she peered at the material in Evie's hands. "A tapestry? Why?"

Evie shook it at her. "Because of what's on it!"

"There is naught on there but a weaving of flowers, lass."

She stared at her as her mouth went dry. Then she glanced down at the material in her hands. "What?" The word came out on a breath.

"Aye, lass. 'Tis nothing but a decorative wall hanging."

But the image was clearly there for her to see. "No…it's…"

Realization dawned. Perhaps Roslyn could not see the images on the wall hangings. She was not of MacLeod or Sinclair blood. Evie needed to test her theory.

"What about those on the wall there?" she asked, nodding toward them.

"Och, lass, more of the same. Nothing more than wall hangings that have been here for years. They're dusty. I should take them out and beat the dust—"

"No!"

When she gave her a look of confused surprise, Evie cleared her throat.

"I mean, that's not necessary. They're not that dusty." She clutched the material tighter in her hands, her mind racing to form some way to get the woman out of her bedchamber so she could find Callum.

Her theory was right. Roslyn couldn't see the morphing images on the wall hangings. But she could see them and so could Callum. It stood to reason Malcolm and Jamie would be able to as well, since they were MacLeod blood.

She tossed the tapestry aside as if it were nothing more than discarded material. She tried her best to act natural because she needed the woman gone.

"Do you think I could have something to eat? I'm famished." Evie plastered on her best endearing smile in the hopes the woman would buy her act and take pity on her.

"There are oat cakes in the kitchen." She pushed up from the chair. "I'll fetch them." Then turned back to her with a stern expression. "Ye stay here, lass."

"Yes, of course," she said, too brightly.

The woman slipped out the door and closed it behind her.

The moment she was gone, she pulled on her overdress and her stockings and slipped on her shoes. Then she snatched the tapestry from the bed and headed for the door.

She pulled it open. The hallway was empty. She had to hurry if she was going to make it to the great hall before Roslyn returned. She dashed out of the bedchamber.

CHAPTER THIRTY-ONE

D OUGAL HANDED CALLUM his claymore with reluctance. A frown of disapproval creased the man's face.

"Ye cannae mean to—"

"I cannae allow him to go unpunished," Callum interrupted, his voice hard and unforgiving.

Duty and honor dictated that he do the right thing and punish Malcolm for his heinous act, but it was difficult for Callum. Even as he stood there with the sword in his hand waiting for his men to bring his brother from his bedchamber.

Jamie arrived first, his face creased with concern as he glanced from the weapon in Callum's hand up to his face.

"What do you intend to do, brother? Run him through?" Jamie demanded.

"What would ye have me do, Jamie? Allow him to go unpunished? When ye ken as well as I do this was an act of war."

"Devil take ye, ye cannae kill yer own blood!"

"Stand down, little brother," Malcolm said as he entered the great hall with two of their men. "I dinnae need ye to fight for me."

The anger flashed across the younger man's face as he stepped aside. He crossed his arms over his chest and watched as Malcolm paused in front of Callum.

Malcolm's gaze was hard and unforgiving as he stared at him. His face was devoid of any remorse.

"So…" Callum began. "'Tis true what ye did."

"Ye were no going to act, so I had to."

"Tell me the truth, brother. I want to hear the whole story."

"Ye were no in yer chamber," Malcolm said with one brow lifted as if he insinuated he was elsewhere—with Evie. And he was, but that was beside the point.

"So ye took it upon yerself to leave the keep and go to the village?" Callum asked. "Because ye thought I had gone to see the chieftain. Ye thought to get away with it, did ye?"

"It was an opportunity," Malcolm simply said. "I dinnae deny I torched the village. Eye for an eye, brother."

Frustration edged through him as he gripped the hilt of the claymore until his hand cramped. "I warned ye no to do anything rash and yet ye did. Who helped ye?"

Malcolm did not shift his gaze, but the imperceptible movement of his men gave away their guilt. Callum remained rooted in place, refusing to look at them though he knew. There was no way Malcolm rode out alone.

"No one." His voice was flat.

"Ye mean to tell me ye acted alone?" Callum asked. He shook his head. "I cannae believe ye."

"Aye, I acted alone."

In a sense, he admired his brother for taking all the blame and not naming those who accompanied him on his reign of terror. He still did not know how many innocents were killed in the razing of the village and he was loath to ask. How much blood was on their hands now? It was bad enough Jamie had shunned the MacDonald lass. Now this.

He huffed out an exasperated sigh.

"Och, by the rood, Malcolm. Why did ye have to act so recklessly? Do ye realize what ye've done? What wrath ye have brought down upon us? Our clan?"

"Do what ye will to me, brother, but I stand accused alone. I accept the consequences of my actions." His gaze flickered to the claymore in his hand for a brief moment before returning back to his face. "No matter what ye decide."

Callum stood ramrod straight. His palm broke into a hot sweat against the hilt as he gripped it. What honor demanded was that he punish his brother by beheading him. A life for a life. One life for the many he took did not seem rational. And how could he? Jamie was right. He could not kill his own blood, no matter how horrific the crime.

As he stood there in indecision, he thought of his da. What would Hamish do if he were the one to mete out the punishment? A fight to the death? A simple beheading? Or nothing at all?

Anger pounded through him as he lifted his sword and swung it in a wide arc, narrowly missing his brother's face. Malcolm did not so much as flinch. His sword came down on the great hall table with a resounding thud, leaving a deep gash mark in the top of it. Jamie's eyes went wide as he looked from brother to brother. Dougal sucked in a sharp breath. The two men who had accompanied Malcolm flinched.

But his brother had not moved a muscle. He glared right back at Callum as if he were in the right.

"Ye missed," he said in a dark even tone.

"Get out of my sight," Callum growled, his voice low. "Ye are hereby banished from Dundale forevermore."

No one moved. The great hall fell into a deathly silence. Callum stared at his brother and his brother stared right back until at last he gave one nod of his head.

"I will gather my things and—"

"Nay," Callum interrupted. "With the clothes on yer back."

His gaze flickered to the two men who stood next to Malcolm. Two of his best men and likely the two who went with Malcolm judging by the guilty looks on their faces.

"And you two as well. Dougal, see them to the stable and make sure they leave. I dinnae want to see their faces here again."

"As you command, my lord."

"Ye cannae do this, Callum," Jamie protested.

"I can and I am," Callum said, his voice unforgiving.

"But—"

"Am I laird or no?" he roared. "Mind yerself, laddie."

"Or what? I'm next? Ye cannae think to banish us both."

Callum remained silent as Jamie gave him a withering gaze. He understood it hurt the lad to see his older brother, whom he idolized led out of the keep, but there was nothing to be done for it. He charged after them. He would not be surprised if Jamie left with his brother. The door banged closed leaving Callum alone in silence. He dropped his claymore. It clattered to the floor.

"Callum?"

Evie's quiet voice rang out into the hushed stillness. He turned to see her standing on the opposite end of the great hall clutching rolled up material, her face devoid of color. Her knuckles were white.

"Och, lass, dinnae I tell ye to wait for me? Where's Roslyn?"

"It's not her fault," she said, quickly. "Don't be angry with her. I slipped out. I had to show you this."

She charged forward. As she neared, he realized she clutched one of the tapestries in her hands.

"What's this?"

"Look at it." She shoved it toward him.

He had no choice but to take it from her. The material unfurled. He held it up to see Dundale with an army charging toward it. And leading that army was Rory MacDonald brandishing his great axe. A cold chill settled through him as he stared at the morphing image.

"I don't know when it appeared, but it wasn't there last night before you…" Her words trailed off. She took a deep breath, expelled it. "Do you know what it means?"

"Aye, lass," he said, his voice quiet and calmer than it should be. "It means we're going to be attacked."

"That's what I was afraid of." She moved closer to him. "What do we do now?"

He stared down at the image of the army that slowly moved across the woven fabric inch by inch. As laird, he had a responsibility to protect his clan and all those who resided within the keep. That included Evie. But Evie didn't belong here. She belonged in another time, another world.

He suspected the MacDonalds were coming for more than revenge. Likely they knew that part of the keystone was somewhere within the keep. If they breached the walls and invaded, they would find it and try to use it.

Though he was not the one to swear to protect the keystone, his ancestor was and he had to honor that. His gaze drifted from the tapestry to the petite woman standing next to him, shivering. Her hair was in fiery waves framing her lovely face which was pinched with worry. He understood then he could not have her here, or the stone. But he didn't want to alarm her. He didn't want to tell her what he was thinking for it would put the fear as well as defiance into her. One thing he had understood about his termagant bonnie lass was that she would never go quietly, even though he was giving her exactly what she wanted.

"We're going to protect the keep."

Roslyn hurried into the great hall then. She came to an abrupt halt. Her eyes widened when she saw them standing together.

"My apologies, my lord, the lass—"

"Roslyn, 'tis all right. Dinnae fash yerself." He rolled up the material and handed it back to Evie. "Take that back to yer bedchamber, lass, and leave it there. Tonight, ye will stay with me."

For a moment she looked as though she wanted to object. He reached for her, unable to stop himself from whisking the wild locks of hair off her shoulder.

"'Tis the way I can protect ye," he said, his voice soft.

"All right," she said at last.

"I'll help ye gather yer things," Roslyn offered. She motioned for Evie to follow her back to the guest bedchamber.

But she remained there, staring up at him with those big brown eyes filled with concern and worry. He brushed the back of his hand over her cheek.

"Go, lass," he said, his voice quiet.

Finally, she nodded, clutching the tapestry in her hands. She turned and walked away, leaving him alone once again.

CHAPTER THIRTY-TWO

I T WAS TO be war. He understood that all too well. And so did Evie.

The moment she saw the image in the wall hanging, she understood. She didn't know if showing him would help. She hoped it would give them a fighting chance to be prepared for whatever may come.

She had never been in a castle under siege which was a silly thing to think. The closest she'd come to being under siege was in the museum the night of the gala when Bruce MacDonald tried to steal the stone from her.

In her haste to get to Callum, she'd left the keystone. She admonished herself for leaving it behind with the door to the bedchamber open. Callum entrusted her with it and what did she do? Left it on her bedside table like an idiot.

As soon as she was back in the bedchamber, she tossed the tapestry on the bed and swiped the handkerchief off the table. She double-checked to make sure the stone was within the folds of the soft material and was relieved to see it was.

The lines were glowing. Faintly. What did that mean?

She hadn't a clue. The keystone was largely a mystery to her. She quickly wrapped it back up and slipped it into her pocket. Roslyn rehung the tapestry on the wall next to the one of her sister, Chloe.

"I've gathered yer things, lass. Shall we move to the laird's chamber?"

Evie stared at the wall hangings one last time, thinking of Chloe and Brianna. If what they suspected was true about the keystone, then both of them would be arriving in the past soon enough, each with a piece of the keystone.

"Lassie? Are ye well?"

"Oh, yes." She turned away from the tapestry. "I'm ready."

Together, they left the guest bedchamber behind and headed for Callum's.

EVIE WAS FULL of nervous energy. To keep herself occupied, she insisted on helping Roslyn in the kitchen, even though she tried to wave her off and tell her the scullery maids would be plenty of help.

"I need a task," she pleaded.

When Roslyn saw her desperate expression, she gave a nod of understanding.

The last time she had helped Roslyn in the kitchen, she hadn't noticed the other maids there to help. Now, though, she was met with wide-eyed gazes of curiosity.

"Back to work now," Roslyn snapped.

The two girls jumped to return to their tasks. One busied herself with scaling a fish. The other scurried out of the kitchen with a bucket to fetch fresh water. Roslyn handed her a basket and asked her to grab the eggs from the hens. Once she'd completed that and returned, the woman sent her to the herb garden to gather herbs for the evening meal.

Evie didn't mind. It gave her something to do while she tried not to fret about Callum, his brothers, and their impending doom.

She knelt and picked the requested herbs—rosemary and thyme—but as she picked them, she got a whiff of mint and something light and fruity. As she paused there, she thought how wonderful it would be to have a cup of herbal tea.

The caffeine headaches had subsided, finally, but she still craved a hot beverage in the morning. It seemed Callum and his household were not that interested in having breakfast on a daily basis and there was for sure no coffee. But perhaps she could find a way to make a pot of herbal tea.

She plucked a few stems of mint and set them inside her basket. Then she inhaled the sweet, grassy aroma of the plant next to it which looked, to her, like a white daisy and seemed to grow wild. As she inhaled it, closing her eyes to savor the scent, she realized with some elation it was chamomile. What she knew about chamomile was that it had calming properties, which she needed. She snipped several of the flowers and placed them in her basket with the mint.

Evie hadn't a clue how to make herbal tea from the items in her basket, but she was going to give it her best shot.

Back in the kitchen, she handed Roslyn her rosemary and thyme.

"What do ye have there, lass?" she asked, eyeing the white daisies.

"I snipped some plants for myself. I hope that's all right?"

"Aye…" she said, sounding wary with one brow lifted.

"Do you mind if I boil some water?" Though she knew next to nothing about fresh herbal tea, she decided the first step would be boiling water.

Roslyn motioned to a pot already over the fire. "I have some there."

Evie looked around and found a small wooden cup. That would be perfect for her hot herbal tea. Then she set about plucking the petals from the white daisies. The aromatic scent wafted to her nose as her fingers rubbed across the leaves. It was definitely chamomile. Smiling, she then plucked a few mint leaves and placed them in a small pile with the petals.

"Do you have a knife I could borrow?" she asked.

Roslyn handed her one of her best chopping knives. By now, Evie realized she had an audience. The two scullery maids had halted their work to gape at her.

She forged on, though, determined to make her tea. With the knife, she chopped up the leaves and petals into tiny pieces. Then she took another glance around the kitchen, looking for something that was akin to cheesecloth. Since they didn't have the modern conveniences of tea balls in this century, she would have to make do.

"What now, lass?" Roslyn asked, a bemused look on her face.

Evie said, "Do you have a small piece of woven cloth? For straining."

She was surprised when Roslyn handed her the small square piece of cloth. It looked like the gauzy woven cotton she was expecting and was surprised to see the woman had a piece. She placed her leaves and petals into the cloth and tied up the corners. Some would likely leak out, but that was all right with her. She dropped it in the wooden cup. Then she took a thick towel and grasped the pot of boiling water by the handle and, ever so slowly, poured it over the cloth. She waited a few minutes before dipping the cloth in and out of the hot water. When she was satisfied it had steeped long enough, she placed the bundle aside.

It was the moment of truth. She took a sip.

And was delightfully surprised.

It had the chamomile flavor with a hint of mint. But it needed something. She didn't want to use sugar as she knew it was likely precious to them. Perhaps a drop or two of honey?

"What are ye drinking there, lass?" Roslyn moved closer, her curiosity evident on her aged face as she peered at her.

"Here. Try a sip." She handed her the cup.

She hesitated a moment before taking it and then giving it a sniff. With a glance back up at Evie, she tasted it. She held the warm liquid in her mouth a moment before swallowing. A smile creased her lips.

"What is this called?"

"Where I come from, we call it herbal tea," she said. "But since there are no tea leaves here, perhaps it's merely herb water."

She almost laughed as she said it, thinking of all the fancy flavored waters, fizzy and not, in her time. What would Roslyn think of that, she wondered?

"The petals are chamomile," Evie said. "It's known to be a sleep aid and to have a calming effect."

Roslyn took another sip. "I've no had anything like it." She paused, then said, "Can ye make more?"

Evie giggled and nodded. "Yes, of course I can."

THAT NIGHT, EVIE made a steaming pot of what Roslyn called her herb water and took it to the bedchamber she now shared with Callum. She didn't expect him to be there. He wasn't at the evening meal, either. She assumed he was brooding somewhere else in the keep and would eventually turn up.

Much to her surprise, he was in the bedchamber sitting in the chair by the blazing fire, looking as though he had murder on his mind.

She paused in the doorway, unsure if she should continue inside the room or not. When he turned to see her, his expression softened.

"Och, lass, dinnae stand there in the door. Come in." He waved her inside.

She kicked the door closed with her heel and moved deeper into the room, searching for a surface to place the tray she carried. When he noticed she juggled, he made a spot for her on one of the tables, then dragged it over to the fire. Then he grabbed the spare chair and moved it across from his. She placed the tray down and noticed he peered at it with some interest.

"What is that?" he asked.

She poured into each cup, then handed him one. "It's something that will help soothe you."

He took it, sniffed, and gave her a wary expression. Then he tasted it. When he swallowed the herbal water, his expression changed to one of surprise.

"Where did ye get this?"

"I made it." Feeling smug, she sipped her own fake tea.

His brows rose. "Ye made it?"

She nodded. "I did. I thought it might help you, especially after what happened this morning in the great hall."

Callum placed aside his cup and glowered. She regretted mentioning it since it turned his mood sour. He didn't know she had been standing there when he swung the claymore in a wide arc, narrowly missing his brother's face. The power of the sword slamming into the great hall table would be something she'd never forget. Then how he had tugged it from the wood as if it was nothing more than a knife slicing butter. It made her appreciate how powerful and strong he was. And it was a bit fearsome.

Hearing him banish his brother and the two men from the keep was a knife to her heart. She imagined how he felt. She took another sip, wishing it was something stronger to give her courage.

"I didn't mean to eavesdrop," she said, her voice quiet.

"So…ye heard then." His gaze lifted to hers. "How much?"

"I know you banished him," she said, unwilling to look him in the eye. She hated confrontation and didn't want to brave a glance at him.

He heaved a sigh, the breath huffing out. "I had to do it, lass."

"I know," she said softly.

On impulse, she placed her cup on the table next to his and reached across to him, placing her hand on his.

"I can't imagine how difficult that was for you."

He seemed surprised by her empathy as he looked up at her. He said nothing for a long moment. Finally, she removed her hand and sat back in her chair, feeling like a fool. She took up her hot tea and took another sip, avoiding his gaze.

"I thank ye," he said quietly. "Ye have a kind heart, Evie."

He had said her name once or twice but hearing it from him now gave her a tingling sensation of joy. She gripped the cup tight and braved a glance in his direction. He'd turned back to the fire, the light flickering over his handsome face. She saw the worry and the torment there and she wished there was more she could do for him.

"I sent scouts," he said. "If the tapestry was right, then I want to be prepared should there be an invasion."

"What happens if there is?" It was a question she didn't want to voice, but she had to know the answer.

"I'll see ye safe," he said then. He lifted his gaze to hers. "Do ye still have the keystone?"

She patted her pocket. "Yes."

"Good. Now, lass, the hour is late. Ye best get some rest."

"And you best drink the rest of that," she said, motioning to the cup. She used her best teasing voice. When he quirked a brow at her, she said, "It will do you good."

"Aye, then, I will."

"Good night, Callum."

"Good night, lass."

CHAPTER THIRTY-THREE

EVIE CLOSED THE thick curtains around the bed for some privacy while she shed her overdress and stockings. In a sudden, strange impulse, she shed her modern undergarments as well. Not that he hadn't already seen her naked—he had—but she felt it was awkward to change with him still in the room. She didn't ask if he intended to sleep in the chair all right—she assumed at some point he'd join her. But what if he didn't?

As she folded her clothes, she recalled she had the stone in her pocket. She fished it out and noticed something peculiar.

The stone was still faintly glowing through the material of the handkerchief. She unwrapped it and stared down at it to confirm it was, indeed, emitting a pale light. What harbinger was this? Why now?

Did it sense something about to happen? Did it know the MacDonalds were on their way?

No, she refused to believe that.

But the niggling sense of *what if* continued to pound through her mind.

She pushed aside the curtain nearest the headboard and placed her clothes in a neat stack on the bedside table. Then she placed the stone on top of that and pretended it wasn't glowing. If she ignored it, perhaps it would go away.

One more glance at Callum who brooded beside the fire with his legs outstretched, the flickering light reflected in his features.

It was disarming how handsome he was and how much he made her pulse race and her heart pound. The image of him there by the fire reminded her of the dream of him, before she met the man in the flesh. Before she traveled back in time. Her blood ran hot for him when she awoke as it did now.

Ignoring the pounding desire through her—or trying to—she settled down on the bed, pulling the blankets to her chin as she tried to sleep. But sleep would not come as her mind raced with all sorts of thoughts of what was to come if the MacDonalds were truly on their way. What, then, would happen to her if Callum perished in the fight?

She shoved that horrid thought away. The last thing she needed was to worry about something that hadn't happened yet. If there was to be a fight, though, it was time for her to tell Callum how she felt. She may not get another chance. She sat up, clutching the bedclothes to her chest with her heart racing.

She was certain he felt the same about her. She was risking her heart if she told him and he didn't reciprocate.

It was worth the risk.

She needed him to know. The best way to tell him was to show him.

She slipped out of bed, standing beside it in nothing but her shift. She was instantly reminded of her dream when she was still in Edinburgh. That seemed so long ago now. Her heart pounding and her hands shaking, she stepped toward him, pausing beside him.

"Callum?"

He looked up at her, his glassy eyes changing from despair to intrigue. Without a word, she shrugged off the shift and let it pool around her feet. Her belly tightened and there was a warming at the apex between her thighs as his appreciative gaze swept over her bare skin glistening in the firelight.

"Och, lass…"

She climbed into his lap, placing two fingers over his lips. "Don't say anything more." Her words shook when she whispered them.

She slipped her hands under his tunic. His skin was warm from the nearby fire, sending a dreamy sensation through her as she pushed up the material. He didn't fight her when he allowed her to take it off him and drop it on the floor. Her hands roved over the hard plains and springy hair of his chest. He tilted his head back as he looked up at her, desire flickering through those deep blue eyes that reminded her of the darkest part of the ocean. She bent to kiss him, their lips melding together. His mouth was sweet and hot against hers. A mewl escaped her.

Callum's hands were on her waist as he positioned her over his lap. She was aware of his hardened length beneath his plaid. The material was still wrapped around his waist despite the loss of his tunic. She fumbled with it to get it out of the way while his hands trailed up her back, leaving gooseflesh in his wake. When she finally had the plaid moved, it was a moment of victory.

He eased inside her. A shuddering breath whooshed out of her as his fingers tightened on her hips, helping her to rock against him. Her breasts brushed against his chest, the fine hairs there leaving a tingling sensation through her nipples. He seemed content to let her set the pace and move against him how she wanted, which sent ripples of pleasure through her.

Evie's fingers dug into his shoulders as every muscle tensed. She tossed her head back as the climax nearly overtook her. He groaned, trying to move her off him but she held fast. Realizing what he meant to do, she tipped her head down to his, their eyes meeting in a blaze of searing emotion.

"No, don't," she panted. "I want to feel you with me."

He stilled for a brief moment, question flickering through the blue depths of his eyes.

"Are ye sure, lass?"

She moved her hands to his cheeks, relishing the roughness of the stubble against her palms. Her lips brushed his. "Very sure."

Their mouths fused together as they soared to heights unimaginable together. She kissed him with a hunger she had never experienced before. In that moment, she understood fully that she would never love another for the rest of her life. Callum was the one for her.

When it was all over, she stilled, unwilling to move from his lap. Her muscles were still tensed, her breath ragged. Their bodies were both slick with sweat from the burning heat of the fire and the torrid fervor of their actions. She refused to move.

And she was glad she didn't when she felt long, slow kisses down her neck, then across one collarbone to her shoulder. Soft, damp kisses that sent her reeling. She clutched him to her, her hands tangling in the long lengths of his hair. Whatever happened, joy shuddered through her that they'd had these moments together.

"I love you."

Oh, God. She hadn't intended to say the words aloud, but they slipped out. She was thankful, at least, she wasn't facing him as he still had his lips against the tender flesh at the base of her throat. He went completely still against her.

He tightened, his arm muscles flexing around her as he gripped her in his arms. He stood up, breaking the intimate contact between them, much to her dismay. But then elation rose through her as he walked to the bed and gently lowered her down. He slid in next to her, pulling her against him and kissing her temple.

"Och, lass, I love ye, too. And now that ye've admitted it to me, I intend to tup ye properly."

She wasn't exactly sure what he meant by that, but she couldn't wait to find out.

CHAPTER THIRTY-FOUR

MORNING CAME FAR too quickly, but come it did. Evie huddled under the blankets, nestled against Callum's broad body, her head on his chest, watching the dawn illuminate the window in his bedchamber. How long would this moment of bliss last until the day interrupted? She savored it.

His hand brushed up the length of her back, sending shivers through her, and a lazy smile crossed her lips.

"Och, lass, I best leave ye before I'm abed all day."

"Would that be so terrible?" She flattened her palm on his chest, feeling the steady beat of his heart.

He chuckled, a rumble deep in his throat that vibrated through her to her toes. He caught her hand in his, lifted it to his lips, and kissed the tips of her fingers.

"Nay," he said, "but there is work to be done."

With some reluctance, he untangled their limbs and left the bed. She remained where she was, watching as he moved around the room gathering his clothes and admiring his strong physique in all his glory. Before he left, he placed more kindling in the hearth and lit the fire.

"I'll fetch Roslyn and have her help ye dress for the day."

If Roslyn were to make an appearance, she had best pull on her shift. "Where are you off to?"

"I go to inspect the crops and the livestock and then take a turn around the grounds to make sure all is secure. Then I meet with Dougal to discuss business." He moved to stand in front of her and dropped a kiss on drop of her head. "Dinnae fash yer bonnie head about any of that, lass. Rest. I'll see ye later."

He flashed her a grin as he turned to go, leaving her alone in the bedchamber. She slipped out of the bed and picked up her shift off the floor, pulling it on over her head. Turning, she saw the neatly folded stack of clothes on the bedside table with the stone still wrapped in the cloth. She was certain she saw the lines emitting their faint light through the linen.

Evie thought about the tapestry of her sister. "I'm not abandoning you," she whispered, as if Chloe could hear her. "If Callum and I are right—and I think we are—I'll see you again soon. I miss you."

She grinned as the thought trickled through her. It gave her happiness and comfort to know that her sister would eventually arrive back in time with her.

A knock on the door sounded. She knew it was Roslyn.

She was ready to start her day.

"Come in," she called.

Roslyn pushed open the door. The moment Evie saw her, she knew something was wrong. She turned to the woman who paused in the doorway wringing her hands.

"Is it true then?" she asked. "He banished Malcolm."

Evie nodded, recalling the way he had swung the claymore through the air as though it weighed nothing, as though it were a feather he flung through the air.

The woman's shoulders slumped as she softly closed the door behind her. A breath shuddered out of her.

"He did what he had to," she said, more to herself than to Evie. "Listen to me prattling on about nothing."

Roslyn bustled over to the bedside table where she had her stack of clothes. Too late, Evie realized her mistake.

"What's this?" she picked up the stone still wrapped in the handkerchief.

"Oh, that's mine." She hurried over to the woman to grab it

out of her hands, but it was too late.

Roslyn pushed aside the cloth and peered down at the keystone. The lines were faintly glowing and pulsing. She glanced up at Evie, question on her aged face.

"Where did ye get this?" she asked.

"I…um…" Evie floundered, unsure how to explain. She huffed out a breath. "It's a long story."

"Mayhap ye best tell me about it, then." She closed her fingers around the stone which told Evie she wasn't going to accept no for an answer.

Evie sagged against the bed and clasped her hands in front of her, defeated. "I'm not sure you'll believe me."

Her face softened as she smiled, the wrinkles crinkling at the corners of her eyes. "I'll be the one to decide that. Now, lass, tell me."

Evie took a deep breath and told her everything. From landing in Edinburgh to see her sister, to being handed the keystone, to the museum, to then falling through time to land here. Roslyn listened intently, her expression never changing or showing her emotions. When she finished, she waited for the woman to respond.

"Sinclair…" She whispered the name as she gaped at her. "Och, I should have known."

"What do you mean?"

"The laird, Hamish, God rest him, spoke of the prophecy many times. Some of us thought he was daft, but others believed." She eyed her, a wisp of a smile on her face before her eyes cast downward to peer at the stone. "And this must be that mystical keystone he mentioned."

"Part of it," she agreed. "There are two more pieces."

"Aye, I see that." She extended the stone back to Evie. "Hamish had the first vision, as he called it, when Callum was a wee one. Jamie was a bairn at the time and the Lady MacLeod had just passed. We all thought he'd lost his mind to the grief. But he continued to tell the story again and again as time went on and the lads grew. Callum never believed but the other two were always asking for him to tell the story of the night the keystone was split."

"The Shattering," Evie said. "That's what he called it."

"Aye, yes, the Shattering. I never did understand it." Her eyes twinkled with comprehension. "Until now. So...yer from the future, are ye?"

"I am," Evie said. "But I'm not going back."

She didn't know what made her say it aloud, but the words spilled out before she was able to filter them. As soon as she said it, Roslyn's brows lifted in surprise.

"No?"

"No," she said, her voice firm.

She was confident in her decision. So confident, in fact, she was certain her sisters would be joining her in time. And their family would be whole again.

Or would it? The question mark was Brianna, the free spirit with a nomadic heart and a love of sunshine and beaches. If she decided not to come, then what would happen to her, Chloe, and the keystone?

"And...how does the laird feel about ye staying?"

It was a fair question and one Evie hadn't considered. She sagged against the bed as she heaved a heavy sigh.

"I hope he's all for it."

"Ah, ye havna discussed it then."

"No," she admitted.

But what she didn't tell the woman was they had professed their love for each other. Would their love stand the test of time and survive a war that was sure to come? Her gaze lifted to meet Roslyn's.

"What do you think he'll say about it?"

"Och, lass, 'tis no my place to say." She reached for the clothes on the bedside table, then added, "But...if I were to guess, I think he'll say he's happy to have ye here." She gave her a wink. "Now, let's get ye dressed. I have a kitchen to tend to."

CHAPTER THIRTY-FIVE

THE NEXT DAYS passed in a blur. Evie spent her nights with Callum and her days wandering the keep. Sometimes, she would end up in the kitchen with Roslyn, looking for something to do. She was becoming an expert at gathering eggs. Her herbal tea was even starting to taste more like real herbal tea as she experimented and learned how to make tea from the plants in the garden. It still wasn't enough to replace her craving for coffee, but it was better than nothing.

Other times, she went to the stable to pet the mare, the one she named Mist, Callum had gifted her. She and the mare were good friends, it seemed.

Every now and then, she spotted Jamie skulking around the keep, brooding. Roslyn told her he was still upset over the banishment of his brother and still angry with Callum for it. She did her best to avoid him.

One morning, after Roslyn helped her dress and left, Evie found herself alone in the bedchamber. She stood in front of the fire holding her modern day undergarments, watching the flames flicker and listening to the faint crackle. She stared down at her old bra and panties with a bit of apprehension sweeping through her. It was time she let go of the past. She wasn't going to return to her old life in the future. If she was going to live in Callum's medieval world, then she was going to embrace it.

She took a deep breath and tossed the material into the fire.

The flames shot up, consuming the cloth.

"Out with the old," she whispered.

It was a moment she was going to savor as she watched her old life—her past life in the future—burn and turn to ash.

After the fire in the hearth had waned, she left Callum's bedchamber and wandered through the keep. Callum was busy with his laird duties, she knew, and she didn't want to bother him. Roslyn was busy with her own duties in the kitchen, preparing for the day. If she went there, she would be underfoot. While she wanted to make more of her faux herbal tea, she didn't want to be a nuisance.

She found herself outside, walking through the courtyard, walking toward the stables. She didn't know why she was headed to the stables. Perhaps a part of her hoped she'd see Callum there. When she arrived, there were a few stable hands hard at work mucking stalls. She walked down the middle of the stable, stalls on either side, garnering a few curious glances from the young men working. She paused when she saw the mare she'd named Gray Mist. It made her smile when the mare poked her head out as if she sensed her there.

Evie paused to pet the mare's nose. "Hello, girl," she whispered.

Mist gave a quiet whicker in response.

"Is there something I can help ye with, my lady?"

The man's voice startled her. She looked up to see Jamie MacLeod leaning against one of the stalls, his arms crossed over his chest and a look of bemusement on his face.

She hadn't seen him come into the stable, so he must have slipped in quietly while she was busy patting her horse.

She had to admit he was handsome with sharp assessing eyes that were different from Callum's. Not blue. Not green either. It was something akin to sea green that seemed to glitter with mirth as he looked at her. His hair, though, was the same as Callum's. Long, plaited on one side. He wore breeches, a long tunic, boots, and a plaid wrapped around his upper body.

"Oh," she said on a breath. "I was…" Her words trailed off as uncertainty hit her.

"Are ye bored then?" He grinned and she noticed a deep dimple in each cheek, which was endearing if he were anyone but Callum's younger brother. "My brother has no been keeping ye busy, eh?"

He sounded like he wanted to volunteer for that job—keeping her busy—as he pushed off the stable wall and sauntered toward her. She stiffened, unsure how to take his comments.

"I'm busy enough," she said, her voice silky smooth as she looked up at him. He was as tall as Callum, but not nearly as strong.

"Are ye?" He paused in front of her, looking her over with an appreciative gleam in his eyes. "My brother told me about yer unusual arrival."

"Callum told you about me?" she asked.

He chuckled. "No. Malcolm did. He told me ye fell from the sky and the prophecy Da talked about was finally coming true."

He scoffed a bit as though he didn't believe in the prophecy. Callum was a hard sell, himself. She couldn't help but think how odd it was that Malcolm had been the one who talked to Jamie about her. She wondered why. What interest was she to him?

"And I know you're the younger brother who spurned the MacDonald girl."

A dark look came over his face as he glowered with the mention of the MacDonald woman. She liked that she needled him. She had the sense that he was up to no good talking to her. As though he were trying to swoop in and steal her out from under Callum.

That would never happen.

She remained where she was, stroking the nose of her horse as she eyed him with a mixture of suspicion and curiosity.

"Aye, well, it had to be done."

"Did it?" she asked. "What did you do? Pack her up and dump her back at her father's keep? And if you did, how do you think the girl felt? Betrayed? Abandoned? Unloved? My bet is she felt all of those things and more."

At least he had the good sense to flush, his cheeks turning a pale pink as he looked away from her.

"Did any of that cross your mind when you decided to break off your arrangement?" She hadn't meant to sound so harsh, but she was willing to bet the younger MacLeod brother needed a good talking-to and by someone not related to him.

"I dinnae think—"

"That's right. You didn't think, did you?"

"I'm sorry, I—"

"Don't apologize to *me*," she snapped. "Apologize to *her*. Though I suppose that ship has sailed by now."

He blinked as he stared at her with an odd look, perhaps not understanding her metaphor.

"My brother said ye were a sharp-tongued lass. I see now he was right." Jamie squared his shoulders as he looked her over again. "He also said ye were the reason Da died."

"Me?" She was shocked as she gaped at him.

"If ye had never arrived with that stone, then Da would still be alive and Malcolm would still be here in the keep."

"How dare you—" And then she cut herself off as she stared at him and straightened with her sudden understanding. "I think I see what's going on here. You're angry with Callum because he banished Malcolm. And you thought coming to me with your charms and your good looks you'd win me over and, perhaps, steal me right out from under your older brother. Well, let me tell you something." She stepped around the horse, who whickered as though sad she'd stopped petting her nose. "Callum is a good, kind, decent human being. He did what he had to do. Your brother, however, made poor choices and now he has to live with the consequences." She wagged her finger in his face. "Like you."

The clearing of someone's throat caught them both off guard. Her head snapped up in the direction of the sound and she saw

Callum standing in the middle of the stable with his feet apart and his arms crossed, looking as though he was spoiling for a fight.

"I thought ye might need rescuing from my knave of a younger brother, lass, but I see that ye seem to have him well in hand." A ghost of a smile flickered over his lips before he managed to contain it and keep his expression stern. But she saw the glint of pride shining in his eyes.

Jamie ambled toward his brother. "Ye should do something to rein her in, brother." Then he cut her a glance. "She's a bit of a wild one."

"I'll do no such thing," Callum said. And this time he did smile. "I like her wild."

He snorted. "I'll bet."

Fury passed over Callum's face and his hand clenched. Jamie turned as if to walk away, but then spun back around, swinging his fist. Callum's reflexes were quick as he grabbed him by the wrist and shoved him backward toward one of the stalls. He slammed Jamie against the wood, which shuddered under the force of the impact.

It all happened so suddenly, she didn't have time to admire the way he was ready to defend her honor.

"Dinnae make me banish ye, too, *brother*," Callum said on a roughened whisper.

Jamie shoved him off. Evie, though, was certain Callum allowed him to do it since he was much bigger and stronger than the younger man. He said nothing else as he walked out of the stable, leaving them alone. It was then that Evie realized the stable hands mucking stalls had paused to watch the exchange. When Jamie was on his way out, they quickly got back to work.

Callum approached her, reaching for her and pulling her to him. That smile was on his lips as he looked down at her.

"Ye do have a sharp tongue, lass."

"You should know," she said.

She was grinning when he kissed her.

"Callum!"

The sharp shout rose up from the courtyard. They broke apart. His brows drew together in concern as he looked at her.

"Go," she said.

Instead of leaving her, though, he took her hand and led her out of the stable. Dougal was rushing across the courtyard, his face flushed and his eyes bright with fear. Next to her, Callum stiffened, his hand tightening on hers.

"What is it?" he asked.

"Riders coming. The leader looks to be Malcolm," his steward said.

"Malcolm? What the devil is he doing back here?"

"Shall we let him inside, my lord?"

Callum was silent for a long moment. "No. I'll ride out to meet him."

"I'm coming with ye, my lord."

Callum nodded as the man hurried off to make the horses ready. He turned to her, gripping her by the shoulders.

"Do ye still have the keystone safe?" he asked, his voice low.

"Yes. In my pocket."

"Good. Find Roslyn. Stay with her until I come to fetch ye."

"But—"

"I want ye safe."

She understood and nodded. "All right. But Callum." She leaned toward him, tipping her face up to his. "Please be careful."

He brushed the back of his hand over her cheek. "Aye, lass. I will."

CHAPTER THIRTY-SIX

CALLUM WATCHED EVIE return to the keep as a deep shuddering fear rippled through him. He had the sense that something terrible was about to happen. He needed her safe and out of harm's way. When she disappeared inside, he turned toward the stables in time to see Dougal leading their two mounts. Concern was etched on the older man's face. The same concern he, himself, felt.

Without a word, they mounted and galloped out of the gate to meet his brother before he arrived at the keep. It wasn't far to meet up with him and the others who accompanied him. As they approached, Callum realized Angus Sinclair was among them. They slowed to a trot and came face to face with Malcolm and Sinclair.

"Brother," Malcolm greeted. His gaze flickered from Callum to Dougal and back again. "I came to warn ye."

Callum shifted in the saddle, unease flickering through him. "Warn me about what?"

"The MacDonalds are on the move," he said. "They mean to attack Dundale."

That niggling fear he sensed when in the bailey returned. "How do ye ken this, brother?"

"I saw them riding out of their keep."

Fury erupted through him as he peered at his brother.

"How many?" Callum asked.

"A thousand strong at least. He's called his banners."

Dougal swore under his breath. Callum gripped the reins tighter in his fists, unable to keep from flinging the accusation. "Ye brought this down upon us."

"I ken that and for that I am sorry, but we havna time to discuss it here," Malcolm snapped. "Not if ye intend to secure the keep and fight back. 'Tis why I brought help."

Angus Sinclair nudged his horse forward as Callum's gaze flickered over to him.

"This isna yer fight," Callum said.

"Aye, it isna," Angus agreed. "But if ye have my kin in your keep, then I thought it best to help defend it."

Evie. The man thought Evie was his kin. And that was his fault when he took her to him intending to leave her there. Looking back on that, he was glad she had remained with him. Before Callum objected, the man continued.

"My lady wife thinks she's related, though I dinnae ken how. Mayhap a distant cousin. At any rate, she insisted we come when Malcolm showed up to beseech us for help."

It occurred to him that perhaps Laird Sinclair wasn't so far off in his assessment that Evie was related to him. Aye, she may be a distant relation—from the future. It made sense Malcolm would seek help from the Sinclairs. They were the nearest clan to Dundale.

They were also part of the prophecy. The words rang back to him. *Two bloodlines. One destiny.*

Two bloodlines coming together to fight side-by-side. Mayhap, Malcolm, too, realized that the Sinclairs were as much a part of the prophecy as they were.

"When will the MacDonalds arrive?" Callum asked.

"With their company and at their current speed, less than a fortnight," Malcolm said.

He glanced at Dougal who listened with rapt attention. His gaze met Callum's, a deep understanding in the depths. He nodded, encouraging him to make his final decision.

"Aye, then," Callum said. "We best get ready to fight."

His gaze landed on Malcolm. They exchanged some silent communication as Callum gave him a nod to indicate he was allowed to return. But it was not the end of it.

As they headed back to Dundale, the overwhelming sensation that the MacDonalds were coming for more than vengeance for the burned village pounded through Callum. He had the distinct feeling they wanted something else—Evie and the keystone. It was something his da had said on his deathbed: that Rory MacDonald knew they had the keystone and he wanted it.

He had sworn an oath to his da that he would protect the stone and the lass. He meant to keep that promise.

When they arrived back at the keep, Callum dismounted and headed straight for Malcolm. He took him by the collar and hauled him away from the others to have a word with him. Malcolm didn't fight back. When they were far enough away, though, Malcolm shoved him off. Anger was etched on his face as he smoothed his tunic back into place.

"I allowed ye back to the keep," Callum said. "But dinnae think ye are forgiven for yer heinous acts."

"Ye allowed me back because ye need me," Malcolm said. "And ye ken that as well as I. MacDonald is coming, brother. There's no stopping it. Call the banners. Bring them here to fight."

Callum clenched his hands into fists and refrained from blaming him. "We havna much time to prepare."

"'Tis why ye need to call the banners. I think ye ken there is more than one reason Rory MacDonald comes to fight."

He clenched his jaw so tight it ached. The thought had crossed his mind, too, but he didn't want to voice it. Voicing it would make it true.

"He wants what the lass has," Malcolm added.

Evie's beautiful face leapt into his mind. He could not allow Rory to take her or the stone. He had to do everything within his power to keep them both out of his enemy's hands.

"And should Dundale fall? What then?" Callum asked. "I cannae protect her if I'm dead."

"Nay, ye cannae." Malcolm stepped closer to him, lowering his voice. There was a seriousness deep within his sea-green eyes. "Call the banners. 'Tis the only way."

Callum nodded. But he had another idea to protect Evie. An idea she would likely refuse. He had to find some way to convince her. "Aye, we will call them and pray they arrive in time to fight."

"Send me and Jamie to bring them back. Sinclair can help ye prepare for what is to come."

It was a good idea, but Callum worried Malcolm would do something that would put them in more jeopardy. He regarded his brother with a lifted brow. Malcolm seemed to sense his apprehension and huffed out a breath.

"I ken ye dinnae trust me, brother. But ye must if we are to survive this fight. Send us to call for arms."

"All right," he said at last. "Bring them. We need the numbers if we're to win."

Malcolm nodded agreement. "Aye. I'll tell Jamie to be ready to ride within the hour. We'll leave at once."

"Good. Godspeed to ye both."

His brother hurried away to find Jamie. As he did so, Callum knew there was one thing left to do—convince Evie of his plan to keep her safe.

He headed inside the keep to find her, to tell her what he intended. She was in the kitchen with Roslyn. When he entered, her face lit into a bright smile. Roslyn gave him a nod of greeting.

"My lord," she said.

"We will need more provisions. Malcolm has returned and brought the Sinclairs with him. There are more men on the way," he said.

Roslyn paused kneading the bread to look up at him, surprise evident on her face. "My lord? We have visitors?"

"Aye. And there will be more coming."

His gaze flickered to Evie. Her bright smile faded into a mask of concern. She sensed what was happening. Roslyn, though, didn't ask questions. She started ordering the others in the kitchen to prepare to feed more mouths. Meanwhile, Evie moved to stand next to him, lifting her gaze up to his.

"What's happening?" she asked.

He took her hand. "Come and I'll tell ye."

They walked out of the kitchen through the keep. She remained silent as they headed back to the great hall.

"It's happening, isn't it?" she asked. "The tapestry image is coming true."

"They are coming," he said, confirming her fears. He didn't want to scare her, but he wanted her to know what was ahead. "A thousand strong heading this way."

She pulled him to a stop and gaped at him with wide eyes. Her face paled. The wild beat of her pulse throbbed in the long column of her throat.

"A thousand? What will you do?"

"Fight," he said. "Defend the keep." He paused, taking her hand once again. "And keep ye safe."

She swallowed hard. "I'm not leaving you."

She suspected his plan. The only way to keep her out of Rory MacDonald's hands—and the stone—was to send her away.

"Evie—"

"No, Callum. I'm not leaving." Her tone was firm as her eyes glistened with tears. "I'll hide in the larder if that's what you want, but I refuse to leave this place. I refuse to leave *you*."

His heart thundered hard in his chest. On impulse, he gathered her to him and held her tight, her head tucked neatly under his chin. As he held her, he felt the pounding of her heart against him. She was determined to stay with him no matter what. He would have to find another way to make sure she was safe.

"We willna talk of this anymore today," he said. Then he pulled back, holding her at arm's length and giving her a faint smile. "I have men to greet and no lady wife to help me receive them."

She flushed, her cheeks turning a pale pink. She shifted from one foot to the other. "If you wish for a lady wife…" She paused, taking a deep breath and letting it shudder out of her. "You have only to ask."

He stared at her in shock. He hadn't meant it to sound as though he were in need of a wife. It was a comment in jest for the most part. She looked up at him with those eyes he was so fond of.

Callum gripped her hands in his. He lifted one and kissed the tips of her fingers. He thought of her desperation to return to her time, to find her sister and wondered when her feelings had shifted.

"I thought ye wished to return home," he said.

"I thought I did, too," she said. "But I seem to have fallen in love with a Highlander."

His heart thudded. "So, ye mean to stay then?"

She moved closer, pressing her small body against his as she tipped her head back to look up at him. "I do. I mean to stay with you."

He smiled down at her. It seemed like the sensible thing to do. "I'll marry ye, Evie Sinclair, if ye'll have me."

She grinned. "I thought you'd never ask."

CHAPTER THIRTY-SEVEN

I T WASN'T THE proposal she had dreamed about. But he was definitely the man of her dreams.

Callum was insistent they not wait. He left to find an officiant to marry them as soon as possible in the keep's chapel. He said it would be a traditional handfasting ceremony—they would be together for a year and a day. When he returned, he would be with the local bishop and they would marry at once.

She recalled that Jamie and the MacDonald woman were handfasted. She wondered if she would give Callum a child within their year and a day and felt giddy at the prospect.

While he was gone, it took all her focus as she cut lengths of flowers from the garden. Then she wove them together in a circle to wear on her head. She hadn't any idea what she would wear to marry Callum and, truthfully, it didn't matter to her. She was never the girl who had a dream wedding with a fancy gown. She thought she would marry someday, of course, but that was nothing more than a wish and a thought.

Now it was a reality.

She placed the finishing touches on the crown of flowers and placed it on her head to check the fit. It would do. She gazed at her reflection in the mirror and grinned. She was pleased with her handiwork especially since she wasn't crafty in any way.

A knock sounded on the door.

"Come in."

Roslyn pushed open the door and paused there, gaping at her for a long moment. She sniffed as a wistful expression crossed her face.

"Och, lass, did ye make that yerself?"

"I did. Do you like it?"

She gave a wistful sigh. "It's perfect." She moved into the room and closed the door behind her. It was then that Evie realized she had material draped over her arm. "I brought ye something."

She brought the material toward the bed and laid it out. The gown was a rich garnet color with long sleeves that had buttons from elbow to wrist and a round neckline trimmed in gold. It was a beautiful gown.

"I thought ye should have something special to wear. It was his mother's," she said.

Evie fingered the material, then glanced up at Roslyn. "It's so beautiful. Thank you."

"Yer going to be the lady of Dundale. Ye should look the part."

Evie froze, her breath catching. The weight of it hit her like a cold gust of wind—she would be the laird's wife, the lady of the castle. A strange mix of excitement and fear fluttered in her chest. Her mind raced, trying to grasp what that truly meant. What duties would fall on her shoulders? The enormity of it pressed down on her, making her pulse quicken.

"Are ye all right, lass? Ye look a wee bit pale."

"I don't know anything about being the wife of a laird."

Roslyn wrapped an arm around her shoulders and hugged her close. "Ye will do a wonderful job."

A sliver of hope settled in her heart. Roslyn would guide her through whatever responsibilities came with being Callum's wife. That brought a small sense of comfort.

"I hope so."

"To be sure. Now, let's get ye dressed. Yer laird awaits, my lady!"

MINUTES LATER, AFTER helping her dress, Roslyn escorted her to the chapel, which was an outer building on the other side of the keep. It was a small stone building with a few windows and inside, rows of wooden pews. She was uncertain how the ceremony would go—after all, she suspected there would be no formal walk down the aisle or wedding march.

When they arrived at the chapel, Dougal waited for her, which was a surprise.

"I'm to walk ye down the aisle, my lady." He bowed low to her, then offered his arm.

She cut a glance at Roslyn, who grinned and then slipped ahead of them into the chapel to take her seat. Evie placed her hand on his arm.

"The laird is a lucky lad," he said.

She flushed as they started down the aisle toward the altar. Surprise flickered through her to see most of the castle had turned out for their impromptu wedding. She thought she spied Angus Sinclair among the guests. Malcolm and Jamie were absent. She knew they'd left to recruit reinforcements for the upcoming conflict.

Callum stood at the front with the officiant. He wore a clean tunic, breeches, and his plaid draped over one shoulder. His boots were well worn but polished. He stood with the bishop waiting for her to join him at the altar. Her heart fluttered like a whispered promise as she walked toward him.

Callum's deep blue eyes sparkled with admiration and love as he looked at her. She gave him a faint smile. Together, they turned to face the bishop.

"We gather here today to witness and celebrate the sacred union of Callum and Evangeline. By the rites of handfasting, they shall be bound together in love and commitment. Callum, do ye come here of yer own free will to bind yerself in love and loyalty to Evangeline?"

His gaze never left hers when he answered. "I do."

"Evangeline, do ye come here of yer own free will to bind yourself in love and loyalty to Callum?"

Her heart pounded so hard she was sure everyone in the room heard it. "I do."

"Join hands and face one another."

When they did, the bishop placed a long thick cord over their joined hands, then bound them together in a loose infinity symbol.

"Your hands and your hearts are now bound together as one. These are the hands that will love ye and cherish ye throughout yer lifetimes.

"Callum, repeat after me. I, Callum, take thee, Evangline, to be my wedded wife. I vow to love and cherish thee, to honor and protect thee, in times of joy and sorrow, for as long as we both shall live. With this cord, I bind my life to thine," the bishop said.

Evie nearly swooned to hear Callum repeat the vows. Then it was her turn.

"Evangeline, repeat after me."

She repeated the same words, pledging her love and loyalty in times of joy and sorrow.

"By the power of the ancient traditions we honor, I pronounce ye handfasted, united in love and loyalty. May yer bond be strong, yer hearts steadfast, and yer love eternal. Ye may seal yer vows with a kiss."

Evie leaned into him, their joined hands between them, as she tipped her head back to look up at him. He smiled at her, sending her heart soaring, and then sealed their vows with the sweetest kiss she had ever had. For the first time in her life, she felt as though she belonged somewhere and to someone and that made her happy.

When they broke, she still leaned into him, looking up at him and feeling the warmth of his body next to hers.

The bishop said, "As yer hands are bound together, so shall

yer lives be bound as one. May ye enjoy a lifetime of love, peace, and happiness. Let us rejoice in their union."

Roslyn sniffed with joy as she stood and hurried over to them. She flung her arms around both of them.

"Yer mam and da would be so proud, Callum." Then she stepped back, her eyes holding unshed tears as she beamed at them both. "Welcome to the family, lass."

Angus Sinclair approached with a faint smile hidden behind his thick beard. "If I dinnae ken better, lass, I'd say ye were part of my family, too."

Evie wasn't sure what to say to that.

"My lady wife thinks ye are a distant relative," Angus went on to explain.

The air whooshed out of her as she gazed at the man whose eyes were the same color as her sister Brianna's. Perhaps he wasn't wrong to think that. After all, she was likely staring at one of her ancestors. She couldn't stop the giggle that bubbled up her throat.

"Indeed, we may be," she said at last.

Angus chuckled, too, then cut a glance at Callum. "May I kiss the bride?"

Callum glanced at her question in his blue eyes. She nodded to signal it was all right with her.

"Aye," her new husband said.

Angus gave her cheek a light kiss.

"An occasion like this needs a celebration," Roslyn said. "Let us feast!"

THEY FEASTED THAT night. Angus Sinclair and his men were in attendance as well as most of the castle inhabitants. It was a joyful time. Roslyn's cheeks were rosy with pure happiness as she bustled about the great hall.

Yet Evie was painfully aware of the knot in the pit of her stomach, a knot of dread for the coming days and the coming fight.

She was also a ball of nerves after their handfasting. It was unexplainable, though, since she and Callum had been together numerous times. What was wrong with her? There was nothing to be nervous about. She had no regrets about marrying him. In fact, elation skipped through her knowing she was his wife and would be here with him. She was at peace with her decision to stay in the past. At peace with the knowledge that her sisters would eventually join her.

It was a long, emotional day. She was exhausted. Perhaps Callum sensed that when he turned to her, grasped her hand and lifted it to kiss her fingertips. A faint smile was on his lips.

"Mayhap it's time to retire for the night," he said, his voice low.

Relief pounded through her as she expelled a sigh. "I'd like that."

"Go. I'll follow shortly."

Evie hesitated for a moment, but finally nodded. "All right."

He released her. When she rose, all eyes in the room turned to watch her go. She was acutely aware of the stares as she made her way through the great hall, leaving behind the noise. Safely alone and in their bedchamber, she leaned against the door and blew out a breath.

Someone had visited the room earlier and started a fire, warming the bedchamber. She was grateful for that. The bed had fresh linens and was turned down as if anticipating their wedding night. Her heart thundered upon seeing that, though she wasn't even sure why apprehension flickered through her.

It was silly.

Would things between them be any different now that they were wed?

She tugged the flower crown off her head and placed it on the bedside table. Reaching into her pocket, she slipped out the handkerchief with the keystone nestled inside, the faint glowing lines evident through the material. Carefully, she unwrapped the cloth and peered down at it. The lines were pulsating and there was a faint humming.

Like the day she used it to go back in time.

With shaking hands, she quickly wrapped it back up and placed it on the bedside table, backing away from it. As if by merely being close to it would send her home.

She didn't want to go home.

This was her home.

The bedchamber door scraped open, and Callum stepped through. She heard bawdy shouts from the other side and down the hall as he quickly shoved it closed. Sweat beaded his brow. His gaze met hers.

"What was that shouting about?" she asked.

"Och, lass, I dinnae want to subject ye to the bedding ceremony."

She flushed, hot, as she peered at him. "Bedding ceremony?"

"Aye. 'Tis tradition the family follow the new couple to bed to make sure they—"

"I get it," she said, cutting him off with a wave of her hand. "You don't have to explain."

She spun around, her cheeks hot. Thank God he didn't allow that. She was grateful to him for saving her from that humiliation.

His movement behind her indicated that he had closed the distance between them. He wrapped his arms around her and kissed the top of her head.

"I ken ye aren't familiar with our traditions."

"I'm not." She turned in his arms to face him, tipping her head back to look up at him. "And thank you for doing that. That means a lot to me."

He cupped her face, grinning down at her. "I'd rather have ye all to myself."

This time, a different type of flushing heat flashed through her. She slid her hands up and over his muscular chest, resting them on his broad shoulders. Her body tingled in sweet anticipation of what was to come.

"I'd rather that, too."

"How does it feel to be a MacLeod?" he asked.

She smiled, warmth spreading through her. "It feels wonderful. Now, we better get on with our private bedding ceremony. We wouldn't want to disappoint your family, would we?"

He chuckled, a rumble deep in his throat. "Nay, we would not."

CHAPTER THIRTY-EIGHT

E VIE HADN'T SLEPT all night. Her eyes, now gritty with fatigue, refused to close. Callum, though, had no problem falling asleep after their many sexy escapades. The curtains were drawn around the bed, making it a cozy hideaway from the rest of the world. She wanted it to stay that way but knew it would not.

Callum asked her how she felt to be a MacLeod. As she laid in bed thinking about that, it occurred to her she was a MacLeod and a Sinclair.

Two bloodlines. One destiny.

And thinking of that made gooseflesh erupt over her despite being burrowed under the thick blankets next to a warm man.

Next to her, Callum stirred. With his eyes still closed, he reached for her, pulling her into his arms and holding her next to him. Her head landed on his chest. Beneath her ear, she heard the soft rhythmic thump of his heart.

She was in heaven.

"Good morning," she whispered.

"Ah, so, yer awake."

"I am." She flattened her palm on his bare chest.

"Ye ken what this means?"

The sultry tone of his voice made her stomach swoop. In that moment, she knew she would never get enough of being with him or loving him. Smiling, she lifted her head and looked up at him, their eyes meeting—his that dazzling blue.

"I'm sure I can guess."

Without waiting for him to respond, she hoisted herself on top of him. His hands landed on her hips, urging her onward. But before they could enjoy each other again, a knock sounded on the door. He growled his annoyance.

"Oh," she breathed. "Are they here to check on us? To see if we completed the bedding ceremony?"

He gave her a mischievous grin. "If so, they can wait."

But the urgent knock sounded again. With a huff, she rolled to her side and landed on the mattress.

"You best answer it," she said. "They'll never go away if you don't."

Callum gave her a quick kiss before sliding out of the bed, grabbing his plaid and wrapping it around his hips as he padded to the door. He jerked it open.

"What?" he growled.

"Ah, begging yer pardon, my lord, but…I thought ye should ken…"

It was Dougal on the other side sounding as though there was dire news. She lifted up on her elbows, the blankets tucked around her and peered through the opening in the curtains on the bed. At the door, Callum stiffened, his muscles in his back going rigid.

"What is it?" he asked, sounding on edge.

"Rory MacDonald and his men approach." His gaze flickered to the bed, making Evie shrink back. "My apologies for disturbing ye both, but—"

"Have Malcolm and Jamie returned?"

"No as yet, my lord."

"Get to the armory. Ready the men. I dinnae want to waste time waiting for them."

Dougal stepped back away from the door as Callum closed it. He turned to her, one hand holding the plaid around his waist, the other scraping over his jaw as he looked at her. She understood, then, what it meant to be the wife of the laird. She would watch him lead his men into battle and she would hate every moment of it.

"Go," she said. "I know you have to."

His gaze softened as he approached her and perched on the bed to face her. He reached for one of her hands, taking it in his and holding it.

"I dinnae want to leave ye this morn."

"But you have to," she said, finishing for him. "I understand. The keystone will be safe with me."

"Good. Keep it with ye at all times. I want ye safe."

"I will be," she said. "I love you, Callum."

He reached for her, cupping her face in his hands, something she had come to love. "I love ye, too, lass."

He kissed her, a long, sweet kiss that she wanted to last forever. But it didn't. He released her and began to dress. When he was finished, he laid more wood and peat in the hearth and relit the fire for her. Then he bid her farewell and was off to see to his men, leaving her alone and bereft in a sea of worry.

By midday, Malcolm and Jamie returned with as many men as they could convince to fight. She didn't know the numbers, but she understood from the tense whispers that they were still outnumbered by Rory MacDonald. She did her best to stay out of the way, but there was an underlying feeling of chaos in the keep. Even Roslyn was dashing about to make sure they had enough provisions to feed all the men.

As the day waned, she took to the garden to find solace. She stuck her hand in her pocket to make sure the keystone was still safely wrapped in the cloth. Relieved it was, she picked her herbs and flowers and returned to the kitchen to make her herbal tea in the hopes it would keep her calm. She needed a distraction to keep from worrying about Callum. She didn't want to get in his way, and she didn't want to hide out in their bedchamber, either.

As she cut her flowers, though, she heard a distant rumble. Glancing up at the early evening sky, she saw it was clear. It wasn't thunder but sounded strangely like it.

Ba-dum-ba-dum-ba-dum.

Snatching the basket, she shot to her feet and hurried inside the kitchen. It was a bustle of activity, as if no one had heard the sound.

"Did you hear that?" she blurted.

Roslyn paused her chopping to look up at her. "What's that, lass?"

"It sounded like…" She paused to think. "Like drums."

The woman dropped her knife and hurried toward the open kitchen door. Evie followed, clutching the handle of the basket as they stood in the garden and listened. She held her breath, as if that would make the sound clearer.

Ba-dum-ba-dum-ba-dum.

There it was again.

Roslyn's gaze flickered to her, worry creasing her face. "Ye best get inside, lass. I'll find Callum."

"What is it?" She followed the woman, still holding on to the basket with her cut flowers as if it were a life preserver.

"War drums," she said, her voice low. Likely so she wouldn't frighten the others working in the kitchen. She reached for the basket and took it from her, placing it on the nearest counter. "We must find Callum. He'll want to see ye to safety."

Roslyn took her by the hand and led her out of the kitchen. Evie didn't have a chance to protest. Her mind whirled with fear of what was to come. All she could think about was Callum going into battle. Callum fighting. She didn't want to think about what would happen to her if he didn't survive.

As they exited the kitchen and entered the great hall, she saw him. He was headed across the great hall, a look of determination creasing his face.

"They're here, aren't they?" she asked as they came to a halt in the center of the large room.

Roslyn released her and headed back to the kitchen, leaving her alone with Callum.

"Aye." He gave one nod of his head. "Do ye still have the keystone?"

Bewildered, she nodded. "Yes."

He held out his hand. "Let me have it."

A trickle of unease went through her as she reached into her pocket and handed it to him. He glanced down at it briefly when he took it. The lines still pulsed a pale light through the cloth. He tucked it into his sporran. Taking her by the hand, he led her out of the keep and into the bailey. Malcolm saw them from across the frenzy of activity and headed for them.

The distant drumbeat pulsed a rhythmic thump under the thunderous vibration of horses' hooves. It was a harbinger of what was to come. Evie clutched Callum's hand, dread shuddering through her.

"I will see my wife safe," Callum said to his brother. "And then I'll join ye."

"Ye cannae mean to—" Malcolm began. His gaze flickered to her and then back again.

But Callum cut him off as he turned to him. "I can and I will."

Confusion slipped through her at his meaning. What did he mean, he intended to see her safe? Was he going to take her away from the keep? She glanced back at the imposing structure of Dundale and wondered if Roslyn and the scullery maids were hiding in the larder.

She looked up at him. Panic skittered through her at what he meant to do. She shouldn't have given him the keystone. There was fire in his eyes as he looked at his brother. Evie trembled. He was determined to make sure she was safe despite Clan MacDonald coming for them. He squeezed her hand, never lifting his gaze from his brother's face.

Malcolm glanced from Callum to her, his gaze lingering on hers. For a moment, his stern expression seemed to soften. His lips thinned as he nodded.

"Aye, go then, brother." He gripped the hilt of his claymore, pulling it from its sheath. "And dinnae tarry for the MacDonalds willna wait for ye to return before they attack."

Then he flashed a smile and went to join Jamie, their clansmen and their bannermen.

"Callum—"

He turned to her. "We dinnae have the numbers to beat Rory MacDonald and his men. I dinnae want to scare ye, lass, but I dinnae want to lie to ye, either."

Hot fear pumped through her as she stared at him. "What are you saying, Callum?"

"I'm saying we are outnumbered. Come." His voice was gruff as he led her through the bailey.

Evie had no choice but to stumble along after him, her breath pluming in the air around her as she struggled to keep up. She didn't have her cloak. They headed toward the outer wall. There was nothing on the other side but rocky cliffs leading down to the craggy shoreline of the loch. An underlying sense of fear erupted through her as a sudden question burned through her mind.

"Where are you taking me?" she panted.

He halted abruptly and turned to face her, taking her by the upper arms and holding her. His sharp blue eyes met hers.

"It will be a bit of a climb, but ye can do it."

She shook her head, panic welling deep inside her. "What are you talking about?"

"I mean to see ye to safety, lass."

"I understand that, but—"

"There isna much time."

He took her hand again and headed for the wall where he rounded a corner. There were several steps leading down to a gate. A gate she hadn't noticed before, made of iron with heavy hinges and, beyond that, the craggy shore and the dark waters of the loch.

Her heart throbbed a mad beat as he led her down the slippery steps toward the gate. Her throat constricted as the threat of tears burned her eyes. At the bottom of the steps, he reached for the gate, then stopped. He turned to her once again, holding her gaze as he gave her hands a squeeze.

Then he reached inside his sporran and brought out the cloth-wrapped stone. She sucked in a sharp breath and shook her head, understanding of what he meant to do dawning. He unwrapped it and discarded the handkerchief.

"No, Callum." Panic clawed at her throat.

"Ye must take this, lass."

He pressed the keystone into her scarred palm, closing her fingers around it. As he did so, she caught a glimpse of the glowing lines etched in the stone.

"I can't!"

"Ye *must*. 'Tis the only way to keep ye both safe and out of the hands of Rory MacDonald." He brushed his hand over her cheek, the tender look in his eyes nearly making her come undone. "I cannae allow ye or the keystone to fall into enemy hands."

Hot tears clouded her eyes. "But if I take it, then I lose you."

"Nay." A smile pulled at the corners of his lips. "Ye can come back to me." He clutched her hands in his. "Come back to me, lass. Promise me."

But what if he died in battle? What if she returned to her future only to have the past reset? What if she forgot her love for him? What if he forgot her? There were so many unknowns.

Her heart thudded as her stomach twisted into a tight knot. The stern look in his eyes told her she had no argument to give him. No way to convince him she should stay in Dundale.

"I promise."

He kissed her, then, his lips warm and sweet against hers. She savored it, knowing it was the last time she'd kiss him. Every moment they had spent together flashed through her mind starting with waking up in his bed wrapped in his warmth. She hadn't meant to fall in love with him. In fact, she hadn't meant to return home. Now, she had no choice.

She vowed to find out the outcome of the battle when she returned home. So many questions swirled through her mind. Questions she didn't have time to ask.

"The shore is a bit rocky, but ye can do it. Get as far from here as ye can. Then use the stone to return to yer time."

"What happens when I do? Will I remember? How will I find you again?"

"I dinnae ken," he said, still clutching her hands in his. "The keystone brought ye to me once. It can bring ye to me again. And keep it out of the hands of the MacDonalds."

She understood, of course, and though she hated the idea, she nodded. Her stomach was coiled into a hot, tight knot. She pulled her hands from his and flung her arms around his neck. He held her tight, so tight, while she memorized every hard angle. They stood there for a moment like that as she fought back tears.

"Ye must go, lass," he whispered against her hair. "Come back to me."

When she left, he would go face the MacDonalds. He would go to war. Her chest tightened as she thought of losing him. That when she returned to her time, he would be dead. Either by old age or by the sword of his sworn enemy. She despised the thought of either one. But he was not immortal, and neither was she. When she pulled away, she placed one palm on the side of his scruffy cheek, holding his gaze and committing to memory every line of his chiseled, handsome face.

"I will find you again."

He smiled, then, his eyes lit with hope and desire. "I ken ye will, lass."

Then he pushed open the gate. The hinges groaned as it swung wide. She clutched the keystone in her hand as she turned to the opening and peered down at the rocky shoreline, the loch lapping against the edges. She gulped in a deep breath, emotions clotting her throat.

"I don't want to leave you," she said without turning around.

She sensed his presence behind her, though he didn't touch her. "I'll wait for ye, my bonnie lassie from the future."

And then he was gone. When she turned, he had disappeared into the deepening twilight, leaving her there to do what she had to do.

CHAPTER THIRTY-NINE

CALLUM RODE OUT to the field on his warhorse, his claymore strapped to his side and his gut twisted into a knot. He did not want to send Evie home, but he needed her safe and the keystone safe and out of the hands of Rory MacDonald.

The rival clan laird knew what he was doing when he arrived at dusk. He intended to attack during the night in the hopes they were unaware of his arrival. The opposing forces sat their horses with their torches blazing like a beacon of death in the night. His one-thousand-strong force was behind him. A few on horseback, but most of them infantry.

Malcolm and Jamie brought a mere three hundred with them. With Angus Sinclair and their men, that brought their numbers to five hundred. Not enough to defeat Rory MacDonald's army.

Callum pulled his horse to a stop between his brothers in front of their line of men.

"Well, brother, I hope tonight isna a good night to die," Malcolm said. His gaze was on the other side of the field, staring at the flicking torches.

Staring at their doom.

"Aye," Callum agreed. He kicked his horse into a trot.

"Where are ye going?" Jamie called.

Callum paused a moment and looked over his shoulder at his brothers. "Let's see how much Rory MacDonald is spoiling for a fight, eh?" He flashed a wicked grin.

"Do ye want to tempt fate, brother?" Malcolm called as he joined him.

Jamie was on his other side. The three of them headed toward the middle of the field. As they did, three on the opposing side headed for them. Callum recognized Rory MacDonald in the center flanked by two of his family members holding aloft blazing torches.

They paused across from each other, sizing each other up. Rory held the great axe that had killed their father. The same one in the mystical tapestries hanging in Evie's old bedchamber.

Rory MacDonald was a brute of a man with broad shoulders and an aged face that was nothing more than a map of wrinkles. His sharp-eyed gaze flicked to Jamie and he scowled, clearly unhappy to see the lad back on MacLeod land.

"Ye dare show yer face here, laddie?" he said to Jamie.

"My brother is my business," Callum snapped, his voice dark and dangerous.

"Och, but my daughter is my business," Rory replied, giving him a wicked grin and showing off blackened teeth. "Did ye think we wouldna retaliate after all ye did to us?"

"Did ye think to attack us in the dead of night?" Callum countered.

"Aye. I hoped to kill ye in yer beds!" Rory snapped.

Fury burned through Callum at his callous reply. He gripped the reins tight until his hand cramped.

"I ken what ye have inside yer keep. I intend to take it from ye."

Callum knew he referred to the keystone but didn't want to acknowledge it. "And what is that?"

Rory frowned, his face going dark. "It calls to us. And we want it."

Next to him, Malcolm stiffened in his saddle.

"And ye intend to kill to get it?" Callum asked.

"Aye, if that's what it takes. Ye cannae beat me, laddie. Give up the keystone…and the lass." He displayed his wicked grin.

Fury erupted through him as he stared at the man who had killed his da.

"Let us settle this like men," Callum said, his tone calm. "I'll fight ye for the stone *and* the lass. If I win, I keep both. If you win—"

Rory barked a laugh. Both Malcolm and Jamie snapped their heads to look at him. But Callum knew that even if he lost against Rory MacDonald, even if the laird killed him, Evie and the keystone were safely in the future. He prayed she had managed to use it by now.

"Ye wish to fight me, eh?" He laughed again. "Hand to hand, sword to sword. Aye, I ken ye'll beat an old man like me. I also ken my army will beat yer army."

Before Callum responded, Malcolm nudged his horse forward. "Ye'll die today, Rory MacDonald."

Then he turned his horse around and galloped back to their waiting men. Jamie hesitated a moment before he did the same, leaving Callum there alone. Anger welled up deep inside him at the hot-headedness of his brother.

"Ye've made yer choice. I've made mine. Godspeed, Callum MacLeod," Rory said.

He and his men turned and headed back to stand with his men. The war drums beat louder. As Rory and his men approached, the cheers of his army went up as if they understood all too well what was about to happen on the field near Dundale.

Clenching his jaw, Callum rode back. He paused in front of Malcolm who remained stiff in his saddle staring straight ahead.

"Did ye mean to pick a fight?" Callum asked.

"I did what ye could no," his brother replied, his voice flat and even. He had no remorse.

If Callum knew his brother—and he did—the moment they charged the field, Malcolm would go straight for Rory MacDonald.

EVIE STEPPED THROUGH the gate, pulling it closed behind her as cheers went up. Her heart hammered like the war drum as she carefully made her way down onto the shore, stepping over large, jagged rocks. The sun had long vanished, plunging the loch and the beach in near darkness.

The light of the full moon rising over the water made it glisten with an ethereal glow. On any other night, she would pause there and think how magical the sight was. But this night was different. This night she was leaving Callum to return to the future.

She glanced down at the keystone nestled against her scarred palm. The lines were still faintly glowing as it emitted a quiet hum, much like the day she used it in the museum to fall through time.

Her throat nearly closed as tears welled in her eyes. She clutched the stone in her hand, careful to keep her thumb from brushing over the lines. She was certain that was how it had sent her back in time.

Evie started down the shoreline, the soft lapping of the water to her left. To her right, the curtain wall of the castle. Beyond that, the fighting men. More shouts in the night air. Her breath fogged around her. Her hands cold. Her feet numb. She managed to keep going, heading away from the castle. Away from her love.

If there was a flash of light, as Hamish had mentioned, she didn't want to bring unnecessary attention to herself. She didn't want to give MacDonald a homing beacon to find her. Or where she was. That is, if he got past Callum and his brothers in the first place.

In the distance, the clanging of swords clashing against each other sounded. She envisioned a horrible battle. She had never seen one in real life. She wasn't certain she wanted to see one.

She was certain she didn't want to see anything happen to her husband.

The thought jarred her to a halt. She stood at the loch, peering out over the darkened water, listening to the battle in the distance.

Callum was her husband.

Hamish had made him promise on his deathbed to protect her—and he was protecting her by sending her away. But he had said something else. Hamish had told him she would do the same for him.

Was protecting him running away and returning to the future? No, it wasn't.

Clutching the stone in her hand, she looked toward the battle, listening to it rage on the other side of the castle.

"This is wrong," she whispered.

"Aye, you have the right of it."

The woman's voice made her nearly jump out of her skin. She spun around to see a woman with long silver hair and eyes like starlight standing on the edge of the loch, the water lapping behind her onto the shore. Her white gown billowed around her in the breeze.

"Moira?"

She nodded, a smile playing on her lips, pleased Evie recognized her.

"I can't return to the future," she said. "I won't use the stone to go home. I can't leave him."

"No, you cannae use the stone to return. For if you do, you will reset Time. Your memories will be erased and all will be for naught. He will not survive this night. Your path is a different one than returning to the future."

Evie's brows drew together in question. "What do you mean?"

"There is another way to use the stone if you intend to save your love," she said.

Evie stared at her in disbelief with hope rising in her breast.

She clutched the stone so hard, the jagged edges bit into her palm.

"Tell me," she demanded. "Tell me how to save him."

Moira grinned. "Aye, then, lass. Here's what you do."

CHAPTER FORTY

IT WAS A hellish battle. As soon as they charged, Callum lost sight of Malcolm, though he suspected he was heading straight for Rory. Jamie would be fighting next to him no doubt.

He didn't have time to think about his brothers as he was trying to stay alive. With every swing of his claymore, he cut down man after man, killing those who tried to kill him. He found no sign of Rory.

Silvery light from the full moon shone down. That, coupled with the few torches burning in the hands of the few who had not yet joined the fray, cast the men's bloody faces in ghastly expressions, their eyes wild as they charged and fought one another.

Callum knew it was hopeless. They could not hope to win against MacDonald and his men. They were outnumbered. They were outmatched. With every swing of his claymore, he cut down one man only to have him immediately replaced by another. And another. And on and on.

All around him was the din of battle. The screams of pain. The clashing of steel against steel. The metallic tang of blood permeating the air. His hands covered in it.

But he could not allow them to breach the walls of the castle and invade his home. He would do everything in his power to keep that from happening.

Near him, a shout rose up. One that sounded like his brother.

He spun in time to see Rory swing his great axe at Malcolm. His brother jumped out of the way, narrowly missing the blade. Callum hacked and slashed his way to his brother's side, ignoring the fatigue pounding through him.

MacDonald swung his great axe again, this time connecting with Malcolm. His brother cried out as he hit the ground. Fueled by the fire of anger, Callum cut down the last man standing in his way. MacDonald gave him a wicked smile, a wild look in his eyes as he charged forward.

Callum didn't have time to see if his brother was all right when his sword clashed against MacDonald's great axe.

"How will it feel to die in the shadow of yer keep?" MacDonald spat.

Callum ignored him, swinging his sword again. MacDonald was a skilled warrior and evaded him.

"And then the lass and the keystone will be mine," he added.

Callum said nothing as he attacked again. As he charged, something strange began to happen. As if the world around him slowed. As though they were underwater. Something was not right. Something was strange. An incessant buzzing sounded.

The swing of his claymore was in a slow, wide arc. He missed his intended target. Even MacDonald's motions slowed down. His eyes went wide as he looked at him, the great axe hanging in the air as though stuck.

It seemed to take eons for Callum to turn his head, his arm falling to his side.

Then he saw her, standing with her fiery hair unbound and whipping around her face. One hand was clutched into a tight fist, light seeping from around her fingers. She held both arms aloft, creating a shimmering bubble around her, him, and Rory MacDonald. The men on the battlefield were still as if frozen in time.

God's teeth, what was she doing?

He knew without a doubt she clutched the keystone in her hand.

She had not returned to the future.

Part of him was relieved. Another part of him was furious.

Though there was distance between them, her dark brown gaze landed on his.

I came to protect you.

It was her voice he heard in his head. His mind had gone blank as he tried to reason through how she had managed to speak into his mind. Was it the power of the keystone? Or something else?

With power thrumming through and around her, she controlled the shimmering bubble that had formed around the three of them.

Images burst through his mind showing him the battle between him and MacDonald. In the vision, his claymore slices through the laird, killing him. Then he is attacked by MacDonald's men and stabbed in the side multiple times.

The vision shifted. The swing of his claymore misses and Rory MacDonald's great axe connects with him, slicing through his gut as it did his da. He falls to the ground, dead.

Another vision. His claymore clashes against the man's great axe; they are locked in battle. MacDonald orders him to give up the lass and the stone. That he wants both of them. Someone stabs Callum in the back. He dies.

His brows knit together, trying to understand.

These are your choices, she said in his mind. *In each scenario, you die. I cannot let you die.*

More images played through his mind. Moira showing him the choices and the ways he and his men fail to protect Dundale. The MacDonalds overrun the keep, taking charge of it and looking for her. That is, a version of her that doesn't have the stone clenched in her fist.

There is only one way to defeat the invaders. There is only one way you will live, she said. She sounded different, not like herself. She sounded more in control, more sure of herself than she ever had.

Show me, he said in his mind, hoping she heard him.

The shimming bubble dissipated and time continued its normal movement. The sounds of clashing swords and screaming men resumed. The smell of death and blood and fear returned.

"Get the lass!" MacDonald shouted.

Callum sucked in a sharp breath when he heard the command. He started to run toward her.

That strangeness of time slowing down happened again. One of his men broke into a run, holding his bloodied sword in one hand as he charged her. But he was running as though he were taking unhurried, methodical steps, as though he had all the time in the world. Callum noticed it wasn't the man who had slowed, but everyone around them.

A flash of light burst from Evie's hand, then, blinding him. He stumbled backward, squeezing his eyes shut to block out the stark brightness. When he opened his eyes to look, the man who had charged her was on the ground, writhing in pain.

Time resumed its normal pace.

All fighting halted on the field.

There was still a great distance between him and Evie, but their eyes met. There was a look of fear mixed with determination on her beautiful face. Her arms dropped to her sides, her one hand still glowing.

Another man tried to charge her. She remained where she was, unmoving. She lifted her free hand up as if to stop him. But Jamie stepped into the man's path, sword raised, and cut him down so fast it was a blur of motion.

MacDonald emitted a cry of frustration. Callum turned in time to see his enemy charge toward him, barreling into him with such a force it knocked the claymore out of his hand. They tumbled to the ground, fists flying. MacDonald punched him in the ribs.

As they tangled with each other, he felt something cold and sharp against his throat.

"Move and yer dead," MacDonald warned.

Callum stilled.

"Get up."

MacDonald wrapped his surprisingly strong hand around his upper arm and dragged him to his feet with him. He kept the dagger at his throat as he turned toward Evie.

"Bring me the stone, lass, or he dies," he called.

Evie remained where she was. Her face blanched as her eyes widened. In her hand, she still clutched the glowing keystone, the white light continuing to seep around her fingers.

"Release him or you and your men die," she countered.

Pride swarmed through him as she lifted her head and spoke loud and clear for all to hear. Behind him, MacDonald chuckled.

"Och, lass, ye cannae beat me or my men."

Evie took long slow steps toward them, her gaze never leaving his captor's face. What was she doing? Was she mad?

"I think I've already proven I can beat your men."

She waved her glowing hand toward a line of men to her left. They cried out, dropping their swords, clutching their middles and falling to the ground.

MacDonald stiffened. The dagger in his hand began to shake.

A smugness swept through Callum, smug followed by a wisp of worry. He wanted to tell her to stop where she was but at the same time, he was intrigued to see what she planned to do next.

"Call her off," MacDonald said, his breath hot in his ear. "Tell the bitch to stop."

That was the final straw for Callum. He didn't have to stand there as his captive. Anger fueled him as he gripped the man's wrist in his hand, jerked his hand away and spun, throwing the older man on the ground. The dagger fell from his hand.

"Dinnae call my *wife* that."

Rory blinked up at him, confusion in his eyes.

Callum turned back toward Evie. She hurried to him, her hand still glowing, her hair fluttering behind her and her face contorted with relieved worry. He caught her in his arms, holding her.

"What the devil are ye still doing here, lass?" He said it

against her hair.

She trembled next to him, her small body shivering as she tilted her head to look up at him. "I couldn't leave you."

He started to reply when a sharp, biting pain lanced through his left shoulder. His back bowed in half. He released her and crumpled to the ground, realizing his mistake—turning his back on his enemy.

"Callum!"

"GIVE ME THAT stone," MacDonald demanded as he stepped around Callum's prone form on the ground.

Evie stumbled back a step, the pulsing, humming stone in her sweat-and-blood-slick palm. The goddess had told her the way to save Callum and his men was to use the stone like a weapon, when two bloodlines became one. Moira had slashed her scarred palm with a knife and said to keep the keystone clutched in her hand. Never let it go.

But that was not all the goddess had taught her. She had shown her how this part of the keystone harnessed the part of time that was the present. Evie understood so much more then about Moira—she was the Goddess of the Present.

Callum groaned. Blood stained the back of his tunic where the man had stabbed him.

The man advancing on her reminded her much of Bruce when he attacked her on the museum stairs before she ran for her life up the steps. Her heart thundered in her ears. Her body vibrated with fear.

This went beyond a clan feud. He must know the keystone was also a weapon, was a way to harness the power of time, and that was why he was determined to get it.

Evie was not going to give it to him.

He reached for her, grabbing her by the arm and dragging her to him. He wrapped his arms around her upper torso, squeezing her and clawing at her clenched fist.

"Give it to me!"

She tried to use the power Moira taught her to slow down time, but she must have expended everything she had. She was unable to create the slow-motion shimmering bubble around them like she had before.

His rancid breath was hot on her cheek. He was stronger than she was and determined to pull her fingers open. She kicked him in the shin with the heel of her shoe which made him loosen his grip enough for her to wiggle free.

But he was fast for an old man. He snatched her by the wrist, dragging her to him once again. The scowl on his face was terrifying as he pulled at her fingers. She tightened her fist and emitted a cry of pain.

At their feet, Callum grunted. He was on his knees now trying to rise, the dagger in his hand. Pain creased his face.

Evie had had enough. With a ferocity she didn't know she possessed, she shoved her fist toward the man and emitted a war cry that came from the depths of her lungs.

Her fist exploded in a blinding white light, the pain of it burning through her palm. She connected with MacDonald's chest, punching him as hard as she could. He flew backward, soaring through the air until he landed with a thud and skidded. He came to a halt at the feet of several of his men who gaped in horror at what she'd done.

She dropped her hand to her side and fell to the ground in front of Callum. With her free hand, she reached for him, placing her palm against his cheek. Dread thumped through her. He reached for her, his hands cupping her face.

"I'm all right, lass," he said. "Are ye?"

She nodded, unable to stop the well of tears pooling in her eyes. She glanced down to see that her hand no longer glowed. The keystone was quiet once again. She opened her fingers to reveal the bloodied stone against the cut on her palm.

They helped each other to their feet and turned to face Mac-Donald who slowly climbed to his feet, his hand pressed against his chest. His tunic was charred where she had punched him.

"It's over," Callum called, wrapping an arm around her shoulders.

MacDonald hunched over, one of his men helping him stand upright. His last words sent a chill through her.

"For now, MacLeod. For now."

Chapter Forty-One

EVIE SAT AT the long table in the great hall, exhaustion pounding through her. Every bone in her ached as she leaned back in the chair, her eyes heavy. Dougal finished wrapping the bandage around her cut hand and tied it off.

"There ye are, lass."

"Thank you. How's Callum?" she asked.

Callum was taken to their bedchamber as soon as they had staggered into the keep. She sent Dougal to him first to dress his wounds, knowing the cut on her hand was shallow and could wait.

"He's a bit of a grump," Dougal said with a grin. "He'll be fine, though."

Malcolm and Jamie returned, mostly unscathed. Malcolm sustained a slash through his upper arm from MacDonald's great axe. Other than that, he was fine. Dougal went to see to them, leaving her alone with her thoughts and the blazing fire in the hearth.

She had never seen so many dead men and horses littering the field. It was a horrifying sight and one she would never forget. The smell of death permeated the air. When MacDonald and his men had ridden away, she had clung to Callum. Another thing she would never forget was the hate blazing in the man's eyes as he left, defeated.

She and Callum both knew it was not the end.

Finally, she pushed up from the table. Her steps were slow and laborious as she headed to the bedchamber she shared with Callum. She needed to check in on him. She pushed the door open to see him sitting up in bed, his head back against the headboard, and a bandage wrapped around his upper torso and over his shoulder. He lifted his head when he heard the door. His face lit with joy when he saw her.

She sat on the bed, reaching for his hand. He held hers, his thumb brushing over the bandage. They hadn't spoken much since they left the battlefield. She sensed he was angry with her for not returning home. But now she was ready to face his wrath.

"Callum, I—"

"Ye dinnae leave," he interrupted.

She kept her gaze fixed on their joined hands. Blood was still crusted under his fingernails. Her hand throbbed from the cut, but at least it had stopped bleeding.

"I couldn't." She refused to meet his eyes. She didn't want to see the disappointment burning there.

Silence stretched between them. The only sound was that of the crackling fire in the hearth.

Finally, he said, "How did you ken to use the stone that way?"

She thought of the keystone, still stained with her blood, in her pocket. Since the final blow she had handed MacDonald, it had remained dormant.

"Moira told me."

She braved a look and met his fierce blue gaze that was full of confusion, concern, love, and a touch of anger. She loved his expressive eyes.

"The goddess?"

She nodded. "She came to me on the beach. She told me if I left, it would reset Time and my memories would be erased. She told me you would die in that battle."

Upon hearing her words, all the fight went out of him. He leaned heavily against the pillows at his back.

"I didn't want to forget you, Callum." Her voice was a roughened whisper. "And I couldn't let you die."

With his free hand, he reached for her and brushed the back of his hand over her cheek. She caught his hand, held it there against her face.

"I understand why ye did it, lass, but—"

"I had to save you."

He looked thoughtful as he gazed at her and she saw he had more questions. "Tell me something, then. When I saw ye standing there with yer hair flying, it was as though everyone and everything slowed around us."

She was nodding before he finished. "Yes, you're right."

"And…ye did that?" He lifted one brow as if he wasn't sure he believed it.

"I did. Moira is the Goddess of the Present," she said. "When she and her two sisters shattered the stone during the night of the Shattering, they put their power within each piece. Her power was the ability to slow down time."

"But that's not all, is it? I had…visions." He sounded as though he were embarrassed by that. "And I heard ye speak in my mind."

"With the power of the stone, I showed you the possible outcomes of your choices. I was able to speak to you in your mind when I did. I don't know how, though. That was unclear to me. And I can no longer do that."

He looked so relieved, she stifled a laugh. She added, "I did what I had to do to make sure you survived."

He glanced down at her bandaged hand, his thumb still tracing over the linen. "And what was that?"

"She said, 'Two bloodlines become one.' She took my hand and sliced my palm with the tip of a dagger with a pearl handle. Then she told me to keep the keystone in my hand and never release it. As soon as I did, it started to hum and glow that brilliant light. She told me to use it and the power within me. I had no idea I was capable of…" She paused, searching for the words.

"Ye saved us. Me." He sounded in awe as he said it.

"I had to." She leaned toward him then, her lips a breath away from him. "You're my love."

"Och, lass. I cannae be angry with ye. *Mo chridhe.*"

She had never heard him speak Gaelic before. The way the words rolled off his tongue sent a tingling sensation through her. It was a beautiful language.

"What does that mean?" she asked.

He took her face in his hands, leaned forward, and gently tipped her head back, preparing to kiss her. "It means *my heart.* For ye are and will always be."

THE END

About the Author

Michelle Miles believes in fairy tales, true love, and magic. She writes heart-stopping urban fantasy, young adult and adult fantasy, and paranormal romance with an action/adventure twist that will leave you breathless. She is the author of numerous series that includes everything from angels and demons to fairies, dragons, and elves.

She is a member of Romance Writers of America (RWA) and Science Fiction and Fantasy Writers Association (SFWA). A native Texan, in her spare time she loves reading, listening to music, watching movies, hiking, and drinking wine. She can be found online at Facebook, Instagram, Pinterest, and more!

Website & Blog: www.michellemiles.net
Facebook: MichelleMilesAuthor
Instagram: MichelleMilesAuthor
Threads: @michellemilesauthor
YouTube: MichelleMiles
TikTok: @michellemilesauthor
BookBub: bookbub.com/authors/michelle-miles

www.ingramcontent.com/pod-product-compliance
Lightning Source LLC
Chambersburg PA
CBHW071248300726
48975CB00002B/591